T0209285

The Shepherd's Voice

MICHELLE NOONAN

This is a work of fiction. All of the characters, names, incidents, organizations, and dialogue in this novel are either the products of the author's imagination or are used fictitiously.

WestBow Press books may be ordered through booksellers or by contacting:

WestBow Press
A Division of Thomas Nelson & Zondervan
1663 Liberty Drive
Bloomington, IN 47403
www.westbowpress.com
1 (866) 928-1240

ISBN: 978-1-9736-5535-0 (sc)
ISBN: 978-1-9736-5536-7 (e)

Print information available on the last page.

WestBow Press rev. date: 6/28/2019

Chapter One

"THANK YOU FOR HELPING me today," Abigail Shepherd said, a smile curving up the sides of her lips, as she watched her daughter Mandy taking the bag out of the trash can at the office where she worked.

"No problem mom," Mandy smiled, her blue green eyes sparkling. "Now that school is out I don't have anything else to do," she teased.

Abigail just shook her head, making her short light brown curls bounce slightly and smiled, "Even on the first day of summer?" she joked back, pulling a rag from her cart.

Mandy bent down, brushing her loosely curled hair, that hung to her waist, behind her as she tied the bag, "Well, not until I get a summer job," she commented wryly.

"Oh, I meant to tell you," Abigail stated, digging a ponytail holder from her pocket, amused that her daughter could never remember to put her hair up. She fished out a black band, with her small rough hand and handed it to her. Mandy paused in what she was doing and looked at her, puzzled for a moment as she began to pull her layered hair into three sections with her slender hands. Abigail smiled to herself as she wondered how long it would be before Mandy took the band back out again. "Do you remember meeting Mrs. Jenson?"

Mandy's thin brows furrowed as she thought, "I only went to one of your janitor meetings," she commented "Was she the older or younger one you sat with?"

Abigail grinned at her kindly way of saying that Mrs. Jenson was absolutely ancient. "The older one dear," she reported, as she began rubbing her rag in small deft circles on the wooden surface of the desk.

Mandy nodded and finished the dark brown braid securing it with the black band. She picked up the bag of trash and took it to the door then headed back to the cart, and leaned down to fix a couple bottles that had been knocked askew. "What did she say?" her daughter asked, "Did she invite me to be a janitor at her office building?"

Abigail shook her head, her blue green eyes peering over at her daughter, "no actually it's a bit bigger than that." Mandy raised her brows and looked at her mother, and into eyes that looked exactly like hers. "Okay, here's the thing, I know you want to earn money during the summer for college," she began, and paused for a moment and her hand stilled, "It would be nice if that scholarship you had the first year lasted longer, or if you'd chosen a cheaper college," she added, then raised her hand as her daughter began to protest, "I know, I know, your school has the best psychology program around, but..."

"In the state," Mandy interrupted a cheeky smile on her pink lips that always seemed to curve up with happiness.

Abigail smiled slightly at her daughter's enthusiasm, then began rubbing again, "The thing is... I don't think just finding a job during the summer will be good enough for your tuition."

She continued rubbing the desk for a few seconds then looked over to watch her daughter's expression. Mandy had paused and stood. She wiped a stray curl off her high cheekbones with the back of her hand then turned to face Abigail. "I know mom," she shrugged, "I already figured I might have to take a year off and just work."

Mrs. Shepherd nodded. "You know dad and I would love to help you..." she began, and began to straighten quickly until the tightness in her back caused her to move slowly. She headed towards the cart.

"You already help a lot," Mandy smiled, "but having five kids is hard on a budget," she teased, and grabbed the vacuum cleaner and began dragging it toward the plug.

Abigail smiled again, thanking God that her daughter had always understood and was always very appreciative, "I thought after Allie got married we'd have a bit more..."

"But newlyweds need even more money than single people," Mandy interrupted again as she stooped to plug in the vacuum.

"Amanda!" Abigail scolded using her rag for emphasis, "You've really got to learn to stop interrupting people, especially adults."

Mandy grinned, trying to look repentant, "Sorry mom. You were saying?"

Abigail tried not to laugh as she picked up a bottle and a different rag. Her daughter was a good child. Course, if truth be told, all her children were well-behaved. She had tried to be a good example of a Christian wife and mother. She had been firm, yet loving, to all of them, and though she kept it to herself, she felt like she had the best family.

She headed towards a nearby nook where several decorations sitting on a small table added to the class of the office building, and continued her appraisal. Her husband was a carpenter, a very good one, and they had a comfortable life, from what he and she provided. They didn't squabble much and she was proud of the example of love they had been able to show their children. With so much divorce, she and Justin, her wonderful, sweet husband, were a rarity.

Her oldest two were twins, Allie and Aaron. They were both very responsible twenty-three year olds. Allie had graduated with a degree in nursing from a Christian college and then married the man she'd been dating since their second year in. He was a Systems Administrator now at the hospital she worked at in Orlando which was only a short drive from where the rest of the family lived in a little town in central Florida.

Abigail pulled out the candle from the holder, sprayed the rag with the chemical, and began polishing the holder. Aaron had joined his father and was learning to be a carpenter. He was the quietest son, and really enjoyed working with wood so much more than he liked being with people. He was a calm, level-headed young man and never raised his voice.

Mandy was the exact opposite. She loved people a lot and enjoyed observing human nature. She could be loud, when play-fighting with her youngest brother, but was also very level-headed. She was nineteen and Abigail knew that even though she was outgoing and loved attention, she had strong morals and wouldn't compromise otherwise she would never even suggest what she was thinking.

She paused a moment to put the candle back into the holder. Her youngest children were good children to, but sometimes she worried that Jenna, who was two years younger than Mandy wanted to be too much like her sister. She didn't know yet what she wanted from life but would have to start figuring that out as soon as she graduated from high school next year. Because she loved attention so much, Abigail hoped that Jenna would never compromise her morals either. She just needed to pray extra hard for that one.

Jason was fourteen and also fairly outgoing. He was definitely the baby of the family and perhaps a bit spoiled, but if his being a bit more babied than the rest was their biggest fault, Abigail knew she had no reason to ever feel bad about her family. He was an athletic kid, with a ready laugh and an easy-going personality. He loved to tease and have fun more than any of them.

Her hands stilled for a moment. Then she removed another candle. If truth be told, all the siblings had had their share of squabbles over the years, but in all they were a pretty close group. She had taught them from the Bible since they had been little, and they had all gone to church as a family. She could say that with God's help, she and Justin had been firm yet loving parents. Now that they were grown she did not need to worry about what they were into like she knew some of her friends did, who were perhaps not so strict with their children. Course there were also the friends who had been too strict with their children. Why couldn't everyone figure out that going to extremes was a bad idea, she began to think when a voice cut into her thoughts.

"Mom?" Mandy broke into her musing with a slight smile. "Are you not going to tell me or just think about it for a while?"

Abigail smiled, "You should work on that impatience too," she teased, and sprayed the chemical onto her rag again then began to polish the holder, drawing out the suspense.

Mandy laughed, "I was going to start vacuuming, should I do something else instead?" Abigail looked over at her daughter standing patiently by the vacuum she'd gotten all ready, and laughed. "Course if you want me to vacuum you could just talk over it," she joked, the laughter causing meniscal smile lines around her bright eyes.

"Okay, Okay," Abigail smiled, and began to explain even as she continued polishing. "Here's the short version. Mrs. Jenson knows a lady named Mrs. Harper, who is the head housekeeper for a wealthy family near West Palm Beach, and she is currently looking for a young lady to hire as a housekeeper for at least a year. It would pay very well, and you would be a live-in staff member, meaning you'd live somewhere in their mansion, or in a place provided for you."

Abigail spoke quickly then paused and looked into her daughter's eyes. Mandy was frowning slightly with her eyes, but her mouth continued to turn up at the ends like she would break out into peals of laughter at any moment. Abigail knew she was taking the idea seriously. She also knew that most people would jump at this chance, but Mandy was not like most people. "When would I get to come home?" she asked her hands no longer on the vacuum, but wrapped around herself slightly. She lifted one hand to her mouth and clicked her thumb nail on her tooth.

"I don't know anything else, but if you want, you can go interview for the job and ask them all the questions you have. The job won't start till June, but I hear a lot of people will probably be applying, so if you like the idea, you may want to call and set up an interview very soon." Abigail stated, looking back down at the table in front of her. She replaced the candle then picked up the last candle-stick holder, removed the candle gently, sprayed her rag, and began polishing.

"Let me pray about it," Mandy said finally. "Anything else I should know before I turn this on?" she asked, a slight grin playing at the corner of her mouth.

Abigail looked over at her and laughed, "Nope, that's all," she said, "though you're going to have to drive that cute car of yours there when you go for the interview, so you may want to practice driving some more," she kidded, knowing how much Mandy loved to drive, much more than anyone else in the family, at least those who could. She shuttered slightly at the thought of Jason driving.

Mandy laughed and stepped lightly on the button to turn on the vacuum. Abigail polished for a few moments as she listened to the familiar whir of the vacuum. She paused a second to watch her daughter diligently get a tough corner. She turned away, knowing that she had taught her daughter to be a thorough person and would do everything possible to get the job done. She was sure Mrs. Harper would be impressed with her daughter, but Mandy was right. They both had some praying to do.

"Lord," she prayed quietly in her mind, "Guide my daughter in every decision she makes. This may seem like a good opportunity, but help her to know if this is Your will."

Mandy listened to the steady drone of the vacuum as she paused to move a chair out of the way. She didn't absolutely love cleaning like her mother, but it was nice to see a place become neat again. Maybe cleaning in someone's home wouldn't be so bad. "What do you think God?"

Didn't it say something in the Bible about cleanliness being next to godliness? She laughed to herself, knowing it was just a saying, but she knew that Jesus loved order. She saw it every day in every little thing that He had made, from the birds that sang in the morning, to the stars at night.

She moved the chair back into place. She knew the only things she needed to worry about were her interactions with those she would meet. Would she meet good people that shared her morals or not? She shrugged. She didn't have to spend a lot of time with people that didn't share her morals, if they only wanted to drag her down. "Help me to be strong," she prayed. Then she thought about the family and their habits.

She wondered if they were a rich family that loved to keep an immaculate home or the kind that loved to throw wild parties and leave a huge mess for the servants to clean up. Despite the new politically correct terms these days, that was what she'd be. Course lumping the owners into those categories was pretty judgmental herself, she scolded. "Will I ever meet the family and is this what you want me to do?" she continued her prayer. It wasn't a bad thing, but did she really want to be away from home for so long?

Mandy moved another chair aside. She'd miss her family and her friends. She could always call her friends from there. Not to mention, she made friends anywhere she went, but family was irreplaceable. "If you want me to do this, help me not to be lonely," her thoughts continued the prayer. She really did want to earn enough money to finish her last four years of college. If she kept cramming as much as possible like she had the first one, she'd be done and have her psychology degree in five years instead of the typical six.

Perhaps if this job paid well enough, she'd be covered for another year or two. Beside this might be a chance for her to study more people. That was always a plus. She had never studied any wealthy or influential people before. She smiled to herself, thinking of the project she was doing. She loved observing people and their behaviors and she'd been jotting down notes for years. If she went, she'd definitely have to bring her notebooks. "Help me to be a good example to all the people I meet."

Mandy moved the chair back into place, and wrapped her long slender fingers around a tall lamp. She lifted it and with the other hand pushed the vacuum back and forth several times across where it had been sitting. Did she really want to do this? "Do You think that I should do this?" She emphasized to God, knowing that what He wanted was much more important than what she wanted.

"I have thought of all the possibilities and as I weigh them back and forth, I don't think that You are saying 'no,' so do I assume that's a 'yes?'" She smiled to herself. She enjoyed talking to God as she went about her daily life as much as her devotions that she had in the morning.

She pushed the vacuum toward the second little nook that her mother had moved to. Her mother lifted the little table with a smile, and Mandy vacuumed under it. She noticed the slight look of pain in her mother's eyes as she set the table back down. She turned off the vacuum with a frown. "Mom, maybe I should have done that."

Her mother laughed and her small light brown ponytail bounced as she shook her head. "I've been doing this for years," she countered, "Don't worry, my back only hurts a bit because Jason convinced me to play soccer with him last night because he has a hard time getting Robin to," she stated, indicating Jason's best friend.

Mandy laughed at her mother, who seemed forever young, despite the small wrinkles beginning to show around her mouth and eyes. "At least it wasn't tackle football," she teased and turned the vacuum back on. She could hear her mother's laughter over the vacuum and sighed happily. With peace in her heart, that she knew was God's way of saying, "Go," she finished up the last corner of the room, and wondered what excitement was in store for her. "And who do you want me to witness to?" she added to God.

Chapter Two

MRS. HARPER PAUSED ON her way to the den to straighten a picture with one hand. She smiled as she pictured her tall, skinny husband walking by and knocking it slightly askew. It was a game they played, one that started with his instance that she was obsessed with perfection. He'd find a picture periodically and slightly tilt it, and she'd find it sometime during the day while she was cleaning, and know he'd thought of her. It was silly, but was his way of showing he loved her.

She clasped her clipboard to her chest and entered the den and watched through her critical eyes as the girl she was interviewing approached her to shake hands. She had two interviews to do in a row, and she hoped that one of these two was more promising than the others she'd met during the weeks previous. Kids were just so untrustworthy these days. She sighed. Mrs. Harper motioned for the girl to sit down with a wave of her thick hand.

The girl handed her a piece of paper and turned towards the sofa. Her name was Alexis Topps and she seemed rather quiet and unassuming. Maybe that was a good thing; at least she'd not be trying to chase Brandon around, even if she was rather cute with her blonde hair and her hazel eyes, set in her child-like face. Her features were round, and light and she resembled a porcelain doll. She sat on the edge of the sofa her large purse beside her, clasping her hands together, her back straight. Her legs were together and she put one brown tennis shoe over the other and then switched them back and forth in nervousness.

Mrs. Harper pursed her lips as she wondered if she could find two girls like this. She put the girl's résumé on her clipboard and sat down in an easy chair. If only she hadn't been forced to fire Cammie last week, she'd only have to be hiring one girl instead of two. One she needed immediately, but the other would start in two weeks, the first of June, when Donna's contact was over. She tapped her pen absently on the clipboard as she looked down at the girl's résumé. Donna had been a pretty good kid, but she needed to go back to school. A lot of them did. At least she still had two other girls this summer that were here on a two year contact.

Mrs. Harper glanced over the résumé trying to concentrate. Alexis had had fairly good jobs before this, and if her references said good things, perhaps she could start soon. She looked up at Alexis who tried to smile slightly. Mrs. Harper put the résumé underneath the other papers on her clipboard. She leaned back, put her left elbow on the arm of the chair, and leaned slightly so that her round cheek was propped up with a few fingers. She poised the pen in her right hand and began.

She asked a few questions, jotting down notes, and then ended with her special eliminating questions, "Do you know Brandon?" Her brown eyes narrowed slightly as she looked for any changes in Alexis' facial expressions.

Alexis nodded slightly, "I have heard of him," she murmured softly, and the muscle beside her right eye twitched slightly and worry lines appeared on her wide forehead. She looked down at her hands and began to twist them together slightly. "He's not here that much right?" she said softly in a nervous tone.

Mrs. Harper sat up a little straighter. "No, not very much," she stated with as little inflexion as possible, but continued to pay close attention to the girl's face. Alexis exhaled slightly and her forehead once more smoothed out to look like porcelain. She smiled slightly and Mrs. Harper sighed to herself, and realized that she had been rather tense up until that point. She willed her arms and legs to relax as she decided that this girl would definitely not be chasing Brandon around.

She finished up quickly, telling Alexis she'd give her a call after checking out her references. The girl smiled nervously, shook her hand and headed out towards the front door. Mrs. Harper sighed as she thought about the girls' forehead. Her own forehead had plenty of worry-lines, but they were a permanent part on her face. If only she were still young enough to smooth them out again, she thought with a grimace, as she set her clipboard down and walked out.

She turned toward the kitchen for a drink when she heard the intercom from the gate buzz, telling her the next interviewee had arrived. She glanced at her watch, and at the hall clock. Ten minutes early. That was a good sign. She'd let Oliver show the girl in while she got herself a drink.

Oliver was a good butler. He was tall, with dark hair and eyes, and most people thought he looked like he could have family in the mob. With a very neutral expression on his face at practically all times, Oliver was serious about his job. That was a good quality to have. Perhaps his seriousness was a bit overkill at times, but it made a very formal impression on anyone who entered for the first time. It was probably good for new prospects to know they were applying for a serious job.

Mrs. Harper grabbed a cup down from the cupboard, and grabbed the juice out of the staff refrigerator. She poured herself some, drank a few swallows then replaced the juice before heading back towards the den. She was surprised to hear that Oliver was still in the room talking to the girl. She walked in and saw him standing near the door with the hint of a smile tugging at the corner of his lips as he said, "No ma'am, I never feel like I'll get lost."

The girl smiled brightly, and light melodious laughter bubbled from her for a second before she turned her blue green eyes toward Mrs. Harper. The girl's long dark curls swirled around her and she immediately moved to close the distance between them and was shaking her hand before Mrs. Harper had a chance to react. "It's nice to meet you, Mrs. Harper."

Mrs. Harper tried not to start in surprise. Her forehead furrowed deeper and she nodded towards Oliver who instantly dropped the corners of his mouth into a painful seriousness before heading toward the door.

"Thank you Mr. Rathers," the girl sang after him. He turned his head toward her and with a smile that only touched his dark eyes, nodded his head slightly before disappearing out the door, which he closed behind him.

"Amanda Shepherd," the girl gushed quickly turning toward Mrs. Harper again, "I am the one that called a few days ago to interview for the housekeeping position that starts in two weeks." She handed Mrs. Harper a piece of paper.

Mrs. Harper nodded slightly and tried to gain control of the interview again, "Yes, of course," she stated blandly, took the paper with one hand, and motioned with her other to the couch where Alexis had been sitting. "I'd written it down, but forgot to check your name before coming in since you arrived early," she added with a little scold in her voice.

The girl smiled almost apologetically, "I'm sorry, I live in a town that the GPS says is two hours away but I left thirty minutes earlier than I should have in case I hit bad traffic. I actually drove around for twenty minutes before I rang," she commented off-handedly and began gazing around as she set her small purse beside her before making herself comfortable.

Mrs. Harper's head was bent over the paper, but her eyes looked up to study the girl. She seemed rather responsible to leave early, but she was far to outgoing and pretty. The girl had long beautiful hair and a face that lit up a room. There was no way this could work. Mrs. Harper sat down heavily in her chair. She was getting tired of these interviews. "So Amanda, what made you apply for this job, since you live so far away?"

The girl had leaned back into the couch, her hands were atop each other in her lap and she had crossed her legs at the ankles. "I usually go by Mandy if that's alright," she replied pleasantly, ignoring the biting tone to Mrs. Harper's words, and turned her attention from the room and looked directly into her eyes, "And actually Mrs.

Jenson told my mother about the position," she continued quickly and leaned forward slightly with another smile, "My mother is a janitor too."

Mrs. Harper started slightly and nodded. She picked up the clipboard beside her chair and clipped the résumé to it as she tried to keep her composure. Getting a recommendation from Mrs. Jenson was no light thing. She'd been into home and office cleaning of sorts longer than anyone else she knew. And like herself, Mrs. Jenson didn't hand out praise or recommendations, for that matter, lightly. She'd have to speak with Mrs. Jenson personally.

Mrs. Harper focused on Mandy's résumé. She would probably not have to train her as much as some of the others. The girl had worked with her mother for several years in high school. Course, when did she start thinking that this girl should even work for her? But if Mrs. Jenson had told her about the job, perhaps it had nothing to do with Brandon. She did live two hours away after all, and not every girl in the world knew about him, no matter what the boy himself thought. But with this strange Facebook the kids were talking about, you never knew anymore. People could be connected over pretty long distances now.

Mrs. Harper looked over the rest of the résumé. It looked pretty good. And the girl had set some pretty high goals for herself. That was always a good sign. She allowed a forced smile to inch onto her lips as she looked up at Mandy. The girl grinned at her. The girl was either clueless to her hostility or she was good at pretending not to notice.

She began her list of questions, jotting down the notes as Mandy answered. She held eye-contact and was polite to a fault. Near the end of the interview Mrs. Harper asked the customary question out of politeness, "Do you have any questions for me?" It was more of a requirement than anything, because very few people had questions beyond hours, pay, holidays, and the like. But Mandy surprised her. Mrs. Harper leaned forward and tried her best to answer all of Mandy's questions. She tried not to smile to herself, because the girl really was taking it all very seriously. Once again a good sign, but not enough.

Mandy paused in her barrage of questions, so Mrs. Harper took the opportunity to ask her eliminating question. She leaned forward, her dark eyes glittering, but she kept her face very neutral.

"Do you know Brandon?" she asked once more paying close attention to the girl's expressions.

Mandy's forehead furrowed and she rubbed her nose absentmindedly. "Brandon who?" she asked and tilted her head slightly to one side.

"Brandon Taylor," she stated still watching the girl's face closely.

Mandy's eyes frowned and she slowly shook her head. "I know that the surname of the family that owns this place is Taylor, but I was not told anything else about them," she stated matter-of-factly, "Is that the owner's name?"

Mrs. Harper paused a moment looking at Mandy's face. She seemed genuinely curious. Her face during the whole interview had been lit up in pleasure, even when she was concentrating, and she had answered each question with frankness. This girl could be telling the truth, "No that is the son," she said and pretended to look down at her papers, but still peeked at the girl's face out of the corner of her eye.

Mandy's face lit up in a grin, "Oh how young is he?" she asked eagerly.

"Twenty-one," Mrs. Harper replied through clenched teeth. Then wonder of all wonders, Mandy's face fell and two small creases appeared between her brows.

"Oh, they don't have any young children?" she finally asked.

"No," Mrs. Harper replied looking up again at Mandy's face and feigning boredom, then rattled off in monotone, "Brandon is the youngest. Charles and Deborah are twenty-six, and twenty-four, and most of the time none of them stay here, except on vacations, or during the winter."

"Oh," Mandy's face lit up again, "So then I will always get to report to you," she smiled broadly.

Mrs. Harper began to chuckle despite herself. She couldn't help it. Mandy was infectious, "Not everyone thinks that's a good thing," she stated dryly.

Mandy's bubbly laughter filled the room, "But why not?" she gushed. Mrs. Harper suddenly knew that despite her reservations, she wanted this girl here. There was something catching about her happy outlook on life. Most people who were constantly chipper grated on her nerves, but she found that for some reason, this girl's joy was just infectious. "I'll make a few calls and then speak with you in a day or two," Mrs. Harper said ignoring the question and stood.

Mandy stood immediately and almost bounded over to shake hands again. "Thank you so much for this interview," she gushed. "And God bless you in your decision making." And with that, Oliver, as if on cue, opened the door, and Mandy turned to followed him out, her curls bobbing as she walked. She turned her face back slightly, smiled and with a tiny wave over her shoulder she was gone.

Mrs. Harper stood for a moment, and allowed a tiny smile to creep up both sides of her lips. "That must be what makes the difference," she thought. It would be good to have a Christian working here. Surely she didn't need to be concerned about Mandy. Then the creases in her forehead deepened. She was a Christian too, so why wasn't she always happy like that?

Mandy smiled to herself as she pushed her suitcase under the bed in the staff quarter's room that would be her home for the year. The permanent staff, had their own houses on the property or nearby, but the temporary staff had what looked more like very nice hotel rooms, with a bed and tiny sitting area and a bathroom they shared with the person next door. They would still need to use the kitchen in what she'd learned was called the villa. She'd have to tell her mother it wasn't a mansion after all, she thought, with a giggle.

She stood and looked around. Her room was small, but nice, done in shades of light blue and deep purple. She looked down at the bed, and then over at the closet where she hung her clothes. Her purse was sitting on a small table next to her bed. She'd put her phone into it after calling her mother to let her know she'd arrived safely. She glanced at her Bible that she had also placed on the table so she could use it every morning and evening for her devotions. She smiled, ran her slender fingers over the cover gently, and then sat gingerly on the bed. Everything was in its place.

Her lips curved into a tiny smile as she thought about the call to come work here. Mrs. Harper was an interesting lady. She had seemed so hostile at the interview, at least at first, but she had finally noticed the woman smiling.

It was nice to leave places and people better and happier than when you arrived. That poor woman must have a lot of stress, she had decided and was just glad that she had called and offered the job. "Help me to do the best job possible," she prayed aloud and her smile widened as she thought about the place she was at.

The villa was enormous, and the Taylor's also had a pool, spa, tennis court, a huge garage, and a rose garden on their property. Their property was located on what was called the Intracoastal Waterway, which she was already familiar with, for it stretched all the way up and down the east coast of Florida, like a huge canal, creating small strips of land like islands, or peninsulas along the coast.

Where the villa was located, there was only enough room for the property and highway A1A between the Intracoastal and the beach. The road was in front of the house on the mainland, and in the back there was a nice little trek out the gate and through some sea grape bushes down to the beach.

Mandy stood again as she contemplated her situation. She clicked her nail on her front tooth as she thought. The place was very beautiful, but rather excessive for only a vacation or winter home, she decided. They also had a yacht that was docked in the canal and she had been told that the area stretching from West Palm, through Ft. Lauderdale, down to Miami was a yachting capital, with all the rich homes, and the network of waterways.

She walked towards the sink, which was located in her room, and wondered absent-mindedly who she would have to share a bathroom with. She turned on the water and splashed some on her face. She didn't have to start work until tomorrow since it was still Sunday. It was nice to slowly get into things. She had also been told that she would only have to work one weekend a month, strictly in case one of the family members showed up unexpectedly, and she could go home all the others. And even the weekends that she worked she would have time off and be able to go to church. That had been her most important question to Mrs. Harper, she decided. So far this seemed like it would be a pretty good job.

She turned off the water and grabbed the hand towel to dry her face. Her weekly schedule was pretty good too. She would be working from seven until eleven, get an hour for lunch, and then work again from twelve to four. During her lunch break and after four, she could go where she pleased. She knew she would enjoy the beach and already planned to bring her notebook and do all the observing she could.

"So God, this is a pretty good place you brought me too," she smiled then looked around. "Are there other reasons you want me here besides the work?" she asked knowing that if there were, God would reveal it to her in time. She hung the towel back up and picked up her room key and slipped it into her pocket.

Mrs. Harper had said that supper was at five every evening, so Mandy decided she had a bit of time to explore. Mrs. Harper seemed strict about meals with the staff, especially supper and their six-thirty breakfast. For those two meals Mrs. Harper had stated, "If you are not there on time, you will have to eat somewhere else." Lunch was the only informal meal, it seemed, and it was fixed at eleven. Maybe she could grab something and eat on the beach during her break, she decided.

She walked the few steps through her room, and opened the door and stepped out. She collided with a skinny body, stepped back and hit something solid. She turned quickly as she heard something clatter onto the ground. "I am so sorry," she began and bent to help the girl that had been behind her. The girl was a cute blonde with hazel eyes and a round face who had been carrying a basket of laundry and a bag. The girl bent down with her to pick up the basket. Long skinny hands reached out to take it from them both.

"Me too," a deep voice stated and Mandy looked up to see that the first person she had run into was a tall lanky guy, with short brown hair and green eyes. "I didn't mean to run into you girls."

Mandy saw the girl start slightly but smiled shyly and let the guy take her basket. Mandy bent and picked up the girls' bag, "Can we help you?"

"Um, I guess so," the girl replied hesitantly and looked down at her feet for a second.

"I'm Mandy," she said to them both.

"And I'm Alexis, thank you," the girl said quietly.

"Donny," the guy stated. "Sorry about that, I guess I was walking out right when you were Mandy."

"And right as you walked between our doors," Mandy added to Alexis with a grin. Alexis smiled shyly again and pulled her key out of her pocket.

"Only two steps and I would have missed you both," she said softly with a tease in her voice.

Mandy laughed as Alexis opened the door right beside hers on the other side. "Oh, so you are my next door neighbor! I guess we share a bathroom."

The girl nodded, opened her door and stepped in then held it open as way of invitation. Mandy stepped in and placed the girl's bag onto her table.

"Are you girls working housekeeping?" Donny's deep voice asked as he walked inside.

"Yes," the two girls replied together, and Mandy laughed again.

"Are you just moving in too?" Mandy asked them both.

"I am," Donny replied and placed the basket on the floor near the girl's bed.

Alexis shook her head, "I've been here two weeks, but I visited my parents this weekend, and brought all my laundry," she added scrunching up half her face into a sheepish grin.

"So I guess you are my other next door neighbor," Mandy stated turning to Donny.

"Yup," his lips turned up into a lopsided smile.

"It's great to meet you both!" she stated and extended her hand. They both laughed and shook her hand in turn. Then Donny turned toward Alexis and began peppering her with questions about working at the villa. Mandy laughed at his exuberance and asked a few questions of her own.

Alexis asked the two to sit, which they did in the couple chairs by the table. She sat on her bed and answered their questions. She described some of the other jobs that housekeepers attended to besides just cleaning, but Mandy only listened with half an ear out of politeness because she had asked Mrs. Harper about all her duties during the interview. Alexis then started describing some of the other staff members, in her quiet unassuming way.

Mrs. Harper was the one directly in charge of them all, and under her was Mr. Rathers, the butler, "Who never smiles," Alexis said a bit in awe.

"Mr. Harper is the maintenance guy," she said, "And Reggie Zeismer is in charge of landscaping."

"Yeah, that's who I'll be working with," Donny grinned as he leaned back in the chair and let his long legs stretch out in front of him.

Donny was eager to hear more about him, but after a while Alexis told them more about the rest of the staff, which was what Mandy was most curious about. She was beginning to wonder if perhaps she should choose one to case study.

The gardener was Edwin Castle, Alexis told them, and he only tended the rose garden. The cook was Andréa Parada, so in all there were six permanent staff members. There were two other housekeepers, an assistant cook, and several security guards that rotated in and out.

"So there are over twelve staff members for this tiny house," Donny teased, and Mandy saw Alexis look down and smile, as a slight change in color stole over her face. She giggled at Donny's joke as she contemplated Alexis. She looked over and saw that Donny's green eyes were on her, and she let one side of her mouth lift into a smile.

She looked down at her watch and realized that it was ten minutes before supper and she still had not explored the house. "Wow, it's almost five," she commented, and stood up, "It was so nice to meet you both."

"Oh yeah!" Donny exclaimed as he stood, "Nice to meet you too," then he turned to Alexis, "See you both at dinner," he added and left.

Mandy smiled at Alexis and also left. She began meandering through the place which was absolutely huge. It had twenty-five rooms, and three stories. Mandy wandered into a hall and noticed several paintings on the wall. There were two rows of portraits, one row on either side of the wall. There were nine. Four on the right side, looked like older people, probably the grandparents, she decided. The two grandfathers' portraits had been placed together and they looked old and gray, and one seemed a bit more regal than the other. The grandmothers, however, looked very different from one another.

One looked older, but had dyed her hair brown, despite the fact that Mandy knew she should be graying. She had short hair, and a very old face which was plastered with make-up in an attempt to make her seem younger. The other one looked more serene. She looked plain, yet beautiful and she had let her hair grow white and long. "Hum," Mandy wondered, "I bet if I studied them more I could figure out which husband goes with which lady."

She smiled to herself then looked across the hall at the last five pictures of the family. Mrs. Taylor was wearing a silk dress that was dark blue to match her eyes. She had brown hair that looked like it had taken hours to put up. Her face was small and she had high cheekbones and a small pointed chin. She had a very pinched expression on her face even though she was smiling.

Mr. Taylor had short blonde hair and hazel eyes, and despite his good looks appeared years older than she knew he had to be. He had a strong square jaw, and a slightly curved up nose which gave him a very distinguished look. His expression reminded Mandy of a man who would bully anyone to get what he wanted and his smile looked like it had taken a lot of force to get there.

Mandy glanced at a picture of a young man who had short brown hair and hazel eyes. He looked almost thirty and she decided that it was probably the oldest son Charles. He had his father's jaw and rounded cheeks and his mother's small nose. He looked almost as hard as his father and knowing that psychological research states that the oldest children are usually fairly responsible she decided that he was probably the one taking over the family business. Course, she didn't even know what that was yet.

There was a girl in the next picture. "Deborah," Mandy said to herself, remembering the name Mrs. Harper had used in the interview. The girl looked like her mother in facial features, with her small nose, high cheekbones, and pointed chin. However she had blonde hair. It was cut up to her chin, and she was quite pretty. The smile that was pasted on her face didn't quite reach her eyes.

The last picture was of a very good looking young man with dark blue eyes and light blonde wavy hair. He had a strong jaw like his father, but the high cheekbones and the slightly rounder face from his mother gave him a softer look than the older men. Being a bust picture she could see that his shoulders were more muscled than the others, and he had a smile that lit up his face in a mischievous way, showing he probably got his way a lot.

"He's probably more spoiled than Jason," she snorted, then grinned to herself and glanced away as she thought of her own family. "You know God," she turned and gazed at each of the five family portraits with a sigh, "Somehow, I think I'm the richer one," she stated then turned and walked away.

Chapter Three

EDWIN CASTLE'S HAZEL GREEN eyes looked over at the girl pulling weeds near him in the rose garden. She paused and wiped the sweat from her forehead with the back of her hand, and smiled at him. He usually hated when the housekeeping ran out of things to do at the end of the week and one was sent to help him. However, this one he did not mind. He smiled back at her, and picked up his trowel.

Mandy bent over her patch again and began pulling at the tiny weeds that were sprouting. She was a cute little thing, and actually helpful. She seemed to be always cheerful, and didn't mind getting her hands dirty. She didn't mind his list of rules and actually seemed interested in what they were doing.

Edwin paused to survey the garden then pulled the new tiny rosebush gently from the pot. He loved his roses and was very particular with them, and she actually seemed to care too, and asked him questions. She was also happy which was considerably different than anyone else who had been sent out to him. That Brandy girl had even complained that she'd been hired to be a housekeeper and shouldn't have to "work in the hot sun like a slave." He snorted, and ran a large hand through his brown hair that had been peppered with gray over the last few years.

He peered at Mandy again as he gently put the rose bush in the hole he had dug then put his gloves back on before putting soil around the bush with his trowel. This was the third day she had been sent out to him, in the two weeks since she'd arrived, and he had decided to request her every time. She looked up at him then and asked another questions about his roses.

"That variety loves the sun more. Because of this tropical climate," he faltered, "they do better than some of the others."

"What about these?" she asked, as she turned to another bush and began pulling weeds from beneath it. He was not use to talking with the other workers so much but found it was a pleasant change. And she was asking about his roses. He loved to talk about them. He dropped his trowel and stood.

"They would like if it were a bit colder," he stated in his gravelly voice, "But I know what to do to make them keep on blooming nicely anyway."

"Really?' she asked and turned back to him her eyes sparkling with a strange pleasure that never seemed to leave her face, "What do you do?"

Edwin looked down and smiled slightly. He began to tell her in his halting way about the ways he coaxed his beloved roses to bloom no matter the climate. When he looked up at her face again he could see that she was concentrating on his words. He smiled again. He liked it when people cared about his roses.

After a slight pause in the conversation Mandy stated, "My older sister loves roses, but she doesn't know anything about them," then she smiled mischievously at him and said with a grin, "Maybe I should write all this down and tell her."

Edwin's lips curled up into a smile and he wrung his hands slightly, "I know some books that she could read to learn more about roses."

"But you know so much more," Mandy protested, and Edwin's eyes creased as he smiled with pleasure at her assurance.

"Maybe."

"So what made you start working with roses?" she asked.

Edwin paused and looked down at the rose bushes in front of him for a moment. He looked at a cream colored rose, and thought of skin that color. He frowned. "My wife," he said faintly, then plodded to get water for his new plant.

When he returned they worked in silence for a few moments before Mandy looked up at his again, concern in her eyes. "Where is she?" she asked quietly.

"She died many years ago," Edwin stated, with a catch in his voice, even though he had tried to state it in a matter-of-fact way.

"I'm so sorry," Mandy began her eyes full of sympathy.

Edwin waved it away with his large hand, "It's okay," he said, "It has been a long time and time heals right?" he grated unable to keep the cynicism out of his voice.

Mandy's eyes frowned. "Mostly," she corrected.

Edwin started at the correction and looked over at her. Did she perhaps understand? "Do you know this from experience?" he questioned.

She shook her head, and smiled compassionately, "I'm going into psychology," she stated, and Edwin felt like growling at the implication. "Besides it just makes sense that the pain of loss can never completely go away, or it would be like saying that you really didn't miss them after all, you know?"

Edwin stilled. She was right. He looked up again, and his large face softened. He contemplated her statement, and nodded. "That sounds about right."

It was strange that this girl seemed to understand things that he had never voiced, but always felt inside. Everyone else had told him that "time heals all wounds" and stuff. He had felt like saying, "So *you* lose someone!"

With her caring questions and quiet prompting Edwin found himself beginning to tell her about his wife. It was odd that he felt comfortable talking about her after staying silent so many years. It was especially strange, he decided, that he could tell this girl, when no other adult had ever listened. She seemed to care.

So he talked about his wife, the beautiful creature with the creamy skin, and dark eyes. They had met when they were so young. She had still been young when she died at the age of twenty-seven. They had never had any children, so he had been quite lonely during the last twenty years. It felt strange, but good, to tell someone about her, and this girl was a good listener.

"She loved roses more than anything," he stated, looking at a red rose and stroking it very gently with one finger. It reminded him of her lips. "And I already loved gardening," His voice stilled as the memories flooded back, "in fact that is how we met," he murmured haltingly.

Mandy asked gently, "Did you both work at a nursery or something?"

He nodded. "We were both eighteen."

He began to talk about their first days together, and the first years, until the cancer had been discovered. He hadn't talked to anyone in so long. Like a lanced boil, he found himself spilling his memories, and with them he felt his store of anger slowly beginning to fade. He had been hanging on to her memories so tightly, as time seemed to make them slip from his fingers like sand on the beach. He had been angrily holding onto all that he could remember, but now as he spoke the simple words, he realized that she could never slip away from him. Her memory would never leave and talking about them made her come alive in a way the memories never had before.

It had been years since he'd had a real conversation with anyone. He had been pushing people away for so long, from fear of loneliness. His fear of being without her had only cut everyone else off from becoming close. He suddenly realized he had missed companionship. How could this girl help him see all this, when all she had done was listen, and be interested in his life?

He stopped suddenly in the cascade of memories and looked over into Mandy's bright eyes. His mouth turned up into a slow, almost painful smile. "I can see why you are going into psychology," he stated solemnly.

Mandy laughter seeped into his soul, "Thank you, I think." Edwin smiled broadened. This girl was good for him. He told her what he had just discovered. "Usually listening is all that is needed," she said, "And sometimes a push in the right direction."

Edwin felt laughter bubbling up inside of him like a long dry stream after a rain. He looked at her and his large face twisted into a mischievous smile, "So how much do I owe you for this session?" he teased. Her laughter like a musical symphony danced around the garden and filled him with a sudden peace. There was something else about her, he decided. What was is that gave her such peace and joy?

Alexis' hazel eyes peered up at the portraits on the wall as she gently rubbed the small hall table. It was almost time for her lunch break, but he was *so* cute.

"Brandon would never go for a servant," Brandy's shrill voice spat out behind her. Alexis cringed and gripped her rag tighter.

"Yeah, but that won't stop you from going after him," she heard Connie's soft teasing and turned to see that the remark had been directed at Brandy. The two other housekeepers walked over and began to stare up at his portrait too. Alexis straightened.

Alexis tried to smile faintly at them both then edged past them as the two laughed about their joke. She felt relieved to see Mandy striding quickly towards her down the opposite hall. It had only been a month and a half, but already Alexis felt quite comfortable around Mandy. She didn't talk to the other two girls much, but she found herself confiding in Mandy.

Mandy was fun to be around and never made her feel inferior like the other two. She couldn't ever be as pretty as the others, but it wasn't fair for Connie and Brandy to make her feel like an insect. Mandy just treated her like a dear old friend. Maybe she should tell Mandy who she liked, but decided it could wait. She wasn't quite that comfortable yet.

"Hi," Mandy greeted her with a small wave and a bright smile.

Alexis felt her lips curl up of their own accord. Mandy could make the grouchiest bear smile. "Are they ogling that boy again?" she snorted in disgust motioning with her head towards the other two girls. Alexis laughed to herself at Mandy's description and nodded, her blonde stringy ponytail bounced around behind her. Then the two turned towards the closet where the supplies were kept.

Mandy just shook her head in disgust causing her gorgeous brown curls, with their hint of auburn that Alexis coveted so much to swish around her like a silk curtain. Alexis tried to ignore the twinge of envy and smiled at Mandy's assessment then scrunched up the corner of her mouth, "He is cute though," she protested lightly. "I've caught myself staring at his picture a time or two," she admitted hanging her head, "especially the one in his bedroom." Alexis set the rag in the laundry basket in the closet and closed the door behind her.

"Beauty is only skin deep," she stated, then added with a tease in her voice, "What sane person has a picture of themselves in their own bedroom? The vanity... don't catch Brandonitis," she pointed an accusing long slender finger at Alexis in play.

Alexis giggled, and walked with Mandy to the kitchen where they picked up the sandwiches that had been made for their lunches. She told Mandy a quick "see ya later," then headed for her room. She knew Mandy would be heading to the beach, but she didn't like going in the middle of the day like this.

Alexis opened her door with one hand and plopped down in a chair to eat her sandwich. After munching on her sandwich a few moments she looked down at her figure in the chair, made plumper by her slouching. She pursed her lips then set the other half of the sandwich on the table. She reached over, retrieved the brand new Kindle she'd gotten for her birthday, and turned it on.

She began reading, trying to ignore the sting in her heart that once more threatened to say, "You are not pretty enough." She wished she looked good enough in a bathing suit to go out during the day. However, her mom had warned her that she still needed to lose a few pounds before she could even pull off a one piece suit. She only went to the beach in the evening when it looked more natural to wear shorts. She sighed, and tried to concentrate on her book.

She loved the way this woman wrote, and pretty soon she was absorbed in the book. Her subconscious need for more food caused her to start nibbling again. Suddenly she stopped and scolded herself, realizing that now there was less than a ¼ of the sandwich left. She stood up from the chair, and headed over to the bed and plopped down.

Her mind, not yet back into the book wandered and she began to think about the other three housekeepers. They were all more outgoing than she was, but it didn't matter. Of the four of them, only Mandy could do a job equal to hers. And while they were here, that was all that mattered. She rubbed her smooth cheek absentmindedly and wished she actually believed it.

She thought again of the picture of Brandon on the wall and frowned at the things she had overheard Brandy telling Connie about the girl who'd been fired for messing around with him. Cammie had been her name, she recalled, and after his parents had found out, Mrs. Harper had to fire her.

"I wouldn't get caught," Brandy had boldly pronounced with a flip of her red curls.

Alexis wondered if Brandon did mess with as many women as the other girls claimed. The other three housekeepers might even be pretty enough to catch his attention, but Alexis knew that she would be practically invisible, and always had been. She sighed, and forced herself to think about her romance novel once more.

Aaron grabbed Amanda around the waist from behind. She shrieked and he chortled loudly. "I hate it when you do that," she slapped him on the arm with a grin.

He just smiled broadly and hugged her. He'd been gone the last time she had visited, and it was already August. She had decided to only come home once a month to save money, and he was glad that he was getting to see her this month.

Amanda stepped into the kitchen to get the rolls for dinner, her curls bouncing. Aaron ran a hand through his thick hair and leaned against the table as he retrieved the silverware he'd set down. "So you like it there Amanda?" he called. He was the only one who called her that.

She smiled, and nodded as she walked back into the dining room. "It's great! Us servants," she said emphasizing the word for Jason's benefit who had just walked in from the kitchen as well, "have the run of the house."

"While the master and mistress are away," Jason teased, his light brown eyes sparkling with mischief as he sat a large salad on the middle of the table.

"We work during the week in the house, and sometimes I get to work in the garden." Amanda stated with that perpetual smile that he loved. "I can't wait to tell Allie more about that."

"Oh, who cares about the boring garden?" Jason's eyes lit up with mischief.

Aaron's blue green eyes danced with laughter as he watched his younger siblings teasing each other. That was what he usually did. They were all so funny to watch and listen to, but he never did quite know what to say to join in, so he always stayed the audience while they bantered back and forth. He frowned momentarily as a memory flooded his brain without warning. He didn't seem to ever know what to say, even when everything had been at stake, he hadn't known what to say. He pushed the thought from his mind and ran a hand through his dark brown hair again and forced a smile. He walked slowly around the table, putting the forks in their place beside each plate, and blocked everything but his family.

He looked over at a grinning Amanda and thought that she looked more like his twin than Allie did. All three, Allie, Amanda, and he had dark hair like their father, but only he and Amanda had the blue green eyes like mom. The younger ones had light hair like their mother, though Jason's was light brown, and Jenna had blonde hair like they all had as babies. He grinned as Amanda walked back into the kitchen to grab more food to put on the table.

Not to mention if he had to choose his favorite sibling it would have to be Amanda anyway. Jason and Jenna were close, and Amanda was close to both he and Allie, though of course he was quieter. It didn't bother him at all though. He was more than happy to miss the silly girly things between the two older girls. He was content with his role in the family.

"But you already told us," Jason protested, as he grabbed a bowl of rice from the kitchen and brought it to the table.

"Aaron hasn't heard," Amanda stated, set down the bowl of mixed vegetables, and bopped Jason affectionately on the head, "Duh?" She giggled at his expression of consternation.

"Alexis is sweet," she stated and paused beside him, "I met her first, oh and Mrs. Harper..."

"Mrs. Harpy," Jason interrupted and moved quickly away from her.

"Oh, she is not," Amanda shook her head and went after Jason again, but he ran around the table. "She's a great boss," she explained breathily as she chased Jason around the table. "And her bosses, the mistress and master," she emphasized to Jason as she grabbed his arm and slapped him playfully, "Are away in like California or New York." She smiled broadly letting Jason go. "Cool huh?"

Aaron grinned at her, "Sounds great," he said, "except for the cleaning," he added with a disgusted raise of his lip and a frown in his eyes and stepped in the kitchen to help Jenna.

Amanda chuckled lightly, "See and you thought you weren't funny," she teased following him into the kitchen, "That was funny!"

Aaron just laughed with her. She'd always been good for his ego, even if he really didn't care about being funny or outgoing like the rest of his siblings. As long as he could keep certain memories at bay, he was happy that he was who and where he was in his life, and it appeared that Amanda was too. That was good.

"What about this Brandon guy you mentioned last time you were here?" Jenna asked, as she spooned the contents of a pot into a dish.

"Didn't you say he was in school in New York," their mother put in from beside her, as she stirred the contents of another pot vigorously.

"Yep," Amanda called back as she set several bottles of salad dressing on the table.

Aaron frowned as he took the bowl from Jenna. "Who is Brandon?"

Amanda shrugged as she walked back into the kitchen, "He's one of the sons that the other girls think is *so* cute," she emphasized dramatically and rolled her eyes. She shook her head in disgust, "It's rather pathetic," she added, "Some of them have never met him, and one girl, I hear, got fired for..."

"Amanda," Abigail said sharply and looked over at her with a frown.

"Sorry, no gossip," she said trying to look repentant, and then smiled slightly at the rest of them.

"He sounds intriguing," Jenna whispered, but Amanda just shook her head and ran a finger down her nose.

"He sounds like a brat," she corrected.

Aaron just smiled, happy to have the family home for dinner again. Even Allie and her husband would be there soon. It felt good to be a part of this family.

Chapter Four

"I'M SORRY," BRANDON SAID matter-of-factly and placed his hands on his muscled biceps.

Lilith just sobbed harder as she sat on the couch in her large penthouse apartment. Brandon ran a hand through his shaggy light blonde hair and pulled at the ends of them. The sides were just to his chin now, and he knew his father would be upset if he grew it any farther. He'd accuse him of being a hippie. He sighed. He hated this part of a relationship; the end.

"I don't want it to end like this," he tried, "I just feel like we both need to move on," he finished walking towards her slightly, his blue eyes frowning.

Lilith suddenly got angry, distorting her usually beautiful face into an angry red puffy mass, "No *you* need to move on," she seethed, "You are so selfish! Just leave!" she ended with a scream as she stood and threw a manicured nail toward the door.

Brandon didn't have to be asked twice. He stepped out and closed the door. He headed down the elevator and walked to his new bright blue Lamborghini and opened the door and got in. He listened to the purr of the motor as he turned it on. At least cars were easier to get rid of than women if he grew tired of them. Course most cars didn't start to grate on his nerves after a while. If he had a reputation for being a player, it wasn't entirely his fault.

He loved flirting, and making out, but he hated the rest of practically all of his relationships. The spark would fizzle out as the girl became a bore, a mooch, or a nag. Those were the typical ones, anyway. He wouldn't mind a serious relationship someday, he told himself, as he drove away from yet another brokenhearted girl, if only he could find one that… but then there probably wasn't a girl in his circles like that anyway, so why think about it. He gritted his teeth and jammed the car into gear.

He saw his relatives, and his friends' parents married and divorced. He saw his sister and her new husband fighting. Even his own parents fought a lot, and even though they were still married now, Charles had always said, "but for how long?" He narrowed his eyes and gunned it as he merged quickly into traffic.

His grandma Rathsmasen always said relationships were hard work, but worth it if you were willing to work for it. Maybe she was right. He sighed and repositioned the rearview mirror slightly. She had been the only one in his list of relatives that had her husband taken through death, and not divorce. He ran a hand absentmindedly up his jaw and into his hair. But then she was a Christian, and he figured she'd say that was the reason. He didn't care for that kind of conservativeness though.

But then again, why was he stressing out. Maybe he'd find a girl to settle down with or maybe he wouldn't. He was still young and he still enjoyed being a player, a very eligible, good-looking one to be exact. He looked at himself briefly in the rearview mirror, and smiled. He knew he had gotten the best features from both his parents. He stared into his cobalt colored eyes for a moment, then pulled his gaze down to his high cheekbones and straight nose. He glanced back at the road, and decided he'd just enjoy the looks and the benefits that came with it for a while.

He thought about how he'd planned to hang out with Lilith over their mid-term break, but now he'd have to think of something different. He had his own penthouse apartment in the city, but with his parents still so close by maybe he should go visit the mansion in California, or the villa in Florida, and get away from the storm he knew was coming.

His father had really liked Lilith, or at least the dollar signs he's seen while Brandon had dated her. Her father owned a very large business that he knew his father would have loved to "keep in the family." His lips moved up into a sneer. He hated that his father used him to get with possible rich relatives. He was used to it by now, but hated it all the same.

It was the end of September so there were still three weeks till his break, but he had best call ahead. So which one should he go to? He drummed his fingers on the steering wheel as he thought. The mansion was great for all the pretty Hollywood-want-to-be babes that flocked the beaches. His brows furrowed slightly. He didn't really need that kind of entertainment though. He drummed his fingers again. The villa was the best one for getting away. He could go yachting which always helped soothe his nerves. Navigating the maze of waterways was so much easier than trying to sort out his life at times. He frowned slightly with his eyes. He'd just go and enjoy himself and forget everything, he determined.

"Call the Villa," he said as he held down a button on his steering wheel. Yes, he'd go to the villa, forget his latest breakup, and relax.

"Come on, it's time for our lunch break," Mandy heard Alexis say behind her. She turned her head and smiled brightly.

"Be there in a bit," she said, then turned to finish polishing the porcelain she was working on.

When she had finished, she ran to the kitchen, grabbed her food, then ran to her room and ate quickly while she changed. She grabbed her towel and her notebook, and headed for the beach. She hiked the seven minutes past the private residences' beaches to the public beach where quite a few people were spread out on blankets and towels, here and there.

She glanced in the water, flipped to the right page, and jotted down an eleven. Only eleven swimming. There were seven people playing in the sand, but all of those were children. She flopped down after spreading her bright red towel out. She glanced around her and counted all the sunbathers. Twenty-nine. She shook her head. So far, her theory that beauty was more important than fun to most people, was holding true around here.

She looked along the beach and decided to observe a child today. It was less depressing. Yesterday she had been watching a sunbathing woman who'd been on her cell phone, and the conversation had been terribly annoying. Apparently the girl on the phone and whatever guy she had been talking to were cheating on her best friend together. Mandy was glad that she didn't know anything else. She ran a finger down her nose and looked around.

She watched a little fair haired boy bend down and pick up something and happily take it to a couple that was lying nearby on a large blanket. The mother said something, but never moved. The father sat up and examined it for a full minute with the child, who chattered happily. Mandy thought of her own parents. She was lucky to have had parents who cared about everything that she and her siblings liked.

The little boy took off towards the water again. Mandy wrote down a few things. He was probably four, and he looked happy and healthy for all accounts. He looked quite brown, evidence that he was a local and was taken to this beach a lot. His parents were also rather brown. Mandy wondered what they did for a living that allowed them to be out at this time of day.

Maybe the father was a business man and the mother stayed at home with the child. Maybe that was why she didn't seem interested, because she was with him all the time. They all seemed to have nice bathing suits on, but then again, she couldn't really tell the cheap suits from the expensive brands. She didn't really care much anyway. She jotted down a sentence and looked up again.

The boy was playing a game with the waves now. He would go towards the water, and then run back laughing as the waves came up onto the beach. Mandy beamed at his antics. He seemed to be having a grand time then he looked back up onto the beach and his countenance fell. Mandy's brows furrowed as she looked back to see what had caused the change.

The father had his cell phone to his ear and seemed to be in a heated debate with someone. He seemed distant and agitated. The boy came up with a new treasure, and this time the man didn't even glance at his son, and the mother sat up slightly to look for a second. The boy seemed melancholy. The father got off the phone and grabbed a few things, kissed the woman, who didn't even sit up. Then he kissed his son, and strode up the beach.

Mandy wondered if he had been called back to work, or had to do some project right then. The boy went back towards the water, and began to make little mounds of dirt that he let the waves carry away. He seemed to have lost his enthusiasm. Mandy glanced at her watch, suddenly wanting to leave too. It seemed like most of her observations had been depressing, and it hurt more to see a child wounded. She still had ten minutes before she usually took her quick swim, but perhaps she should take a longer swim today.

She closed up her notebook and ran a finger down her nose. People like these made jobs for people like her, but it still didn't feel good. She went into the water, smiling at the little boy on her way by, and swam for fifteen minutes before getting out and heading back. She jumped into the shower for two minutes, rinsing off the salt water, and then changed for work.

They all met together before going to work each morning and afternoon, so Mrs. Harper could go over the job schedule and any changes that had occurred. Mandy sat quickly beside Alexis and grinned at her. Then the girls all sat quietly as Mrs. Harper went over their normal chores.

When she was finished Mandy began to stand when Mrs. Harper said, "I have a quick announcement."

Everyone paused to look at her. Mandy sat back down. "Brandon will be here in two weeks..." a couple squeals from Brandy and Connie interrupted her for a moment. She frowned at the two, and then continued, "So we need to do an exceptionally good job cleaning his bedroom before he comes, and any other places he will be in. He will be coming in on Friday, and staying a week. Connie," she said, looking at the girl, "that will be your weekend to work, but I need someone else to volunteer to..."

"I will volunteer to stay and work," Brandy proclaimed quickly trying to look less excited than she obviously was.

"Fine," Mrs. Harper growled with a nod and Mandy could see her clenching her jaw. "You are all dismissed."

Mandy shook her head on the way out. Those girls were just as bad as the self-absorbed individuals she observed every day on the beach. She grabbed a rag from the cleaning supply closet as Mrs. Harper walked out of the room they had all met in and closed the door behind her. Now she at least seemed to have some substance to her, Mandy thought. Even Andréa the cook did. Perhaps it was just because they were older. Mandy frowned slightly with her eyes. But then again, there were people of all ages that acted like Brandy and Connie. Well, at least she wouldn't have to be here over the weekend to see those silly girls flirting with their employer's son.

The drive from the airport wasn't long and Brandon was glad. He liked to be the one driving, but all his cars were at the villa. Oliver had brought the limo to pick him up at the small airport that serviced the millionaires'

private jets, like theirs. He turned his phone off, leaned back, and tried to relax.

He knew he had been a bit earlier than expected, but he had also known that Oliver would be there waiting for him anyway. He often wondered if the man had psychic powers, but knew that in reality the man was just good at his job, which meant learning about the certain quirks that each of the family members possessed. Brandon ran a hand through his wavy hair and pulled at the ends slightly and looked out the window.

There were many nice homes along this stretch, but none nearly as nice as his families. His mouth turned up into a proud smirk. It took another five minutes before he saw the brick home by the road, meaning the villa was next. It could only partially be seen from the road, thanks to the thick vegetation the landscapers had put around at his mother's insistence. She hated nosy neighbors, she had said, but Brandon didn't really care one way or the other.

The drive was short, but meandering. The landscaping really was beautiful and lush. It had always reminded him of stepping onto a tropical island, secluded from the rest of the world, if he so wanted. And right now, that is what he wanted, though there would be certain distractions from a few of the staff members, he thought with a smile. There had been a redhead in particular last time that had encouraged his flirtation along with Cammie. What was her name? He shook his head to clear his thoughts. No matter.

He stepped out of the limo when Oliver opened his door and looked up at the terra cotta colored home that towered above him, and smiled again. He strode up the couple steps and opened the front door, leaving Oliver to worry with his luggage. He walked into the marble foyer and then glanced around. The den was directly in front of him, the balcony above that. A little sitting area was also visible above. He could see one of the housekeepers working there. She didn't look familiar, but not a bad looking blonde.

He strode up the stairs and smiled at her as he passed. She blushed furiously and he chuckled to himself and headed to his room. He saw the door was open, telling him that someone was still in there working. He stepped in and stilled as he looked at the profile of the beauty dusting his dresser. Her eyes seemed to be looking at his picture, and what beautiful eyes they were. Even at this distance he could see that they were a bright blue green. All of her was quite breathtaking actually. He ran his eyes down her perfectly slender body, and the dark brown mass of curls that hung down her back and wisped about her softly as she worked.

She had to be staring at his picture, he decided, but who didn't when they came into his room? He smirked to himself, and decided to joke around with her, since he'd caught her staring. "That's a bad picture of me," he stated with a smile playing at the corner of his lips.

She started slightly, but after the first second or so passed with no apparent response, he was about to say more when she turned her bright eyes on him. She looked up at him for a second, with hardly any emotion, just like he'd seen Oliver do when greeting someone of little importance. Her eyes ran over every inch of his face a moment then she turned back to his picture, as if studying it. He watched her with furrowed brows, not sure what to make of her.

His eyes wandered over her while she was turned from him. She had a perfect straight nose, full lips, and she was built like a model, tall and slender. She had dark hair, but he noticed a hint of auburn in the layers that swished around her from the quick turn.

She looked back at him again and frowned with her eyes at his perusal, and he dragged his eyes back to her face. “Yes,” she stated matter-of-factly, “it makes your nose look big.” His eyes widened. Then she turned and breezed past him. When she got to the door, she said over her shoulder, “Your room is clean now,” and then she was gone.

Brandon was stunned. No girl had ever reacted that way to him. Was she really that stoic about his good looks or was she just strange? She’d almost seemed disgusted, but that couldn’t be right. His nose was big in the picture? He’d never noticed that before! He walked over to examine his picture and frowned. Who was that girl?

Chapter Five

MANDY'S EXPRESSION AS SHE'D left Brandon's room was a puzzle. Mrs. Harper walked down the stairs and decided that Mandy had looked almost disgusted. Then she had glanced her way and the look had vanished, replaced by the bright smile. It seemed odd, because no one had ever met Brandon for the first time, and come away looking like that. Mrs. Harper was quite curious.

"Harper," she heard behind her, and turned to see Brandon striding down the stairs behind her.

"Yes?" she paused and looked up at his tall frame.

"There was a girl in my room when I got here. Who is she?" he asked in one breath.

"A housekeeper, a new temp," she barked, keeping her voice neutral, but eyeing him closely. "Is there a problem?" she added.

"Oh, no" Brandon shook his blonde head then he raised one brow, "What's her name?"

"Mandy," Mrs. Harper replied looking the boy over. Brandon had never bothered to ask her anything about the employees before. Had something happened or was he simply just curious? So why didn't he just ask Mandy?

"Where did she go?" he inquired, and she pointed in the direction Mandy had vanished in. She watched Brandon stride in the direction she had indicated momentarily wondered if she should worry. She thought of Mandy's expression and grinned to herself. Mandy was a level headed girl. She wouldn't do anything to compromise her job, she decided, and headed in the other direction.

Mandy shook her head again as she cleaned the crystal. The nerve of that guy! He'd assumed that she'd been staring at his picture because he was cute. She'd really been trying to analyze him and boy had she been right on all of her assumptions. That boy was conceited! "Course, that wasn't a very Christian way to respond, was it," she silently scolded herself as she prayed.

She absent-mindedly ran a finger down her nose then pushed a strand of hair back behind her, and paused. She should really have her hair up for this job. She put the crystal down, and split her hair into three sections, and began braiding.

"Need help?' she heard the same deep voice interrupt her thoughts for a second time.

"No thank you," she replied stiffly without turning around, and finished braiding her hair. She pulled the ponytail holder off her wrist, where she kept it, and put it on the end of her braid. Then she picked up the crystal candle holders again.

"So what's your name?' she heard him ask, this time from much closer and she glanced up to see his deep blue eyes looking into hers. Her heart skipped a beat and she quickly reminded herself that it was a proven fact that after looking into someone's eyes for three seconds you had the urge to either kiss or kill them. Course, she didn't feel like it was that extreme, but it was a good phrase.

"Mandy," she stated blandly and looked back to what she was doing.

"So you're new here right?" he asked and sat down in a chair next to her and right in her line of sight.

"Yep," she quipped, wishing he would leave. She set the candle holder back down and picked up the candle. Did he interrogate all new employees like this, or just the females? She set the candle back in its holder.

"When did you start?"

"June."

"How old are you?" he asked running a hand through his wavy hair. Mandy looked up at him momentarily then picked up a wooden music box sitting on the same table.

"Nineteen," she said, then added, "I am really supposed to be working. If you interrogate all new employees, perhaps you should do so during my break."

He began to chuckle, which was a rather pleasant sound, "And when will that be?" he asked, a maddening smile playing on his full lips.

"At eleven," she stated, and then looked back down at the music box as she began to polish it, hoping he's leave.

He sat still for a moment and Mandy could feel his eyes on her. It made her uncomfortable. She looked up, a questioning look on her face. He was looking down at her body.

"Sorry," he said unapologetically looking back up at her face. "Oh, and I don't interrogate all new staff," he added.

"Then I guess there is no reason for you to be here," Mandy retorted bluntly, wondering if she'd gone too far, and offended him, but also hoping he would leave.

"You're very interesting," he commented, the maddening smile still playing around the corners of his lips. He didn't seem to be offended in the least.

"Well can you possibly stop distracting me from my work?" she snapped.

"I'm distracting am I?" he teased an amused light in his blue eyes.

She refrained from snorting in disgust, and simply replied, "I work best alone."

"Fine," he mused, and finally stood. "I'll see you later," he crooned.

Brandy couldn't believe that Mandy had practically dismissed Brandon. Was she crazy? He was walking out the door now. She yanked the ponytail holder out of her short red curls, and sped up enough to bump into him.

"Oh, so sorry," she cooed up at him making her curls dance around her face ever so slightly. He had to remember her. They'd flirted so much the last time he'd been here. She was sure there had to be action soon now that Cammie was gone.

"It's okay," he said, not really looking down at her. He turned towards his room, and didn't even look back at her, but he did glance back into the room Mandy was in, a strange smile on his face, before he strode down the hall. Brandy gritted her teeth. Determination coursed through her and she sped up.

"Brandon?" she said sweetly, hurrying to catch up with him.

He paused and looked back at her finally. She came close and batted her eyelashes, which accentuated her brown eyes. She brushed her red hair down her neck as she looked into his eyes for a second before speaking. His lips pursed into an amused smirk and he looked down her body then up at her face. "Yes?" he asked, a bit more flirtatiously.

"If you need anything," she said, with emphasis, "Anything at all," she smiled suggestively, "just let me know."

He nodded with a grin then looked down a second, "Brittany right?"

"Brandy," she corrected. "Rhymes with handy," she teased.

"And Mandy," he stated softly and looked past her. "Thanks," he stated with his beautiful grin then turned away.

Brandy stood in shock. How could he not remember? And then to mention Mandy? So what if their names rhymed? Mandy had practically dissed him anyway.

Brandon stretched his shoulders back slightly as he entered his room. Why was Brandy not as interesting now that he had met Mandy? And despite the apparent hostility she had to be bluffing, because she'd almost asked him to meet her on her break. He snorted then grinned absentmindedly. He was sure of it.

He headed to his closet. Maybe she really was just worried about her job. And as he thought about it, he really didn't like when girls got fired on his account, like Cammie and Samantha, and what was that blonde girl's name? Oh well. That had been a year ago, or was it two now? No matter!

So, she had a break at eleven. He wondered where she'd meet him. Maybe he'd have to go find her. It was a good time to change into his shorts while he waited, he decided.

He contemplated her as he removed his designer pants, and polo shirt, and pulled on some Tommy Hilfiger shorts and a blue tank top. She was simply stunning. He wondered why she'd been so brusque even if she had only been trying to protect her job. Maybe she already had a boyfriend. He paused and frowned slightly. He didn't like that thought, but then that had never really been a problem for him either. Many girls would dump their boyfriends if there was even the slightest chance that Brandon Taylor would go out on a date with them.

He grinned to himself. He didn't need to worry about it. Most girls tried to get a job here because of him anyway, he knew. He slipped on some flip-flops and checked the clock. Fifteen minutes till. He headed out the door. Maybe he should grab a bite to eat first. He headed to the small dining room and on the way told Andréa to bring whatever she had prepared that day.

He flopped down and pulled the phone from his pocket while he waited. A moment later, Elise, the cook's assistant, who was another two-year temp came in and brought him something to eat. She was a stocky lady in her thirties. She came in quietly and left just as quietly. He didn't even smile at her, but did manage a quick "Thanks" before she left. He ate quickly, but it was still ten minutes after eleven when he left the dining room and went searching for Mandy.

He had searched for over five minutes when he decided to ask someone. The blonde girl he saw when he had first arrived was getting a soda from the refrigerator in the kitchen. "Where's Mandy?" he asked her, trying to sound nonchalant.

"Uh… on… on break," she stammered softly, looking down at her feet. She was biting her lower lip softly. She was probably nervous to be talking to him, poor thing.

"Where does she go on break?" he asked with a slight smile trying to put her at ease.

"To the beach," the girl faltered as she tried to look up at him.

He smiled lightly and she blushed again and looked down quickly. He thanked her, and grabbed some sunglasses as he headed down to the beach. He stopped and surveyed the sandy beach after he had headed through all the sea grape trees. He didn't see anyone, except his neighbor two doors down, sunbathing.

He was puzzled for a few moments, and then looked back at all the tracks from his pathway. They all headed back and forth to the right. Maybe she had friends that she met at the public beach every day, he decided, and headed off at a sprint. He was not going to be exercising over his break anyway, so this jog would be good for him.

When he was almost there he slowed down and searched for her with his eyes. He spotted her on a purple towel, probably sunbathing, he decided. She was on her stomach, her head propped up on her left fist. He noticed that she had a notebook under her right hand, and a pencil in it.

Maybe she was drawing or writing as well as sunbathing, he decided and walked within two feet of her before she looked up at him. She frowned slightly with her eyes, "I thought you said that you didn't interrogate your employees?" she said.

He chuckled, lowered the sunglasses to look down at her then plopped down in the sand beside her. "What cha' doing?"

She glanced over at him then closed her eyes for a second. She let out a sigh, opened her eyes and stated simply "Observing."

"Observing what?" he asked watching her lithe body move up and down slightly as she breathed.

"People"

"Why?"

Mandy looked into his eyes for a second searching them before she answered. "It's a hobby." Brandon wished she hadn't looked away so soon. Her bright blue green eyes were captivating and she appeared to have a smile playing at her full lips even though her brow was puckered in a frown.

He waited to see if she would go on. She didn't. He was used to people that loved to talk about themselves. He pursed his lips a moment. "What exactly do you do?" he finally asked jovially trying to draw her out of her somber mood.

"I choose someone and watch them. I jot down notes that I might someday use in my classes or something," she stated quickly and wrote something in her notebook.

"Classes?"

"I'm taking psychology," she admitted, and added nonchalantly as she stared down the beach towards a couple playing in the water, "I like to read people."

Brandon smiled quite impressed. Most people that he knew were going into psychology for the money. She honestly seemed interested in it, especially since she spent her break observing human behavior.

"See that couple," she stated, her eyes still studying them, "She is deeply in love with him, you can see it in the way she keeps looking at him. He, on the other hand," she continued, her voice growing harder, "he doesn't seem quite as interested and you will notice that he keeps staring at all the pretty girls that walk by. Now some couples are perfectly comfortable talking to each other about those they find attractive but he obviously doesn't. He's sneaky about it. If they get married and he still sneaks around, he'll probably cheat on her."

Brandon looked down at Mandy for a moment, surprised at her passionate remark then stared at the couple for a few minutes, trying to see all that Mandy had pointed out. All the glances she referred to were quick, too quick, to be noticed unless one was watching for them. The guy would look at other girls so briefly that Brandon didn't realize that he was checking out other women until the second time it happened. He was impressed that Mandy could catch all those things and knew what was going on. His eyes shifted back to her with renewed awareness.

"So can you observe anyone and know things about them?" he asked.

"For the most part," she replied still not looking up at him.

"Could you observe me?"

"Possibly," she stated her eyes still on the couple.

"So do you have to take a few minutes to get it, or does it only take a few seconds?" he asked scooting a bit closer, willing her with his eyes to look up at him again. He put his sunglasses on the top of his head.

She half chuckled, "Well, it depends," she began and looked out over the water, "I can usually learn a lot by observing a person's picture too."

Brandon let his eyes wander down the rest of her body since she was obviously not going to look at him. She looked way to appealing in her blue two piece bathing suit. Her curls were falling down beside her face on the left side over her fist, and spread out on her towel. With the sun beating down on them the auburn highlights in her hair stood out even more. "So what did you find out about me from my picture?" he teased realizing that was what she was trying to say she had been doing. He smirked to himself, knowing that it was just an excuse.

She went still from a moment, and finally dragged her bright eyes up to look him in the face. Brandon's breath caught momentarily. Her eyes were frowning at him though. "I don't think that this is such a good idea," she stated finally and Brandon realized he'd actually been holding his breath. He exhaled.

"What do you mean?" he inquired looking away momentarily. For some reason it was hard to breath looking into her eyes like that.

"I mean that I don't think that me telling you what I think of you is such a good idea," she implored looking back down at the couple quickly.

Brandon stilled. Was this a good thing or a bad thing? Surely it couldn't be bad. He cleared his throat then looked back at her. She had turned away again and Brandon found a sudden longing sweep over him to turn her face back towards him. He kept his hand still. She had to be playing with him. He grinned to himself. "Okay, so you won't tell me, because you can't handle the sexy," he asked provocatively while motioning toward his body.

Mandy looked at him again, one eyebrow raised. She shook her head and rolled her eyes. "In case you are wondering, you are taking up my lunch break," she declared, pulling herself up to a sitting position.

Brandon frowned. Maybe she was playing hard to get or something. His eyes followed her movement as she sat up wishing he could brush the hair from her shoulder, just to feel it. Her shoulder looked way to soft. "Okay, tell me what your first impression was when you saw my picture and I'll leave you alone," he lied knowing he never would.

"Really?" she turned back to him a smile beginning to light up her whole face.

Was this girl for real? He swallowed hard from the impact of her smile. It was the first one he had really seen and it made her all the more irresistible. "Yes, for now, but later you'll just have to go out with me when you have more time to talk," he teased and batted at her hair lightly. It was silky and clung to his fingers. He pulled his hand away when he saw her frown again.

She put her pencil away, and closed her notebook. She stood and shook out her towel. Brandon just watched every part of her body as she moved to pick up all her stuff. He could feel himself growing a little hot. She finally had all of her stuff together then turned towards him. "My first impression?" she said, "In one word?" She looked down at him for one moment contemplating. Would she really tell him, he wondered, and once more realized he was holding his breath.

She looked into his eyes for one moment and some strange emotion flickered in her eyes momentarily before they hardened. "Spoiled," she stated and turned. Brandon froze. Was she teasing? After walking three steps she flung over her shoulder, "And no I won't be going anywhere with you tonight!"

Brandon's eyes widened. Had she really just rejected dating him and called him spoiled? He watched the gentle sway of her hips as she walked back down the beach away from him. She was so beautiful. It had to be that she was already dating and she was trying to keep herself from temptation. That must be it, he decided. Well, he had to admire her determination. He eyed her back as it grew smaller with the distance.

Or maybe when she'd said, "tonight" she meant only *this* evening. Perhaps she was one of the girls going home during the weekend. He knew that some of them did, but why anyone would want to do that was beyond his understanding. He snorted. He should go find out, he decided, and pulled himself up.

Chapter Six

MANDY STRODE BACK TO the house and headed into her room, upset that he's come out. She'd not even been able to swim. She had noticed his subtle glances as he checked her out. It made her flush just thinking about it. She did not need advances from a guy like him. She couldn't believe he'd tried to ask her out already. She sighed and began changing. There was no need to shower today.

She took the last few minutes of her break to look through the last half of her notebook. She had done a lot of observing in the last four months since she'd arrived. She thought about Brandon momentarily. He was definitely cute, but he was so conceited, and he had different morals than she did. Mandy looked down as she thought of the tingles down her spine that happened every time he looked into her eyes. "Oh God, please help me," she breathed and closed her notebook. She had avoided his eyes as much as possible, but he was like a magnet. She sighed and headed to the staff meeting. "Does he even know You?" she prayed quietly on her way, determining not to think about him.

After the quick meeting she headed back to work. She worked quickly and thoroughly and tried to watch out for Brandon, but he found her once. “Stalking is still a crime,” she quipped, when he walked in.

He just laughed, “So you got a boyfriend or something?” he asked.

“No”

“You going home this weekend?”

“Yes”

He nodded twice seemingly lost in some thoughts of his own. Maybe he would leave now.

“You done with your inquisition so that I can get back to work?” she retorted looking over at him.

“Will you go out with me sometime when you get back?” he asked his eyes on hers. A tingle ran up her spine. She tried to swallow and dragged her eyes away.

She sighed. He was definitely very persistent. Maybe he didn’t take the hint easily. “Doubtful,” she replied, “Can I work without your questions now?”

He stood up. Maybe she’d finally gotten through. “I’ll see you later then,” he whispered from a foot away and she stiffened. Her breath caught and she fought to keep from looking up into his blue eyes. She could hear his brief sigh then he walked out the door.

Mandy sighed herself and dropped her shoulders, loosening the tension that had caused them to be rigid while he was hovering over her. She didn’t like being rude to people, even annoying, conceited ones like Brandon. Mandy thought about him for quite a while after he had departed. She tried hard to be objective. Maybe the environment he grew up in was the biggest problem. Would he still be so stuck on himself if he’d grown up say, in her family? Or would he be more like Jason? He was fairly amusing and seemed interested in what she thought. He'd even seemed impressed with the things she knew, but that wasn't enough to build a relationship on. She smiled to herself. "God what am I thinking? Please help me to see him the way You do."

He was also conceited, spoiled, and way to aware of himself. He had completely different morals and important things in her life were not to him and vice versa. Not to mention, if he didn't have a relationship with God, there was no way she was going to allow herself to be "unequally yoked." She sighed. He wasn't thinking of marriage anyway, she scolded herself, but refused to think too deeply about what a guy like Brandon was really after.

The twinkle in his blue eyes rose up in her mind and she couldn't help smiling slightly. She had to admit that she could understand why all the other girls thought he was irresistible. He certainly had a charming personality that drew people to him. Not to mention he was very good looking and when he looked at her.... Mandy stilled. She knew he did this a lot, and every girl he looked at probably felt the same. She gritted her teeth. She would not be sucked into his game. "Thank you for opening my eyes to this," she prayed, "Help me not to let my feelings get in the way of who I need to be when he is around."

Mandy picked up the supplies she was using, and headed out the door towards the supply room. "Help me to be a good example to him," she added as she put her supplies away and headed out to help Mr. Castle in the rose garden. When she got to the door she heard a motor start up. It was a very low rumble, one that she had not heard before, and she glanced in the drive as she made her way out to the rose garden.

A black Ferrari pulled from the garage and headed down the driveway. Mandy ran a finger down her nose and wondered absentmindedly where Brandon was going as she headed out to the garden. "Keep him safe," she breathed, then let God take her thoughts to the peace that the nature of the garden provided.

"So how is that sexy Lilith doing?" Trevor Duritzen asked. Brandon has been almost moping since he'd arrived almost an hour ago at the club where they were.

"I broke up with her," he stated pulling at the ends of his blonde hair.

"Sorry man," Trevor furrowed his brows then patted him twice on the back.

"No problem," Brandon said with a shrug. "Got tired of her wanting to control my life." He wrapped his long fingers around his glass.

Trevor nodded. He didn't actually expect Brandon to be with any girl for very long anyway. He sipped his Scotch. They were a lot alike in that respect. "Next one found yet?" he asked eying his friend.

"Yep," Brandon's lips rose upward on their own, as if pulled by a string, and he got a far-off look in his eyes. Then his eyes frowned slightly.

"Problems?" he asked, remembering the few times when they had come up with plans to get girls that were either taken, or otherwise unavailable. He frowned slightly. Strange how they'd come up with even more ways to get rid of some of the very ones they had schemed to be with, but he didn't want to think about that. He shrugged the thought away.

Brandon looked up at him, and his frown increased. "Yeah," he stated and looked down a second, staring at the alcoholic beverage in his glass. Then he looked back up at him, a fire burning in the back of his eyes. "Hey, maybe you can help me figure something out?"

Trevor laughed, "So what kind of girl problem do ya got this time?"

Brandon raised the right side of his lips and his eyes didn't focus on anything as he stared off to the left. "I'm rather confused by this one. She's totally available, but she acts like she is not interested."

"Playing hard to get?"

"I don't know," his brows furrowed, "Maybe, but she's really good at it if she is."

Trevor listened as Brandon explained how he'd met some housecleaner named Mandy. She sounded gorgeous, yet if she was only a housecleaner shouldn't she be all over this chance to better her station? Maybe that was it. "Maybe she is not used to those above her station giving her this much attention," he suggested when Brandon was done talking.

Brandon frowned, and Trevor looked around at the people drinking around them despite it being the middle of the day. His gaze swept behind him for a second as he checked out a couple of blondes. Maybe some of the girls in here could distract Brandon from his problem.

"So you think she's confused or something?" Brandon asked him.

"Sure," Trevor answered, watching the sway of a girl's hips as she walked their way, and not really thinking about Brandon's problem anymore. He let his gaze travel up the girl's body to her face. She had a sultry smile on her full red lips and Trevor started momentarily with recognition.

Now here was a girl that could take Brandon's mind off his problem. He grinned. "There are lots of fish in the sea," he mused, smiling in Emily's direction, and motioned for Brandon to look her way. "Now there's a girl that can help you forget Lilith *and* this other chick,"

Brandon turned to watch Emily approach them too, a slight smile forming on his lips.

Emily Jones brushed her long dyed blonde hair behind her and consciously swayed her hips even more. She had known that Brandon would have to notice her eventually, and he finally had. She liked being noticed first before enticing her latest prey. She smiled at Brandon as she sat down beside him. "How are you boys?" she asked sweetly. "Enjoying yourselves?"

"We are now," Trevor teased and she smiled up at him. He was cute too, but not as cute as Brandon, and not nearly as rich either. She turned back towards Brandon and leaned in closer to him.

"Yeah, we're doing pretty good," he commented, "And you?"

She smiled up at him, "Oh you know me! I'm always good," she commented with a suggestive smile and laid a hand on his heavily muscled arm.

"Still with Eddie?" he asked and drummed his fingers on the table.

Good! He was still interested. A twinkle lit her eyes. She was worried that he would give up too soon, and she liked being hard to get. "No," she said slowly. "It was mutual," she added. It was best for all involved that everyone believed that.

"I see," he stated and took another sip of his alcohol. It was half empty already. Good! She hoped he had been drinking a lot. She liked being in charge when a man had lost himself. Her lips turned up, and she stroked his hair for a moment.

They talked for a bit about her recent relationship and then he told her about his recent break-up. She smiled to herself. She already knew. She made it a point to know what Brandon and several other sexy, single, rich guys did and how their relationships were going. Social media was the perfect tool when used right.

She feigned sympathy and encouraged him to tell her about it. This one talked even more when he was drunk. His voice sure was deep and sexy, and even if she really didn't care what he was saying, she enjoyed listening to him talk.

Trevor finally left them and Emily snuggled up closer in the booth. She cajoled and soothed. He would be hers very soon, she knew. Maybe she would be the one to finally pin down this legend. Everyone in their circles knew his ways, and every eligible girl tried to be the one, but none of them could.

He needed something that no one else could figure out, and she was determined to try. She could be whatever he wanted her to be. All she had to do was figure out what that was, and with him drunk, she could learn more. He guarded himself to much when he was sober.

"And she said I have a big nose," his comment snapping her to attention.

"Who?" Emily asked, stroking her long hair with one hand and tried not to seem more interested than she was before. Who would ever tell him that? Especially if it were a girl?

Brandon looked at her and seemed confused a moment. "I need to go talk to her," his words slurred and suddenly he stood and swayed slightly.

"Why don't you stay a little longer," she cooed, grabbing his arm, "and tell me about her," she added.

Brandon looked down at her for a moment, and then looked around the room, alive with people dancing and talking. It was a very nice club, and only the wealthy and influential could get in.

"Stay a little longer, so the alcohol can wear off," she tried again and pulled on his arm. "You are too drunk to drive."

Brandon plopped down beside her for a moment and nodded. "Maybe I should order coffee," he slurred slightly.

"Tell me about her," Emily tried again, twisting a strand of hair in her fingers.

"She's pretty," Brandon garbled his blue eyes starring off into space.

Emily frowned. He couldn't still be talking about Lilith. Who was he talking about then? She yanked on her hair slightly as she brushed it behind her ear. She waited for him to go on, but after several minutes gave up that he would. "What did you say her name was again?"

Brandon eyes swung back to her. Then they seemed to be looking right through her. Suddenly he leaned forward and kissed her cheek, then stood up. "I've gotta talk to Trevor," he stated and was gone.

Emily was too stunned to react. Who was making Brandon act so oddly?

Brandon rubbed his eyes with one hand as he drove carefully home. Emily was gorgeous, there was no doubt, but for some reason all he could think about was Mandy. That was wrong, all wrong. He shook his head trying to focus. He'd only just met her. Course she'd probably be like all those other girls that intrigued him until he finally got a taste of them. He frowned. That was the way girls were for him. Amused him, then used him. None of them had ever really been interested in who he was, and if the truth be told, he had never really cared about them either.

He pulled into his driveway, and up to the garage. It was after four in the afternoon, and he wondered if Mandy was leaving to go home yet. There were several staff cars in the extra parking lot, but he didn't know which one was hers.

He pulled into the garage, closed it and headed inside. He went towards the kitchen knowing he really needed that coffee now. He'd feel this in the morning. He opened the door and walked right into a mass of dark brown curls that stepped forward immediately and turned towards him.

Brandon smiled at Mandy wishing he'd been able to drown himself in that beautiful mass of curls for a while. She smelled wonderful. "Sorry," he said with a bemused look.

"My fault," she commented walking around him. "I was not looking where I was going," she added, and went out the door.

Brandon noticed Andréa watching them from the other side of the counter, and then he turned and followed Mandy out the door. He sprinted to catch up. "You leaving now?" he asked.

"Yes," she replied hurrying out towards the back. "Andréa was sweet and packed me some food for the road," she declared.

"Hey," Brandon stated and grabbed her arm, "I just..." he stopped short as she turned to face him. She was so beautiful. She looked into his eyes with her blue green ones, and he was mesmerized. He couldn't remember what he was going to say.

She frowned and Brandon realized how close they were. "Please...." he breathed, not sure what he was going to say, but suddenly her nose wrinkled up and a frown appeared in her eyes. She took a step back.

She must not like the smell of alcohol, he thought. "Did you need something?" she asked her expression strangely neutral.

"I'll see you when you get back," he sighed with what he hoped was a convincing smile, but suddenly he felt weary and tired. Weary of chasing. Tired of running away and tired of drinking to forget it all.

He turned slightly but a hand reached up and stopped him. Her gentle soft touch on his face rooted him to the spot and he looked down into her bright eyes. Mandy smiled slightly with the corners of her mouth, but her eyes held his with their tender concern. "Maybe you should try going after something worthwhile for a change," she breathed softly, and then she turned. Brandon couldn't move. He couldn't breathe. Had she been reading his mind? Other hands had touched him, softer even, so why did she feel so different? What was it about her that captivated him so?

Chapter Seven

WHY DID HE HAVE to seem so vulnerable at times? Mandy sighed. It was easy not to care about that rich, spoiled brat when he was acting like one, or when he came home drunk, confirming all she'd decided about their differing morals. But it was hard not to sympathize when he seemed like a lost child, chasing after pretty toys that were eventually meaningless. God wanted her to help people like him which was why she was going into psychology. But she had to be careful. "Oh Lord, please help him see."

It was like he had suddenly realized what he was doing and yet he didn't really have a clue. She probably shouldn't have said that though. Knowing him and his conceited ways, he had probably thought she was hitting on him, when she'd really been referring to God. She sighed. That would be a good line though, she thought, and began to laugh to herself. "Help him to understand," she breathed through her laughter.

She passed another car on the road and glanced over. She liked to see what kinds of people drove what kinds of cars. It was a black Ford Taurus and inside four guys were all looking over at her. She smiled faintly and pulled ahead of them.

She was glad that she was going home this weekend. She missed her family, especially when she was confused like she was now. She knew enough to steer clear of Brandon, but when she began feeling… feeling like what? Feeling sorry for him? That had to be it, she decided. When she felt sorry for him, she somehow didn't want to be as far away from him. She groaned at her thoughts. "Lord help me too."

Mandy ran a finger down her nose as she thought. She knew thinking this way about Brandon was a bad idea. "Help me to be a good example for him, and not to get involved in the way he wants me to. Help me to cling to my morals, and cling to You," she continued praying out loud.

The black Taurus pulled around her. The guys were all smiling at her, and she grinned to herself. Her exit was coming up soon and these poor teenagers would have to find another pretty girl to amuse themselves with. It was interesting observing teenagers' behavior. It was even more extreme than human behavior in general. She was close to leaving her teenage years behind, but didn't recall being as rebellious or crazy as some of her friends. One had grown up a severely conservative Christian, which probably accounted for her swing in the other direction. She was glad for the way she had been raised, with firm love, and yet understanding.

She smiled as she wondered what Brandon had been like as a teenager. He was probably rebellious, she decided. She shook her head, deciding to stop thinking about him.

She was glad she was going home. She needed a good grounding in reality.

Justin leaned down a few inches to kiss his wife as he came in through the kitchen. She scrunched up her nose looking as cute as the first time he'd seen her do that over twenty-five years ago. "You smell," she teased.

He grinned knowing she loved the smell of wood, but not the sweat. He was too happy to care though, because his family was together for the weekend. He headed into the dining room and hugged his tall middle daughter who laughed and laughed as he tickled her with his whiskers. "Mom's right," she teased, "You smell!" She bat at his chest playfully.

He smiled broadly and pulled away, "Then I'll go get a shower while you women cook," he turned up the side of his mouth into a grin waiting for the retort that was sure to come.

Mandy snorted, "Men cook too," she replied.

"Not this one," he stated, ending their age old joke. He thanked God every day that he had a wonderful wife that didn't mind that despite it being a new century, didn't expect him to cook. He was terrible at it. He was also glad that at least one of his sons hadn't inherited his cooking skills. Jason was able to cook like his mother, and someday he'd make some lucky girl very happy. He smiled to himself as he walked through the hall.

He stopped to watch Robin grabbing her stuff from the living room coffee table and grinned. For a while it had been odd that his youngest son had a girl as his best friend, considering how different they were. But now he thought of Robin as part of the family. "Good evening Mr. Shepherd," Robin smiled and pushed a black strand of hair behind her ear.

"Hi," he responded, "helping Jason with his English homework again?" he asked.

Robin shook her head, "Chemistry this time," she stated as she tried to scoop up another book and ended up fumbling it then dropping it instead. Jason laughed at her clumsiness from the floor beside her then grabbed the book, a few notebooks, and loose paper for her.

"Be right back dad," he stated as he pushed himself off the floor beside the coffee table then headed out the door to carry Robin's books across the lawn to her house. Justin shook his head and laughed again. So strange those two, he thought. So different.

After his shower, Justin went into the living room and sat down with Aaron and talked about their business before Allie and her husband showed up. Soon the ladies called them to set the table for dinner.

"Where's Jenna?" he asked Abigail with a frown as they were headed to the table.

"Right here daddy," he heard her call from the doorway as she came inside and closed the front door. "Called mom and told her I'd be late," she commented and went to kiss him on the cheek before heading to her place at the dining room table.

Most people thought them old fashioned, and one of his customers teasingly referred to them as the Brady Bunch, but Justin didn't mind. He smiled as he propped his elbows on the table and extended his hands. He liked having a good Christian family.

Mandy and Aaron who were beside him took his hands. He'd never regretted his decision years ago when he'd broken up with his fiancé to date Abigail. He'd been blessed because of it. She was a wonderful wife and mother. He smiled at her, as she was clasping Jenna and Jason's hands down at the end of the table.

Once all the hands were clasped they bowed their heads and he said a quick prayer of thanks. "Amen," he said and heard it echoed around the table. He raised his head and noticed the look of concern in Mandy's eyes before she smiled up at him. His light brown eyes studied her as she laughed at something Jason was saying. He should talk to her after supper, he decided then grinned. She was her daddy's little girl, after all.

They started passing food around the table and he smiled to himself, and joined in the lively conversation that was going on around him. As soon as the meal was over, he sent the others to help clear the dishes with Abigail, and asked to speak with Mandy.

"Am I in trouble?" Mandy teased as she snuggled down beside him on the couch.

"That depends," he put a thick arm around her and eyed her with mock suspicion, "Have you been behaving yourself?"

Mandy's bubbly laughter filled the room, "I've only stolen two paintings, slept with five guys, and done pot thrice," she held up three slender fingers.

"Losing your edge are we?" he raised his brows.

Mandy shook her head in mock horror. "I need to steal more don't I?"

Justin laughed with his daughter, glad that they could joke about such things because she was such a good kid. "You seemed a bit distracted tonight," he commented the laughter lines around his eyes smoothing out a bit. "Anything wrong?"

Mandy grew still and looked at her nails then brought one up to click against her teeth. He frowned as her bright eyes clouded over and she looked up at him, "Daddy?"

"Um-huh?"

"I met Brandon and he's like I thought," she began and tightened the corner of her mouth.

"So what's the problem?" he asked.

"Well there's not one really..." she faltered then frowned. "I actually feel sorry for him," she added, looking up at him, "And I've been praying for him too."

"Too much sympathy?" he eyed her closely.

Mandy laughed, "It's not a problem really," she stated, "I was just thinking about it because today is when I met him."

"Oh," Justin nodded his dark head, and smiled down at his daughter.

"So tell me all about it," he heard Jenna gush as she rushed into the room and jumped onto the couch beside Mandy.

Justin frowned, "Were you being nosey?" he asked propping the arm that wasn't around Mandy on the arm of the couch and leaning his fist against his cheek to look over at Jenna.

Jenna looked a bit sheepish and ran a hand through her blonde locks and smiled apologetically. "I only heard her say that she met him only today and I figured that she meant Brandon?"

He pursed his lips trying not to smile and Jenna leaned closer to Mandy. "Not much to tell," his older one stated.

Jenna sighed dramatically. "You are so boring?" she teased.

Justin smiled again, as Jason came in next, a snooty expression on his face, "So how is the little minion doing?" he teased Mandy in a pathetic attempt at a British accent.

Mandy suddenly jumped up, "A lot better than you are doing little insect," she hooted as she chased Jason into the other room.

"Running around the house still?" he heard Allie teasing from the kitchen. "I thought you had finally matured!"

Justin heard a shout of protest from Jason.

"He started it," Mandy joked then came running out squealing, jumped onto the couch, and grabbed his arm, "Ahh, save me daddy," she shrieked.

"I'm Switzerland," he joked raising both hands. "I'm staying out of this." He looked over at his wife as she stood in the kitchen door, drying her hands on a towel and grinned. He was glad to have another member of his fun, crazy family back for the weekend.

"So tell them about meeting Brandon," Jenna teased Mandy as they sat with three of her sister's friends from college in Starbucks.

"Brandon?" Devon's brown eyes narrowed.

"So you met him?" Susan cooed. "I've seen his picture… so hot," she murmured.

"What's he like?" Evelyn asked with a grin.

Mandy smiled slightly and Jenna studied her carefully. "Like I thought he'd be," she answered. She looked over at Devon, "Brandon is the owner's spoiled son," she explained, "And yes," her eyes moved over her friends, "I met him, just yesterday."

Jenna smiled wistfully. Her sister's life seemed so much more interesting than hers. It would be so exciting to date a rich boy like that, but Mandy acted like she wasn't interested in the slightest. She frowned slightly. Something seemed strange though. Mandy was acting slightly odd. She studied her sister pondering when to ask her exactly what had happened.

"So what happened?" Susan asked, mirroring her thoughts.

Mandy looked over at Susan and smiled. "Nothing much," she teased, "I only insulted him and that was pretty much it."

Jenna's mouth dropped open. "You're kidding," she inquired her light brown eyes widening.

Devon laughed, "Not afraid of being fired?"

Mandy giggled and explained how Brandon had come in while she was analyzing his picture and what she'd said to him. Jenna smiled to herself. So maybe this was more interesting than if Mandy had encouraged his advances, she had to admit. Mandy told them about how he'd followed her and a little bit of their conversations.

"Oooh," Evelyn leaned back a delighted look on her narrow face, "Roasting the rich kid!"

Mandy infectious laugh burst out. "He followed me to the beach also. I guess rich spoiled brats don't get the hint easily."

Jenna watched her sister as she laughed and talked with her friends. She got off the topic of Brandon rather quickly and Jenna was left feeling like her sister was leaving something out. She frowned.

Shortly they all headed home and Jenna rode with her sister, and Evelyn. She pulled out the new cell phone she'd just purchased with the money she'd saved up for six months and began to play a silly game while Evelyn and Mandy talked. After they dropped Evelyn off at her house, Jenna put her phone down and turned to eye Mandy.

Mandy shifted her bright eyes from the road to her and gave her an inquisitive look. “What?”

“So what else happened with Brandon?” she inquired.

“You don't give up do you?” Mandy laughed and looked back at the road, “Why do you always think you are missing something exciting or romantic?”

Jenna frowned. Sure, she liked to turn things romantic in her head if she could, but she knew that wasn't what was going on here. She knew something else had happened. “Mandy, I know something else happened,” she stated. “I may be younger than you are, but I do know a thing or two, and I know you!”

Jenna had always felt closest to Mandy and always confided in her. Mandy had shared her secrets too, at times. Why wouldn't she now? Her brows furrowed and she stuck her bottom lip out.

Mandy looked over and laughed at her pout then her eyes grew serious. “Well, it's not very exciting,” Mandy replied and looked back at the road.

“So,” Jenna said, “If it's not that exciting then you should have no problem telling me,” she concluded with a shrug.

“What if I said I don't think he is a Christian?” she commented a crease between her brows.

Jenna shrugged, “It's not like you're marrying him,” she reasoned, “So what is it that actually happened?” she persisted.

Mandy laughed with an odd expression on her face, then her eyes once more grew concerned. Jenna waited for several minutes wondering if her sister would tell her or not. She frowned and looked out the window at the scenery. Just as she was about to question Mandy again, the quiet voice lifted over the drone of the car. "He came home drunk."

Jenna stilled. All of her allusions vanished. She sighed and met Mandy's eyes with remorse. Well, there went her great idea of Brandon being an exciting date!

Brandon paced in the yard as he waited. He wondered if she'd come back in the afternoon or evening. He wanted to wait where he could watch for her and stay away from Brandy and her little friend. He gritted his teeth. They were getting on his nerves.

He strode towards the rose garden and stopped to admire a few of them. He ambled toward the bench in the middle of the garden. It sat beneath a trellis that the climbing roses had crept up in a profusion of color. The bench faced the fountain with another plethora of roses growing around it. He stopped. Edwin Castle was standing beside the bench starring at the fountain.

He had the urge to turn and leave, but the man's hazel green eyes turned toward him and Brandon decided it would be rude. "Mr. Castle," he nodded toward the older man. Mr. Castle eyes lit up slightly and he nodded back. Brandon was surprised to see it. Mr. Castle hardly ever smiled.

Of course, Oliver didn't smile much either, but for an entirely different reason. Oliver had been trained in old-fashioned etiquette where a servant must not show emotion. Mr. Castle, however, was a different matter. It had been whispered in hushed tones for as long as the man had been working here that Mr. Castle was depressed. As a child he had hardly ever come out to this garden, because of his fear of the older man's brooding anger.

On the other hand, Oliver's serious expression intrigued him, perhaps because he'd always been so serene. Plus, Brandon had always been a favorite with the man. And Oliver had smiled on occasion, with the family, and especially with Brandon. He had never seen Mr. Castle smile for any reason.

"Did you need something sir?" Mr. Castle gravely voice broke into his thoughts and he turned to face the man. The man's eyes were still smiling, so Brandon flashed a quick smile in return.

"No, I was just admiring the roses," he stated and let his gaze drift over the plethora of color around him. Brandon felt the urge to talk with the man, but wasn't sure what to say. He shifted his weight from one foot to the other realizing he had never really been at a loss for words before. The awkward silence stretched. Finally he pointed to a rose nearby. "What's this rose called?" he asked as he looked at the peach and pink colored rose before them.

Mr. Castle chuckled, "Suddenly interested in roses are we?" he teased. Brandon eyes widened and he gazed at the man in astonishment. Since when did Mr. Castle have a sense of humor? "Those are Tiffany Roses." Mr. Castle stated, "Mandy's favorite actually," he added in his soft voice.

Brandon eyes widened again. "You know Mandy?" he began then tried hard to calm his face, "I mean, she comes out here of course," he tried to make it seem less like a question.

Mr. Castle chuckled again, "Yes, she helps me out here sometimes."

"Really?" Brandon mused softly mostly to himself, wondering if this was a chance to find out more about her.

"Yes," Mr. Castle tilted his head to one side and eyed him strangely, "She is a sweet girl," he added then looked back out over his roses. "I request that she always be the one sent out to help me."

"Why?" Brandon asked as casually as he could but he felt his heart begin to pound with excitement.

Mr. Castle slow smile began in his eyes and then spread over his whole face. Brandon furrowed his brows. Now this had never happened before he was sure! Mr. Castle's hazel green eyes suddenly turned and stared deeply into his as if contemplating him for a moment. Then he lowered his eyes and replied softly, "She cares."

Brandon's eyes frowned. "About roses?" he asked, letting his curiosity get the better of him.

"Yes, and about people," Mr. Castle answered and lowered himself onto the bench and gazed out at the fountain.

"She going to be a psychologist," Brandon stated nonchalantly, but kept an eye on the man.

"Yes," Mr. Castle smiled again, a strange light in his eyes, "she told me." He paused and looked up at him again, a peculiar peace in his expression. "She's a good listener." He added, nodding his head and pursing his lips slightly into an amused expression.

Brandon looked over at the man and suddenly felt as if he'd been kicked with the realization that Mandy was the reason Mr. Castle was smiling. Had someone finally cared enough to ask about his depression? Everyone had known that Mr. Castle's wife had died, but no one cared enough to talk to him about his pain. He looked down at his hands and frowned. He felt guilty that he'd known this man for over ten years and never been anything but scared of him.

His mind switched thoughts. He looked down again at the rose Mr. Castle had stated was Mandy' favorite. He smiled thinking of how the peach coloring would look great against her fair skin and pink cheeks. Maybe he should bring her a rose. He grinned to himself. "Do you have clippers?" he asked suddenly.

Mr. Castle mouth turned up slightly into an amused smile and he leaned forward to retrieve some clippers from his back pocket. He stood and handed them over. Brandon clipped off a half opened rose and handed the clippers back. He said his goodbyes and headed back towards the front of the villa. He walked towards the other side of the house where the staff parking was, behind their huge garage.

Brandon leaned against the edge of the garage, wondering how long he'd be there. As he waited, he thought about Mandy. He raked his fingers through his blonde hair and pulled subconsciously at the ends of them. He'd never given a girl a flower from his own garden before. He'd always bought expensive roses and flower arrangements for all the other girls he'd liked. He wondered if she would like it, and yet at the same time, it seemed the right thing to give her. She didn't strike him as someone that would be impressed by a huge flower arrangement.

His thoughts shifted and he folded his arms across his chest and drummed his left fingers on his right biceps. He looked down at the peach rose in his right hand and wondered if Trevor was right. Was it true that she was not accustomed to getting attention from someone like him? His brow furrowed. He doubted it. He wasn't sure if she were trying to save her job or really trying to reject him. Though the latter was highly doubtful, he smirked to himself.

Almost a half hour passed and he stood there wondering if it were worth the trouble, when she pulled into the drive in a little red Toyota Celica that looked about ten to fifteen years old. She was in a green sleeveless cotton shirt and dark jean shorts and when she stepped out of her car and her dark curls swished around her slender body, Brandon decided that it had definitely been worth the wait. His heart began pounding.

He pushed himself off the wall casually and sauntered over towards her. She was closing her car door with a hip, and balancing a bag in one hand and a purse and several books in the other. As he came closer, she shifted her bright eyes toward him. They were the same blue green color as glacial lakes. He swallowed hard when her eyes met his, but he couldn't read her expression. He hurried to her, and handed her the rose. She looked down at the items in her hand, and began shifting the books over when he took the bag from her.

She smiled slightly and reached out to take the rose he offered. He suddenly felt nervous, because her eyes were frowning. "A Tiffany Rose," she stated as she reached to grasp it. Their hands touched briefly and Brandon felt a strange jolt run through him. "Thank you," her voice sounded almost gravely. He looked down at her, but her expression hadn't changed. She looked up at him and one side of her mouth turned up into a tentative smile. "If you'll excuse me…" she muttered softly and reached out to take the bag back.

"Let me help," he stated, and walked past her towards the temporary staffs' quarters.

"That's not necessary," she countered, but hurried to catch up with his long strides.

"It's no problem," He slowed allowing her to catch up so he was walking beside her towards her room. She stopped at one of the doors and turned and held out her hand once more for the bag.

He tightened his grip, "There are still a few hours until dark," he began and watched her face, "After you put your stuff away, would you like to go out somewhere?"

She had been staring at her bag as he spoke, but she looked up briefly and shook her head.

He frowned. "Why not," he asked, "Do you already have plans?"

"No," she stated, "no plans, but I don't think going out with you is a good idea."

"Why not?" Brandon asked, wondering what excuse she could possibly make that he couldn't counter. If she brought up her job, he could say they'd be away from the house and besides she wasn't working currently. If she really was worried about him being in a class above hers, he knew just what kinds of things to say to dispel her fears. He smiled to himself as he watched strange emotions play on her face.

Mandy looked down at her feet then up into his eyes. There was a strange longing in them, and Brandon's heart lurched. He found himself pulled closer as if attached by a string. Then she looked away quickly and stated, "We have different morals." She grabbed her bag, opened her door and walked in before Brandon could even think.

Brandon was rooted to the spot. He felt like he was on an emotional roller coaster. What did she mean? Did she mean that his standards weren't up to hers? First he'd felt fire and now ice. He didn't know what to say. He'd never thought there was anything wrong with his habits. But then again, is that what she was really talking about? She had confused him again. What did she mean? He frowned at her closed door, deciding it would not go well if he pounded on it now demanding answers. If she was just playing games still, he knew what to do. There had been desire in her eyes, he was sure of it. He felt the heat washing over him again. He'd figure her out eventually. He turned to leave. She had to be like all the rest.

Chapter Eight

OLIVER'S DARK EYES GLITTERED with amusement as he looked down the stairs at Mandy working in the foyer. He smiled to himself. He'd been good at making a very formal impression on anyone that had walked through those doors into this house, except her. She'd been so sweet with an almost childlike boisterousness, and called him Mr. Rathers. Everyone else called him Oliver. It left him feeling amused and he couldn't help smiling at her. She was always so cheerful.

He placed a bony hand into the other behind him. In the months that followed he had learned what a great girl she really was. She always spoke to everyone with respect. A lot of younger adults and teenagers thought they knew it all and didn't listen. Mandy listened a lot. She listened to everyone actually.

He straightened slightly as he thought. He'd noticed the changes she'd made around here. Edwin's was the most noticeable. He'd always been kind to the man, but Edwin had never let anyone close. Perhaps he should have tried harder, but it was in the past now. He pursed his lips slightly. And now she'd come along and helped open him up and he seemed like a new man. He'd even noticed Edwin talking with Andréa on occasion and wondered what sparks were flying between them.

Oliver's dark eyes took in the girl as she worked below him polishing the hand railing on the steps in the foyer. Andréa had always been slightly hostile. She had come directly from South America several years ago and knew hardly any English. She had always felt like people looked down on her, Oliver reasoned. Mandy had somehow softened even her. His lips curled up.

Mrs. Harper loved the girl, he could tell, and she seemed to be more relaxed. Reggie and Mr. Harper weren't inside much, but the very atmosphere of the place seemed nicer somehow when she was around. She had an infectious smiled and people laughed more when she was with them. Sometimes when she was working he would hear her humming to herself.

Donny tramped through and gave her a goofy grin. She smiled brightly and said a quick, "hi," as he walked through. Connie also came through on her way to another room. Oliver's expression became neutral and his black eyes glittered. He turned from the far railing where he was standing and headed deeper into the hall, when he heard Brandon's voice.

Oliver paused and looked down into the foyer. The kid had stopped near Mandy his eyes on her.

"I'm doing okay," he heard Mandy say, as if in answer to his greeting.

"You were humming," Brandon stated, and Oliver smiled. So, he wasn't the only one to notice.

"Was it bothering you?" she asked but continued to watch her hands as she worked.

Brandon shook his head, and continued to watch her. Oliver noticed a certain gleam in the kid's eyes and a frown creased his own brows. She stopped and looked up at Brandon her lips pursed together tightly.

"Sorry," Brandon stated, and then grinned impishly, "I forgot this distracts you," he emphasized with a sight lift of his brows.

Mandy rolled her eyes and went back to work. Brandon turned with a smile and walked away, but not without a look over his shoulder at Mandy. There was a question in the kid's eyes and a strange longing.

Oliver understood that look. She was very intriguing. Oliver turned as well, but his thoughts stayed on Brandon. He'd always liked the kid the best. He had a lot of potential and talent, as well as a good sense of humor. He wasn't as serious and demanding as the rest of his family.

Then Oliver frowned again. Course that hadn't always been a good thing either. He didn't take dating seriously enough. And over time Oliver was no longer seen as a sort of father figure but became just the butler. Oliver sighed. He thought about Mandy again and paused. A smile lit his eyes. Maybe she could make a change in Brandon too.

Mandy pulled into the theatre parking lot, and got out of her car. She decided to go see a movie by herself tonight since Alexis was busy. She needed to get out of the house so Brandon couldn't try to ask her out again. He'd asked Sunday night, and despite her reasoning he'd asked again last night too. "Help me stay strong," she breathed.

She thought about the rose he'd given her and tried to keep from smiling. She'd put it in water and set it in the windowsill to get light. Every time she'd walked into her room she couldn't help but smell the sweet fragrance and then she'd look at the peach beauty and remember his face when he'd given it to her. He'd seemed unsure of himself and vulnerable. It was like catching a glimpse of the man behind the façade. "Help me to see him as You do," she prayed the same prayer for the millionth time.

She was more concerned about him than she cared to admit, but she was concerned for his spirituality more than anything. She kept trying to tell herself that she wasn't interested in him in any other ways, but her mind kept drifting and she'd grow warm thinking of the way he looked at her. Then she would scold herself and pray furiously about it.

She went up to the window, and bought a ticket, wishing Alexis had been able to come with her. She was only slightly fond of going to movies by herself. She had decided that she would see a romantic comedy this evening and think about what a good guy was like. She scrunched her nose. Course movies weren't all that realistic anyway, but no matter. She did like romance, she reasoned. Maybe not as much as her sister, but she did like it. She just wanted romance with the right guy.

She went into one of the smaller theatres and found a seat near the middle. The movie started shortly and Mandy became interested in the plot line. The girl was a good character and the guy was a terribly unrealistic romantic, but she liked him.

"So it's not that you don't like going out," she heard a deep voice whisper in her ear from behind her. Brandon! Her heart began to beat harder. Did he have to scare her?

"What are you doing here?" she pursed her lips and turned to look behind her. Her heart began pounding faster. His face was inches away and she could feel his breath on her.

His blue eyes bored into hers a moment before he answered, "I like movies too," he breathed.

Mandy broke the spell, and looked back at the screen. She crossed her arms and decided to ignore him. "You like romance?" his voice hissed in her ear and she felt herself shiver.

"Shhh," she hissed. "I'll miss something!"

She heard his low chuckle and she resisted the urge to think about the tingles that ran up her spine from the vibration. Persistent thing, she thought seething. If she were the kind she'd really think about getting a restraining order. She smiled at the thought. Actually that would probably be an irony for him. She shook her head, trying to clear her thoughts. She needed to concentrate on the movie.

Brandon left her alone for a moment and then she heard movement and turned to see his tall muscular form coming down her row. She looked at the screen again, determined to ignore him. He was a large guy and when he sat down beside her his arm pressed against hers. The heat burned into her and she moved her arm quickly.

She looked over at him with a frown but he was watching the screen, so she decided to enjoy the reprieve and looked back at the screen herself. He broke the silence moments later. "Do girls really do that?" Brandon asked as the main character and her best friend were thinking of a plot to get the guy together with her.

"Some do," she murmured never looking over. She didn't want him to think that she did though, so after a few seconds she leaned over slightly and added, "I don't."

"Never?" she heard him whisper in her ear causing her hair to bounce slightly from his breath. She could feel the sensation going down her spine. Her face was growing warm. His voice was deep and soothing, and she knew she had to stop reacting to it.

"Only twice," she answered trying to remain calm, but deciding it was best not to look at him. "In sixth grade and once in high school."

Brandon was watching her, she could feel it. Her heart beat faster, but she kept her eyes glued to the screen. Finally he looked away and was silent for a few moments. Mandy sighed to herself and sent a quick prayer that God would help her. She decided to try to enjoy the movie. The characters were quite silly though, in their terribly predictable plotting. All the girl had to do was honestly tell the guy how she felt and the two would be together. She giggled to herself. Course, the movie would only last twenty minutes if that were the case.

"What's so funny?" she heard Brandon's deep voice ask gently in her ear. Why did he have to do that? She pulled away slightly annoyed with the feelings he was causing.

"Nothing," she hissed back.

Brandon gave her a look that said, "Yeah right," but he didn't say anything.

In fact he was quiet for the rest of the movie, except for a few moments of laughter and other expressions of excitement or outrage as the movie called for it. As soon as the credits began rolling, however, he asked again, "So what was so funny?"

"The movie," Mandy replied, grabbing her purse and getting up. Brandon's muscular chest stood between her and the exit. She looked up into his eyes. They were full of laughter. She looked away.

"Come on tell me?" he pleaded. She frowned. He was obviously not going to move until she did. She grinned to herself and thought, "Maybe I should scream."

"Now what?" he asked, seeing the twinkle in her eyes.

"I was just thinking that maybe I should scream and say you were stalking me," she blurted out unable to resist the joke.

Brandon smirked, "Go ahead. That might be amusing." He crossed his arms accentuating his muscles, a solid wall between her and the exit. Oh why didn't this row have two ways out? She looked away from his chest and arms. They looked to nice.

Mandy groaned and asked through gritted teeth "Are you always this annoying or only when you don't get your way?"

Brandon chuckled. "Only when I'm provoked." He teased, and moved one hand to lift her chin up towards him. "So what was so funny?"

Mandy tried hard not to feel his hand and stared straight ahead. She groaned. That wasn't working either. She was staring at his tight chest. She crossed her arms over her own chest pulled her face away, and decided to admit defeat. Reluctantly, she looked back into his eyes and stated, "Honesty."

Brandon's eyes frowned. "And that's funny how?"

"If they'd been honest in the very beginning they'd have never needed the silly games they played," she replied and shrugged.

She looked up into Brandon's eyes and saw the he understood what she was saying. He still didn't budge. His eyes were playing games with her heart. She looked down as he said, "So how is that funny?"

She smiled slightly, "How long do you think the movie would have lasted if that were the case?" she replied looking over toward the theater's exit which was mostly clear of people now.

Brandon's slow grin was amusing to watch, and out of the corner of her eye she saw it. He began to laugh and then turned and stepped out of her way. Mandy hurried by him and quickly walked out the door and toward her car.

"What's the hurry?" she heard Brandon saying behind her. His strides were longer. She'd known that she couldn't get away from him, but she'd almost been hoping. She didn't need this... this annoying distraction.

"God help me," she whispered, before she turned around, "Stalking is illegal," she stated blandly.

"So you told me," he chuckled. "And some girls think it's romantic," the side of his mouth turned up into a mischievous smirk.

Mandy glared at him, then opened up her car and got in. She put the key in the ignition and turned. Best to keep on ignoring him. The car stayed silent. She turned the key again. Still nothing. Great!

"Oh Lord, not this," she prayed. This was exactly what she needed she thought sarcastically and clenched the steering wheel. Especially with the spoiled brat standing out there watching her. He just kept on smiling. She gritted her teeth and turned to look at him.

She rolled down her window, "You didn't touch my car, did you?" she accused looking into his face trying to read if there was any guilt there.

Brandon shook his head, "Thanks for the idea though," he teased.

Mandy rolled her eyes. He could be very exasperating. She tried the key again, this time praying the whole time the car would start, but it still made no response.

"Battery dead?" she heard Brandon ask, and felt like whipping out a sassy retort.

"Sounds like it," she replied instead as she prayed that she would stay calm.

"Can I help?" Brandon's maddening grin widened.

Mandy paused to cool off. Why was he being so infuriatingly nice? She had been cold and annoying to him, and he kept on being sweet and persistent. She wondered why he'd gone after other girls that had acted this way, girls that were *really* playing hard to get.

She sighed, knowing she had no choice but to accept his help, "Thank you," she said finally and tried to smile, realizing that God must have other plans.

Brandon grinned and ran towards his Ferrari. Mandy watched him and ran a finger down her nose. Maybe this was God's way of letting her witness to him, she thought. But why was he so exasperating and why did she let him affect her? She wondered if all those girls that played hard to get had suddenly changed when he "got" them. Was that why he'd lost interest? And why was she even thinking about it? She didn't care, she told herself, and again reminded herself she was only worried about his spirituality.

Brandon drove his car over and they hooked up her jumper cables between the two cars. He was quiet as he helped her and Mandy wondered if he was finally changing his mind about chasing after her. Good! That would definitely be for the best.

Mandy tried to start her car again after a few moments had passed. The car tried to start and then a loud crunching sound startled them both.

"Turn it off," she heard Brandon shouting as she found her instincts doing that very thing.

"What was that?" she asked her face a mass of confusion as Brandon came to her window, his blue eyes wide.

"I don't know, but I don't want to chance anything," he replied. "I don't know enough about cars to tell you much."

Mandy frowned a moment and looked down at her car. Then she looked back up at him and smiled slightly with her eyes, "Well thanks for helping anyway," she stated and then turned away to get her purse out of the seat.

"I guess this means that I'll have to drive you back," he stated matter-of-factly, a hint of a grin forming at the right corner of his lips.

Mandy sighed, and took the key out of the ignition and put it in her purse. It would be easier to get a ride with him than to get a taxi. She pursed her lips and looked up at him as she got out of the car. That maddening grin was lighting his whole face. She was tempted to accuse him of tampering with her car again, but refrained. She unhooked the jumper cables and put them back in her trunk.

"So if you want me to witness," she prayed silently, "help me to say the right things." Then she walked back around the car and smiled up at him hesitantly. "Thank you," she said again, and turned to lock her car door. Brandon was already walking to the Ferrari. When she turned she saw that he was standing there with the passenger side door open for her. She swallowed hard, and thanked him again as she got in, very careful not to touch him in any way. She looked back at her car as he got in beside her. She'd have to call a tow truck in the morning.

The two drove in silence for a while. Mandy was trying her best to figure how much this would set her back. She'd probably still have plenty for school, at least the first year, but she hated thinking that this would take any money away from her school funds.

Suddenly her thoughts froze. She didn't recognize this road. "Where are we going?" she asked turning narrowed eyes on him.

Brandon maddening grin returned. "I think your car wanted us to go out together, so that is what we're doing," he announced looking at the road.

Mandy groaned, and made a fist with her right hand. "That still doesn't tell me where we are going?"

Brandon's blue eyes suddenly turned and perused her khaki pants and maroon tank top. Mandy grew hot as his glance assessed her. Why did he have to do that? "A restaurant," he finally stated, "not extremely fancy this time," he began a half smile on his lips, "we're not dressed for it... this time." His emphasis was clear.

Her glare would have stopped most people in their tracks. "No restaurant," she barked, "and we are not going out," she seethed.

Brandon just laughed ignoring her discomfort, "And what can you do about it now?" he teased, "Just face it, this is fate!"

Mandy glared at him again, "Stalking me and forcing me to go to a restaurant after my misfortunes is not fate. I don't even believe in fate!" He threw back his head and laughed.

She didn't know what to do. She could go and not eat, but that would seem childish. She could get out when the car stopped and call a taxi, but that would waste even more money. She sighed. Maybe she should just resign herself to it this once and never allow herself in this position again. And once again maybe this was how she was supposed to witness. "Help me Lord!"

Brandon stopped at a restaurant, true to his word, and stepped out. Mandy sat for a moment contemplating wastefulness and childishness, when her car door opened. She looked out to see Brandon grinning from ear to ear his hand held out for her. His blue eyes were sparkling. Why did he have to look so irresistible like that?

He looked almost like a little boy who'd just received everything he wanted for Christmas. She could almost see the look he'd have had as a child and knew he probably always got his way. She sighed. She stepped out without taking his hand. She knew what touching him did to her. He closed her car door behind her and touched her elbow gently to lead her in. She felt the warmth creep up into her face and dropped her arm and furrowed her brows. She turned towards him. "This is not a date," she glared.

He just grinned again and dropped his hand. "Maybe, maybe not," his deep voice whispered in her ear, sending delightful shivers up her whole body. He strode past her and Mandy knew she needed to say another quick prayer before she went in with him. This witnessing was going to be harder than she thought!

Brandon stretched as he lay in bed. He enjoyed laying here thinking before he got up. He'd enjoyed last night immensely, even if Mandy had seemed annoyed.

He'd taken her to Antonio's and the food had been as good as always, despite it being one of the cheaper restaurants he frequented. She'd been upset about her car and upset that she'd been forced to rely on him. He had doubted that she'd stay upset all evening. He'd seen to many "damsel-in-distress" acts, but strangely she had not seemed to relax the whole time.

She was a puzzle to him. She'd said that their morals conflicted that first night and again when he'd asked her again the next night. So he'd decided to just wait her out. She'd change eventually wouldn't she? All the others had. This had to be a game. He'd seen the way her body reacted when they'd been so close, looking into each other's eyes. He snorted. Hah! And she said that she didn't play games.

He sat up suddenly. She'd talked of being honest while they were in the theater, but he didn't quite believe her. She had to be playing hard to get. Maybe she was even trying to change him. Everyone wanted something from him, but everyone did want him. This girl was no different, he was sure. He frowned and picked up his phone from the table beside his bed and unplugged it.

He twisted his torso slightly and put his feet on the floor. They had not talked much in the restaurant. She'd been polite, but not open when he'd asked her questions, almost as if she had resigned herself to the fact, but didn't like it. He was sure that couldn't be it though. He'd even begun to think she'd messed up her car on purpose, but it was odd she'd asked if he'd done something. His eyes glittered. Maybe that was part of her plan to throw him off. But then, how would she have known he was going to follow her? He opened his phone up and checked his social media pages absent-mindedly as he thought of her.

Finally he stood up and got dressed. He headed to his little desk in the corner and plopped down in the chair and picked his phone up once more. He could always help her along with the damsel-in-distress act by this bit of kindness. He frowned as he dialed the mechanic. They had discussed where she should take her car last night. He had this strange impression that maybe she wouldn't like if he paid for it all. The line picked up and he began talking. Perhaps he should just pay for part of it. He smiled to himself as he thought about telling her. Surely she would be happy. Then he thought about their meal together. He drummed his fingers on the desk.

She had been upset that he had wanted to pay for their food last night. She kept insisting that it wasn't a date and she could pay for her own food. He frowned. He got his way of course, but she had seemed genuinely upset. Maybe he shouldn't tell her about this. He finished his discussion with the mechanic and stood, not realizing that this would be the first time that he hadn't used his financial gifts as a way of showing off.

Brandon thought again about Mandy's car as he stuffed his phone in his pocket and headed out the door and down the stairs. He was sure that she was still playing with him though. He smirked to himself. He'd go find her and see if she was ready to stop playing her little game, and go out with him for real tonight.

He glanced at the hall clock. It was after ten. He went to eat, and then decided he'd wait somewhere for her until she went on break. He headed to the path's entrance that led to the beach, deciding to catch her there. He raked his hand through his hair and whistled under his breath as he spotted her. She always sent delicious emotions coursing through his whole body.

Brandon smiled to himself. She just got prettier and prettier every time he saw her. She was wearing a red two-piece bathing suit, with a navy towel draped over her shoulder. She froze when she saw him and frowned with her eyes.

"Aren't you done stalking me yet?" she muttered sullenly, then walked around him towards the beach.

"Not until you're done playing hard to get and go out with me," he teased and fluffed her hair gently as he turned to walk behind her.

She stopped suddenly and he found himself colliding with her back, his face in the top of her mass of curls. He breathed her in deeply before she moved forward suddenly and turned on him. "I already told you…" she stammered, unable to look at his face.

"Yeah, yeah," he said, holding up his hands, "Different morals right?" his sarcastic tone definitely said otherwise and she looked up at him with a scowl. "So let's be open and honest, like you were saying yesterday and get down to the real reasons."

Her sigh was palpable. "Okay, you want me to be honest?" she asked, and looked down at her feet. She seemed to be muttering something under her breath and then her face grew suddenly serene. Brandon felt his eyes softening in response. He couldn't be angry with her. Not really. He moved a half step closer.

"Will I lose my job?" she asked suddenly and her eyes bored into his.

Brandon's teeth clenched and he looked away with a sigh. "No," he ground out, and bit back a snort at how predictable all this was. She'd better be worth this hassle.

"Fine," she spat out, and began quickly, "I will not go out with you because you are a spoiled brat who thinks he can have anything he wants." Brandon froze. "Well, you can't! Plus, you don't believe in giving yourself to only one person and I do. And you were drunk," her voice steadily growing louder with emotion. Brandon looked up into her eyes that seemed to shoot out fire. “I could never, ever go out with someone who drank like that.”

Brandon felt emotions swirling around him. He felt like he was at a firing squad, or like he’d just been punched. She spat out her words quickly and then she was gone, stalking up the beach. His mouth opened and then shut. No one had ever treated him like that. No one had ever made him feel like he was the lesser person. His face grew hard and his eyes glittered. How dare she! He could get any girl he wanted and he didn’t want her anymore! She was more trouble than she was worth.

He stalked back up the trail and into his house. She really had dissed him that first night. He’d begun to think it had all been a mistake, but no, she really had stated this time loud and clear that he was not up to her standards. Well fine! She wasn’t up to his anyway. She was just a stupid housekeeper after all!

Chapter Nine

JOHN MOBY GRINNED. IT was good to see Brandon back to his old self. Trevor had called him on Monday asking if he'd heard from Brandon. That had been news to him. He'd not even known Brandon was in town over break.

Brandon was here drinking and laughing like they had all done in times past. It was a good sight, especially after the moping he'd done the last few days.

He'd gotten the beginning of the story from Trevor, but Brandon's drunken depression had filled in the rest, the rejection. He couldn't believe Brandon had been put down by some self-righteous girl. Brandon had never been told "no" before. Course his list of rejections was low too, but it *had* happened. The first time was always the hardest though.

What he couldn't understand though was how a housekeeper was his first. They were usually all over Brandon. John had only been rejected by girls above him, never below him. How could someone below their social class reject Brandon, the best of them all?

She sounded pretty. Maybe that was it. She thought herself better looking. But no, Brandon was the best looking guy any of them had ever seen. Maybe she was just a self-righteous conservative girl that needed to loosen up.

Brandon laughed and whispered something in Sonya's ear. Emily and Desiree were on the other side. John could tell that Emily didn't like being one of many girls. She'd probably leave soon. Maybe he should try for her. She might not go for him though. There was only one way to find out.

He stood up, and slid in next to her running a hand over his short spiky hair. She smiled at him. That was a good sign. Brandon looked over at him and grinned. That was also a good sign. "Want to dance?" he asked.

"Sure," she cooed. Maybe she'd allow him to be a good second, if she couldn't have Brandon. He didn't mind. He'd done this a lot. He enjoyed the girls he'd gotten that way, because he could make them feel better again. It was odd the power they allowed Brandon to have over their feelings, and he could take that over. He'd never been rejected by one of the girls he'd gotten this way.

"Oh you brute," Desiree teased as she playfully slapped Brandon away. She loved all this attention. Usually some of the other girls got it, but now it was her turn, and she planned to make the best of it.

It was Friday and tomorrow Brandon would be heading back, so she didn't have the time to worry about taking things slow, and being subtle. She got guys to stay longer that way, but this was Brandon. She'd throw all caution to the wind to get this one.

Brandon kissed her neck and she touched his face softly. He looked up at her and suddenly stilled. His eyes were unfocused but strange emotions were playing there. He tried to smile and said, "I need to head home." He looked upset and she frowned.

"Aw, It's early yet," she protested and batted her eyes up at him. She had to keep him here a little longer.

Brandon tried to give her an enticing smile, but it fell short. He frowned. He seemed distracted. He'd been that way the last couple days and Wednesday when he'd taken friends yachting, he hadn't invited any females. Maybe he was still sore from his break-up with Lilith. "I really need to go," he said.

"Oh," she pouted, then put her hand up and softly touched his face, "I can help you forget," she crooned.

Brandon stilled and she knew her offer was sinking in. She put the other hand behind his head and gripped the back of his blonde hair in her fingers. She ran her fingers through it gently.

A muscle in his jaw jerked. "What if I don't want to forget," he suddenly declared, and stood up.

She couldn't let him leave so soon. She grabbed his arm and began stroking it softly. "Please don't leave," she implored. "You have plenty of time to go home and do your remembering later. One quick distraction won't hurt anything."

Brandon clenched and unclenched his jaw. "Actually it might," he replied and walked away.

Mandy sighed as she slipped into the deserted kitchen. She grabbed a glass and filled it with water from the tap and sat on a barstool to sip it. It was getting rather late and she needed to be in bed.

She wrapped her slender fingers around her glass. She was glad her car was fixed and the bill had been rather inexpensive. She momentarily wondered if Brandon had anything to do with it, and then put it from her mind. She had no way of knowing for sure.

She lifted one hand and stroked her nose once and sighed. She felt bad about her words to him three days ago, but he had left her alone. Course she wanted to help people, not hurt them, but the brat just wouldn't take a hint. He even accused her of playing games with him. Of all the nerve!

She stilled. The boy was aggravating, but she still wished she could go back and say it nicely. As a psychologist she would meet a lot of aggravating people that needed to be set straight and she needed to learn to be objective and kind. Course with Brandon it was a personal issue. He wasn't asking for her help. He was asking her out and she didn't know what else she could have done to make him understand the facts.

She gripped her glass tighter. Worst of all was that she had totally forgotten all about her plans to witness. When she'd told him about her reasons, she hadn't told him the most important one of all; he didn't believe. At least he didn't act like he did. She frowned. She should have found out at least and gone from there. Oh why had she let her temper get the better of her. Not many could anger her as he had.

Suddenly she felt uncomfortable. Someone was watching her. She turned around quickly and saw Brandon leaning on the door jam. He looked defeated. She half smiled, and then turned back to drink more water, her mouth suddenly dry.

Brandon trudged past her and she could see that he was starting the coffee machine. She refused to watch him and looked back at her glass of water. She took another sip of water. She didn't like being here with him, but she didn't want to be a coward and run either. She sat quietly.

Why did Brandon have to be so rude at times and then helpless at others? She'd seen his face after she'd spoken her words and felt sorry until his face had grown angry instead. He needed help, of that she was sure. And here he was coming home drunk again, proving her theory. How could she help him, yet keep her distance? Several moments passed and she found herself praying.

She felt more than saw when Brandon sat down beside her. She looked over. He was gripping a cup of coffee. He quickly looked at her with an odd unreadable expression. Was he upset, hurt, or simply going to ignore her? They sat for several moments only the sound of their sipping disturbing the quiet.

"Drinking water?" he asked in an almost monotone voice, breaking the silence.

"Yes," she answered, "Drinking coffee?" she asked in the same tone.

He looked over at her, and she saw a slow smile creep onto his lips, "Yes."

Mandy's eyes softened and she half smiled back. "I'm sorry that what I said to you the other day came out so rudely," she said before she lost the nerve.

Brandon stilled. "So are you changing your mind?"

"No," she answered quickly, "but I could have said it nicer, and I'm sorry." She looked down at her glass.

Brandon nodded and sipped on his coffee. Then she heard a slight chuckle and turned to see a twinkle in his eye. "I like being a spoiled brat." He was trying to grin, but it was only half-hearted.

She turned up one corner of her mouth, "I guess some people like it," she teased back.

"Why not you?" he asked huskily.

Mandy looked into his eyes. They were deep pools of questions and emotion. She pursed her lips, realizing that he didn't know where all the hurting came from. Maybe now was her chance to say what needed to be said politely. She breathed a slight prayer for help in her mind and began. "My brother is a brat," she started, and smiled up at him. His eyes frowned. She added, "But he still follows the rules."

Brandon looked skeptical. "The rules?"

Mandy hesitated, knowing that she needed to word it just right, so he would understand it, "There is a rule to life that you never take more than you give," she stated, running her finger along the top of her glass. "My brother may get a lot because he's the youngest and he's spoiled too, but he never uses people." She knew that just stating she was a Christian would not get through to him, but perhaps the logic of a Christian lifestyle would make sense.

Mandy looked over to see if he was offended. His frown had deepened. "People use me," he retorted.

"But does that make it right?" she asked softly hoping he wouldn't get offended.

Brandon took another sip of coffee and looked down at the table. She let her words sink in a few moments and then went on. "The same thing applies for being with so many women," she remarked, "People get hurt and eventually it's hard to trust anyone." Brandon turned startled eyes on her and she knew he understood completely. "Do you trust anyone?" she asked softly.

He looked into her eyes, the depth of his thoughts revealed in his dark blue ones, "I know no one trusts me," was all he said.

She nodded. "Trust has to go both ways," she replied, and again let silence hang for a few minutes. "The last thing I mentioned was drinking," she said.

Brandon snorted, "It's fun," he commented and drank another sip of coffee.

"Is having a hangover fun?" she asked, taking a sip of water. "Is losing your control fun? I guess I'm not a fan of destroying my liver and waking up in the morning hurting so bad, wishing I could remember what I'd done the night before." She set her cup down a little too hard.

"I don't get that drunk," he protested.

"Yet," Mandy replied, "Drinking, like all addictions start out small and simple."

Brandon sipped on his coffee and didn't answer. She bit her lip momentarily, hoping she hadn't upset him to much but wanting him to understand her point. "I'm not trying to be mean," she added. "I only want you to understand why I don't drink and why I can't get involved with someone who does."

He turned hooded eyes in her direction. "So where did that rule come from?" he asked, "The one about not taking more than you give?"

Mandy stilled. Here was the chance she had been waiting for. She sent up a silent prayer for her words to come out right, then said softly, "It's a Biblical principle actually," then added, "It's the rule of love. God is love which is why He follows the rule and wants us to as well because He knows it will make us happy."

He looked away and his jaw tightened slightly, but said no more about it. After several moments went by he looked over at her and nodded. "Well, you were right about honesty being quick."

She nodded once and stood up, satisfied that he understood, at least part of it. She was wishing she could say more about God, but knew it wasn't the time. He had to realize he was hungry first.

She put her glass in the sink and walked back to Brandon. He looked up at her with an emotion she had never seen before in his eyes. Her eyes held his and she put the palm of her left hand on his cheek and stroked it softly, pitying him. "I'm sorry that I didn't mention that honesty can also be painful," she murmured and dropped her hand.

She sent up a quiet prayer of thanks to God for being able to see him as a hurting child and nothing else at this moment. She turned and walked towards the door praying silently that he would start to hunger for the truth. She stepped out the doorway and looked back. Brandon's eyes were watching her. They were full of emotion. Mandy felt her words catch in her throat as she whispered, "Goodnight Brandon."

Brandon stretched out in the jet's comfortable chair and reclined. He couldn't relax though and for once his phone sat turned off on the small table beside him. He couldn't stop thinking. Her last words, so soft, her whispered, "goodnight Brandon," resounded in his mind. He'd wanted to see her once more before he left today, but he had not had time to find her.

Her last words felt like a "goodbye," and for once in his life Brandon hated the thought. She'd said his name so softly and sweetly, like a caress. And her touch had been better than anything he'd ever felt. His hand absentmindedly reached up and cupped his cheek where she had caressed him.

It was strange. She was no softer than any other girl who'd touched him. In fact her hands were rougher from the work she did, but somehow it was sweeter, better. In some way it was like she was giving him something and not requesting. Everyone else touched him to get something. He sighed. That was why she was different. She actually believed and lived the words she had told him. He didn't know many others like that.

What she'd said about drinking was true and he knew it, but he'd been ignoring the facts for years. But what she'd said about trust had surprised him and he understood suddenly why he'd never stuck with anyone. He didn't trust anyone but himself and no one trusted him either. Not that he could blame them. He knew he was guilty of using others as much as they used him. He drummed his fingers on the arm rest.

The part about God had confused him though. All the things he'd heard about God were rules, a list of "do's" and "don't." No one had ever given him a reason for them though. Perhaps she was trying to give him a reason, but he shook his head, not quite ready to accept it all. God wasn't for him.

He groaned to himself. At the bar that evening he had thought about her as Desiree had tried to woo him. She had touched him and somehow that had reminded him of Mandy's first quick stroke on his cheek when she'd told him to chase something worthwhile.

He'd been trying to forget her all week, but couldn't. After the initial hurt and anger had left him, he had been almost curious about her and why she'd believed so strongly that his looks and money were not enough. He shifted uneasily in his seat.

She'd explained it to him quite well last night and he was left feeling like he really wasn't good enough for her. She wanted a guy who would give and take equally, but all he knew how to do was take and take without any thought for his partner, while someone else did the same thing to him. He put his head into his hands.

When he'd walked into the kitchen last night he'd paused to watch her. Despite the hurt and anger, she was so lovely to watch. Everything she did was so graceful and deliberate. But something else had pulled at him too, was it a peace that radiated from her? He wasn't sure, but something about her drew him.

And then she had noticed him and the spell was broken. He'd been ready to chew her out, but she'd stayed, almost like she was willing to take anything and he could not go through with his desire to hurt her. But he had wanted answers, and that is just what he'd gotten. He sighed.

Why did she have to be so right about him? It was her psychology, he knew, which meant that she probably thought of him as someone to help and nothing else. No wonder she had not responded to his advances. He gritted his teeth. But then why had she seemed to feel... why did her eyes...? He sighed. Maybe it had been his imagination. Why couldn't he just forget her? He'd never measure up and he wasn't sure if he even wanted to if it meant he had to be a Christian.

It was fun chasing after many different girls. He'd experienced many different "flavors," he thought with a grin. Then her comment about going after something worthwhile crept into his mind again and he realized that all his chasing had really only left him feeling empty and almost drained. He sighed again and raked his hand through his hair. Maybe this girl was like his grandmother. He smiled as he thought of her and pulled at the ends of his hair.

As a child his Grandma Rathsmasen had been his favorite. She always gave him so much love, and yet she wouldn't let him get away with things that he shouldn't. No one else had earned his respect like she and strangely that was the way Mandy was now. He hadn't liked his grandmother's ways as a teenager, but he'd always respected her. And now he even admired her for standing firm in her beliefs despite the family she was a part of.

No one else in his family was a Christian, except for his grandma. Was that what made her and Mandy different? They both seemed so peaceful and content despite how much less they had than he. He frowned. Did God really give peace? He pursed his lips, and was he actually willing to give up all his fun for that? He shook his head.

Then a smile played on his lips. He did miss his Grandma Rathsmasen. Maybe he should go pay her a visit. She still lived in California, but going to see her over some weekend might be a good idea. Maybe they had a long weekend coming up soon. He tugged harder on the ends of his hair as he thought.

His mind shifted to Mandy again and he wondered if he shouldn't just forget her entirely. He wouldn't see her again for months, as the family was going to California for Thanksgiving. Maybe he'd just have to wait and see his grandmother then too. He frowned. They'd be in Florida for Christmas though. Two months. No girl was worth that wait, he decided. He might as well get back to his life in New York, he thought as he picked up his phone and began to post some pictures to his social media accounts, but the whole way home all he could think about was a girl with dark brown curls and blue green eyes.

Chapter Ten

GARY EVERETT LAUGHED AS Brandon snubbed Rachelle's attempt at trying to get his attention. They hurried to their class and sat down in the plush chairs that only a college of this caliber could afford. "Want to come to Michael's with us tonight?" he asked Brandon, nodding slightly.

"Maybe," his friend grinned, cocking his head to one side. "Who's going to be there?"

Gary smiled mischievously. Girls, the right ones anyway, could always entice Brandon.

"Bianca, Lilly, Allison..." Brandon waved his hand cutting him off.

"Derek coming?" he asked.

Gary frowned rubbing his chin. Usually Brandon was more interested in what girls were going to be there, and not which friends. "Uh, yeah, I guess."

"Cool," Brandon said, looking up at the door as the teacher entered, "Maybe I'll come when I get my load of school work done."

Gary frowned again as Brandon began watching the teacher turn on the Smart Board. Brandon was also usually more concerned with parties than with schoolwork. True he had to maintain good grades to keep his folks happy, but he never let it interfere with his social life. Maybe his father was coming down on him again.

"So did you enjoy break?" he asked nonchalantly.

Brandon looked over at him and smiled slowly. For a moment there was a strange longing in his eyes, and then it vanished and he said mischievously, "Got away from my parents."

Gary laughed. Now that sounded like Brandon.

Brandon had to come to Michael's party, Allison Prety thought, as she scanned all the men. She finally saw him. Her dark eyes glittered, and she pounced the moment he got near. "Brandon, it's been awhile. How are you?" she cooed sweetly leaning into him.

He smiled down at her, his blue eyes playing games with her heart. "How are you Allison?" he asked letting her lead him to a couch where several of her friends sat.

Allison smiled up at him. "I'm doing well now that you've decided to grace our presence," she teased fingering her black hair, "And you?"

"Good," he answered and plopped down beside the girls, "Ladies," he said and they all giggled, and said, "hi Brandon." A few other girls were heading their way and Allison was glad that she'd grabbed him first.

"How was your break last week?" she asked twirling a strand of her silky straight hair in her fingers wishing that Brandon would do it instead.

"Pretty good," he droned tonelessly, "You?"

"Good," she answered repetitiously.

He nodded and looked over to the sliding door going out to Michael's pool, his eyes searching. Quick, she had to think of something to talk to him about before he left, her mind screamed. He was already searching out a new place to go.

"So tell me about your new Lambo?" she inquired putting a hand on his arm.

"It's now really new anymore," he commented. "I've had it three months now."

"Oh, but I haven't seen it yet," she purred. "Tell me about it."

Brandon smiled and then looked up as Devon walked over with a beer.

Allison saw Brandon pause for a moment before he reached his hand out to take it. He had seemed uncertain and she'd never seen him uncertain about anything. Then he began telling her about his car.

She half listened, wondering if she could get him to take her for a ride. That would really boost her reputation, even if she never did get him to go out with her. She tapped her foot on the floor as she thought.

"It's a Gallardo but next time I think I want a Murcielago," he stated.

"Oh yeah," Allison crooned feigning interest.

Brandon nodded and smiled at her.

"So is it a V10?" Brenda asked.

Allison frowned to herself. Brenda actually liked cars and could keep this conversation going. Better to get them on a conversation that she liked. She waited for Brandon to finish. She stared at his large muscular hands. He was gripping the glass of beer, but he hadn't taken a sip yet.

"So how are your classes going?" she asked the moment a lull in the conversation appeared.

"Good," he said. "Liking my afternoon classes better than my morning ones though," he added with a grin.

"I know what you mean," Danielle smiled sweetly up at him, "I hate mornings."

Allison gritted her teeth and pursed her lips. She'd brought him over here, not them. She'd love to get him into a private booth. "Me too," she added. "I love all my interior decorating classes," she commented as a way of shifting the topic, "but I also have two generals left that I'm taking this semester. I'll be glad when they are over."

Brandon lips turned up, "I never liked generals either," he agreed and Allison watched as he lifted his glass slowly. He stared at its contents a moment as if in contemplation, the muscle in his right jaw twitching slightly and then set it on the coffee table in front of them without taking a sip.

"They probably have wine too," she commented.

Brandon looked down at her and smiled a slow sad smile and shook his head. Allison was puzzled. She'd never seen Brandon look like that. "I gotta go," he breathed and stood up and left them before she could protest. But he didn't go to another group. He headed for the door. Brandon had never left this early before. She looked down at his beer. And he'd never refused to drink either. What had happened to him over the weekend?

Mandy sighed as she dusted around the picture. Brandon's smirk starred back at her when she looked down at it. She had made herself scarce that last day, wanting to leave Brandon with no more thoughts of her. He'd go and hopefully the only thing he'd remember was her comments about God. That was for the best.

If she'd helped him understand a few things then that was good, but it was best that he leave and forget about her. He lived in a different world than she did and she would be better off with him gone too. He had been gone almost two weeks now. She pursed her lips. Why did she have to think about him?

She studied his picture a second longer and turned. Well, she'd have to stop this nonsense and get back to her job. She'd forget about all this soon, just like he would and maybe she could use their encounter as something else to add to her notebooks. Even as that thought entered her mind, she instinctively knew that it would never enter there. For some reason she just couldn't use that as research.

She twisted the rag in her hands as she walked. It had been good to see him really contemplating her words. It was best for him if he did change a few things, but whether or not he did was not her concern. Only God could help him now. Mandy glanced at the hall clock and headed for the cleaning closet. She put her rag in the basket then went into the kitchen.

"Hey Mandy," Donny called out from behind her.

Mandy turned and grinned. "Having lots of fun playing with mulch in the sun?" she teased.

"Loads," he countered, "You having fun with your Windex in the cold house?"

"Of course," she answered with a mock British accent, "My darling Alexis and I," she began and draped her arm around the girl who had just entered, "are having a delightful time at our teapot cleaning party."

Alexis giggled, and Donny roared with laughter, "You're a trip," he teased.

"What's so funny?" Connie asked as she walked in.

Mandy smiled at her, "I was just making a dumb joke, but I guess it was funny to these two," then turning to Donny she gave him a mischievous look and added, "Course he could have simply lost his mind after being in the sun for so long."

She heard Alexis laughing behind her as she turned and raced out of the kitchen. "Hey," she heard Donny calling, but she didn't stop. This was almost as much fun as teasing Jason.

"Watch it," she heard Brandy scolding as she raced around the corner.

"Sorry," Mandy called out over her shoulder and slowed down on her way out. She wondered if Brandon and his brother and sister had ever chased each other through this house. Then she scolded herself. No more thinking about Brandon.

Mrs. Harper paused with a smile to straighten the slightly tilted picture. She almost jumped when she hear a voice behind her. "It's like a shmily."

Mrs. Harper turned to see Mandy smiling at her, "A what?" she asked gruffly.

Mandy grinned, "A shmily," she repeated and then laughed as Mrs. Harper furrowed her brows. "It means See How Much I Love You! SHMILY!" she added.

Mrs. Harper frowned. What did Mandy mean? What was like a SHMILY?

Mandy smiled at her again and nodded toward the portrait. "Your picture tilting. That's a really cute way to say 'I love you,'" she stated, shifting the chemicals in her arms.

Mrs. Harper's brown eyes glittered with understanding. It was interesting all that this girl picked up on. "Thank you," she said curtly, and walked slowly up the steps with Mandy.

"Would you like to hear the story about the SHMILY?" she asked. "It's really cute too."

Mrs. Harper shrugged.

"It was about this couple who left these SHMILY's for the other to find in all kinds of strange places. One would like write it on a slip of paper and put it in a book the other person read a lot. When the other one found it they would write it and place it under a candle, or on the last sheet of a roll of toilet paper," she giggled and Mrs. Harper looked at Mandy as they plodded up the last step. The girl's face was alight with pleasure and Mrs. Harper's eyes softened.

"It was a really cute story," she added, but her face fell slightly. "The end was kind of sad though. The man who wrote about it was writing about his grandparents, and said that when his grandmother died, his grandfather left one in her casket."

Mrs. Harper looked over and nodded, a strange sheen in her eyes causing the girl to blur slightly. "That is a sweet story," her voice came out hoarsely. She wondered if Mandy had always had this way with people. She had a way of pointing out the best in people and putting others at ease. She sniffed and rubbed her eyes with the back of her sleeve.

It was strange that she hadn't been affected by Brandon. She'd noticed that boy always following her around, but she didn't seem interested in the least. Her lips curled slightly. It was probably good for the boy. It was definitely good for her. She needed more workers like Mandy. She continued walking down the hall with her.

It was almost the third week since Brandon had gone and Mandy was still the same cheerful, helpful girl she'd always been. There had been other workers who had become depressed after the boy had left, because he hadn't paid enough attention to them, or simply because he was gone. But Mandy was still the same. Good! Brandon hadn't affected her in the slightest. She smiled ruefully.

"I like sweet stories," Mandy stated, replying to her comment, "With all the divorce and hate in this world I like to see couples that really love each other."

They stopped beside the supply closet. "It is good to show each other in little ways, or the spark dies," Mrs. Harper stated gruffly.

Mandy laughed, "That's very true," she said as she switched out the bottles in her hand then added, "Would you mind if I wrote down what Mr. Harper does, you know the tilting pictures, in my psychology notebook? I would like to use you both as an example someday, you know, of a healthy relationship."

Mrs. Harper raised her thick brows, pleasantly surprised by the request. "Of course," she agreed grabbing a broom, "that would be fine." She had a hard time not smiling at the girl.

"Thank you," Mandy replied with a pleasant smile lighting her face and turned to go. Mrs. Harper began to head in the opposite direction then paused in mid stride. It would be a shame to lose this girl.

"Mandy," Mrs. Harper turned towards the girl who stopped and whirled around, her brows raised.

"Yes?"

"I was wondering if perhaps you might think about staying on a second year?" she asked sternly.

Mandy's eyes clouded slightly. "I'm so sorry, Mrs. Harper. I would love to stay here longer, but I really do want to finish my degree even more," she added apologetically and wrung her hands.

Mrs. Harper huffed slightly. "It's okay dear," she said brusquely and turned to go.

"Thank you for the offer though," she heard Mandy call out behind her.

Mrs. Harper could hear the smile in her voice and couldn't help smiling herself. "You're welcome," she answered her voice much lighter and headed out. At least she would have one year with a good worker.

Ryan Cavanaugh ran a hand over his short textured brown hair and scanned the beach with his light brown eyes. It was a habit, despite the fact that he hadn't been a lifeguard for two years now. He clenched his teeth. Why did he have to think about that now?

He liked having a good reputation, whether he deserved it or not, and that job had put a black mar on his otherwise perfect reputation. So what if he'd been caught making out with his girlfriend during the shift. It was a calm day and he'd still been keeping an eye on the water, when he could.

He put a hand on his hip. Best if he stop thinking about the past and focus on the beauties currently on the beach. He looked good, he knew, with his muscular chest and broad shoulders. He smiled to himself, as he unconsciously flexed a bicep. He didn't have to be to his next class for an hour, if he was even going to go today. He should enjoy himself.

Ryan strode down the beach. There was another public beach only a minute's walk from here and perhaps between here and there would be a girl pretty enough to warrant his attention. He needed a distraction today. It had been over a month since he and Christine had broken it off and he was getting lonely.

Then he spotted her. She was a beautiful sight, with a perfect body and bright eyes. He couldn't see the color from here but her long brown curls that spilled all over her were all he could stare at anyway. Her hair looked soft, and Ryan narrowed his eyes. Soon, he vowed to himself, he'd be able to touch it.

He studied her for a moment deciding on the best approach. She seemed to be writing something furiously in a notebook of some sort. Studious, he decided. He knew how to handle the type. She seemed to be watching a little girl playing. Maybe she was going to be a teacher, or perhaps she just liked kids. He'd better pretend to like them a lot. He could tell her about all the children he'd rescued as a lifeguard. He smiled dryly.

If she was going to be a teacher she was probably pretty responsible. He could be responsible and good for a while at least. He could go to all his classes and stay away from the clubs, at least until they broke up. Course she didn't have to know if he strayed a bit. Hey, and maybe she would even like going to clubs. One could never stereotype completely these days. He'd find out. He flexed his fingers and rested the tips on each other.

He liked having girls and he liked the fact that he could be anything they wanted him to be so that he could get what he wanted. He didn't keep girls very long, because he never liked sticking with just one. He grinned to himself as he approached her.

"Hi," he said as he stood beside her, arms folded and looked out over the sea.

She looked up, her eyes bright, and smiled, "Hi," she repeated. She had a nice smile. She seemed use to people talking to her. She probably knew she was pretty. That would definitely work to his advantage.

"It's a calm day isn't it?" he asked. She nodded her face alight. "This is good weather for a lifeguard," he mused and watched her expression out of the corner of his eye. She simply smiled again. He frowned to himself.

"I suppose it would be," she stated, "Are you currently a lifeguard or used to be?"

His eyes widened momentarily then he slipped his calm mask back on. She was better at this game than he'd thought. Had she read him that quickly? "Used to be," he replied, "A couple years ago."

She looked up at him, her brows furrowed. "Why not anymore?" she asked.

Best not to reveal the truth if she were the responsible type. "It was interfering with my schoolwork," he lied with a shrug.

"Um," she nodded, "What are you taking in school?" she asked.

"Business," he answered, "I'm also on a sport's scholarship, football," he stated, "so I have to keep my grades up to keep the scholarship, you know?"

"I see," she nodded looking over at the ocean. A couple seconds passed and Ryan plopped down in the sand next to her. He looked over at her from the corner of his eye.

She had a perfect model's body, but she certainly didn't act like one.

"Didn't bring a towel?" she teased, glancing over at him briefly.

Ryan shook his head, and smiled, "I only came for a little walk before my next class," he admitted. She nodded. He purposely ran a hand through his couple inches of hair, which always drew attention to his biceps. She looked away briefly. He grinned to himself. "Oh, sorry for my manners," he said suddenly, turning to her and extending his browned hand, "My name is Ryan."

She tentatively shook it, "Mandy," she responded gently her face still slightly closed, "Nice to meet you."

"And you," he added.

A moment of silence hung in the air and he looked down at the notebook that she'd been writing in. She closed it and then looked at him with a slight smile. "What's that?" he asked, "Doing homework on the beach?"

She laughed blithely and he rather liked the sound of it, "Yes and no," she replied. "It's a notebook with observations in it that I will one day use in some of my classes," she stated sitting up. He inhaled at the sight. All of her was very nice.

"I see," he acknowledged looking away least she suspect, again wondering if perhaps she was going into teaching or some profession with children. "And what classes might those be?" he asked.

She smiled for a moment and picked up her notebook, "Psychology," she said and Ryan nodded, understanding how she'd read him so easily. At least she didn't play games like he did, or he'd have to be even more careful than usual that he wasn't caught. As it was he would have to be extra cautious around this one.

He paused and leered as he discreetly assessed her supple body while her face was turned, "Neat," he replied, "But what's with the 'one day' statement? Are you not in school right night?"

"I've been taking a year off to earn money for school for next year," she commented looking back over at him. Her bright eyes sent little waves of delight through him. Then she began collecting her things. "Speaking of which," she began, as she stood up, "I need to get back to work now."

"Where do you work?" he asked and stood as well. She paused and looked over at him. She smiled gently and then her eyes clouded over.

"Bye," she said with a little wave.

"Will you be here tomorrow?" he asked.

She shrugged and then turned away. Hum? This one was cautious, but she had definite potential. She was tall, perfectly shaped and her hair was absolutely stunning. Even her eyes, a bright blue green were perfect. He wanted her. His eyes narrowed. He was up for a long game, he decided with a sly smile because, in the end, he knew he would have her.

Chapter Eleven

CONNIE KRUTHERS FLIPPED HER light brown braid behind her and looked down the stairs with her green eyes. Mandy and Donny were at it again. It wasn't that she really wanted Donny or anything, but it wasn't fair that Mandy got so much attention.

It wasn't like she was ugly or anything. In fact with her long straight brown hair, green eyes, and petite figure, most guys found her quite attractive. Brandy was a good friend to remind her of that on occasion.

Just yesterday even Brandy was saying, "With my vibrant red hair, and your brown hair, well with your green eyes anyway, we could have our pick of guys. Did I ever tell you about all the guys that wanted me when I worked as a waitress before coming here?"

Brandy was always telling her stories of all the men she'd been with and she even had pictures of them all over her social media pages to prove it. It was all very fascinating. Course it was odd that Brandon had paid more attention to Mandy when he was here since Brandy was prettier. Brandy had said so.

Connie walked into the kitchen to get her lunch and saw Mandy's head thrown back laughing. She always seemed to do that. It would be a nice sound if Brandy hadn't mentioned how grating it was. Even though she knew Brandy didn't really like Mandy, she kind of did, but more than anything she wanted to know about Brandon. And Mandy had talked to Brandon. She had to think of a way to get Mandy to tell her about him.

Alexis and Mandy were the only ones in the kitchen and Alexis was just heading for the door. Now was her chance.

"So you like Donny?" she asked, as the door closed behind Alexis, trying to think of a way to start.

Mandy grinned. "He reminds me of my little brother," she admitted.

Connie half smiled back at her, "That's cool. So you don't have a boyfriend or anything?"

Mandy beamed, "Nope," then added as she grabbed some juice out of the refrigerator, "Don't really need one."

Connie's brow creased. Not need one? She frowned at Mandy's back as she was putting the juice away. What did she mean? "What about Brandon?" she asked, trying to sound nonchalant.

"Yeah, what about Brandon?" she heard Brandy repeat in an acid tone from behind her and Connie cringed.

"What about him?" Mandy asked, her face open and questioning, despite the smile that stayed pasted there. She began sipping on the juice.

"What was with him chasing you around three weeks ago?" Brandy snorted, and Connie could tell she was looking away to seem uninterested. Brandy was just as curious as she was, but jealousy had kept Brandy from asking before and Brandy had kept Connie from asking.

"I don't remember him chasing me around," Mandy began with what looked like a genuinely puzzled expression, "but he did keep asking me questions," she added. She finished the juice and put her cup in the sink. Then she smiled, "See you girls later," she announced and picked up her sandwich.

"Um, sure," Brandy muttered and faked a smile. Then Mandy disappeared out the door.

Connie grabbed her food and plopped down at the barstools. Brandy got hers as well then headed for the refrigerator. "Well, what was that all about?" she seethed.

Connie shifted uncomfortably, wondering if Brandy meant her or Mandy. "I don't know," she replied, and swallowed down the acid in her throat.

"She thinks she's so much better than us," Brandy fumed, yanking open the refrigerator, and Connie face softened, glad the wrath was not directed at her.

"Yeah," Connie asserted.

"What did that mean anyway, 'he kept asking me questions?'" Brandy mimicked Mandy in a rude way as she came and sat down then glared at her food as she took a big bite of her sandwich. Then she pulled her phone from her back pocket and began scrolling through something.

Connie looked over at her friend. She sighed and the two ate in silence for a few moments.

"What did you say to her before I got there?" Brandy looked up from her phone with a menacing glint in her eye.

"Oh, I just asked if she had a boyfriend," Connie started casually, glancing over at Brandy out of the corner of her eye. She was never brave enough to carry her phone on her all the times like Brandy since it wasn't allowed on the job.

She wished she'd had time to go get it to hide behind when Brandy asked her questions like this.

Brandy nodded, a sinister gleam lighting her eyes, "She doesn't have one does she?"

"No."

"I didn't think so," Brandy smiled smugly then looked back down at her phone.

Connie watched Brandy for a moment, glad she was happy again. Maybe she should invite Mandy to see a movie with her and learn more. Perhaps she could find out something that would make Brandy really excited.

Soon they were done eating and Brandy and she were off to Brandy's room to look through Brandy's social media sites which were all much more colorful than hers. Sometimes they went out on their breaks, but usually they waited until after work to leave the property. They didn't want to have to rush back, and Brandy was a stickler about being to work on time, if only so that she would not lose her job because of its proximity to Brandon.

As soon as break was over and everyone was back to work, Connie found an excuse to go outside. It was Thursday and Mandy always worked in the rose garden on Thursdays and Fridays. That was one good thing about Mandy working here. Brandy and she no longer had to work out in the heat and dirt.

"Mandy," Connie called as soon as she saw her. The girl was down in the dirt, pulling weeds. Connie wrinkled her nose slightly.

Mandy turned and grinned, from her kneeling position on the ground, "Hey Connie, don't tell me you got sent to help me?" she teased.

Connie couldn't help but smile in return, "No," she answered, "I was just wondering if you were doing anything tonight?"

Mandy shook her head, "Nope."

"Well, I thought maybe the three of us could go out to see a movie or something."

Mandy face brightened, "That's sounds fun. Sure."

"Great," Connie smiled, hoping Brandy would see this as a good idea too.

"Hey, would you mind if perhaps Alexis came too?" Mandy asked quickly.

Connie paused, not sure that Brandy would like that at all, but knowing she needed to keep Mandy happy. "Um, sure," Connie conceded, biting her lip slightly and turned to leave, "See ya later. At the end of work perhaps?"

"Sure," Mandy answered. "See ya at around four."

Connie turned, "Okay bye."

"Bye."

Mandy smiled again, Connie noticed, as she left. She was always smiling. But why was she always so happy? I mean, she didn't even have a boyfriend!

Brandy grit her teeth as she smiled at Mandy and Alexis as they came hurrying up to meet them at the theater that evening. She was frustrated that Connie had done this yet secretly she was glad too. This was a good chance to observe Mandy and learn about Brandon while making Connie think that she wasn't interested. After all, she had appearances to keep up with.

Last year had been better. Cammie had been her friend, even if she had been jealous that Cammie got Brandon's attention first. Served her right for getting caught. Cammie should have shared and should have been more careful. She would be careful. But then Mandy came along.

Brandon had been scarce the whole week he'd been here. First she had seen him talking to Mandy or he'd been asking where she was. Then he'd just been plain gone. She was so curious, but kept trying to tell herself that she wasn't.

She studied Mandy as they bought their tickets and went to find seats. Mandy was no prettier than she was. Why would Brandon choose her? Everyone told her that guys liked redheads, and with her short curly red hair and puppy-dog brown eyes which she knew how to use to her advantage, what guy could resist her? She'd proven the fact that men liked her looks time and again, so why not Brandon anymore?

Mandy laughed readily at all the funny moments in the movie. She laughed a lot. What did she have to be so happy about? Connie had told her that Mandy had no boyfriend and when asked about it on their way in, Mandy had said that she hadn't had one since high school. But what was with her saying that she didn't need one? That was the oldest excuse in the book, but it didn't seem like Mandy needed to use an excuse.

After the movie the girls decided to go to an ice cream parlor before calling it a night. Several male heads turned to look at them when they entered. That was just the way she liked it.

"What kinds of questions did Brandon ask you?" Connie asked Mandy after they had their ice cream and began sitting down.

It was nice to have someone ask the questions for her. "Nothing exciting really," Mandy began and Brandy held back a snort. She narrowed her eyes slightly. "He asked why I have some of the beliefs I have, my morals and stuff, because I had told him about them earlier. And he asked me about my interest in psychology and stuff like that."

"Oh," Connie said and Brandy would have liked to know more, but Alexis asked a question.

"Um, you told me about meeting some guy on the beach yesterday." The girl was quiet and Brandy almost didn't hear her. "Did you see him again today?" she asked her face turned up in a shy grin.

Brandy looked at the two. She frowned with her eyes. What guy, she thought. Were these two purposely trying to get onto a new topic of conversation?

"All I said about that," Mandy began with a bubby laugh, "was that some guy named Ryan interrupted me yesterday."

Alexis smiled almost in wonder, and Brady gave a condescending look when the girl's back was turned. That girl had probably never had a boyfriend in her whole life. She probably didn't even have a Facebook page. She was hardly pretty and she barely talked. Well, she talked to Mandy, but that was about all. "So did you see him again today?" she asked hesitantly.

Mandy eyes flickered momentarily and then she smiled, "Yes."

"So what happened?" Alexis asked, with a bit more courage.

"Well, he came up to me yesterday and talked about the weather and I discovered that he used to be a lifeguard."

"Oooh," Connie squealed, and Brandy frowned. "Was he hot?"

Mandy laughed, "Now that you mention it, I guess so. He was quite good looking."

"And ripped?" Connie asked again her green eyes sparkling.

"Yes," Mandy added with a little laugh, "He said he was in college on a football scholarship, so I guess he probably works out."

"How old did he look?" Alexis asked in her quiet way.

"It sounded like he was maybe in his third year," Mandy answered.

As the girls giggled and carried on about this guy named Ryan that Mandy had met, Brandy began to seethe. It wasn't enough that Mandy got Brandon's and even Donny's attention, but now she had some new guy's attention as well! And he sounded really hot. He had been coming out to see her for two days now, and was bound to keep coming back.

Even here there were more guys watching Mandy than her, and the girl never seemed to notice. Or maybe she was just pretending that she didn't. Brandy's brown eyes glittered with rage. Well, if this were a game, she could play too. She could work just as hard as Mandy pretended not to, to get every guy away from Mandy. And even if Mandy wasn't playing a game, Brandy was determined to get them all anyway!

Lilly Rathsmasen smiled faintly at her grandson and braced herself as she slowly sank into the couch. It had been one year and nine months since she had seen him last, on his twentieth birthday. It seemed as if her daughter and son-in-law avoided her, which meant she didn't see the grandkids either. Now they were all grown.

She had been flabbergasted and a little weary when she'd heard from him a few weeks ago when he'd asked if he could visit. Brandon had always been a selfish child and very spoiled too.

"Grandma?" Brandon exclaimed getting out of her easy chair, "Would you rather sit here?" he asked concern in his eyes.

Her brown eyes opened slightly in surprise then she quickly forced the amazement down. "No dear, the couch is fine," she stated and folded her gnarling hands in her lap. She was already seventy-eight, for her daughter had been the youngest, born when she was thirty-one, and this was her daughter's youngest son. Sometimes she felt so ancient. When she'd turned seventy-two she had not actually felt old until her husband had died later that year. Loneliness had a way of aging a person.

Lilly frowned, and again wondered if Brandon wanted something. It wasn't that she had a lot of money like his family did, though she was well enough off. She had never spoiled him, because his parents already had, so it couldn't be that he wanted something his parents had refused him. It was a sad day and age when you had to worry about what motivated your favorite grandson's visit.

Brandon smiled at her, "I'm sorry I haven't visited in so long," he confessed, pulling slightly at the tips of his hair, "but we will be coming here for Thanksgiving," he added.

"Here to my home, or to your parent's home in the valley?" she asked, knowing that the last two times her daughter had visited their California home they had not visited her.

"I don't actually know grandma, but I may not be with my family for Thanksgiving…" he added letting the sentence trail, and shifted uncomfortably in his seat.

Lilly looked at him in surprise, her pale eyes frowning slightly. The family was usually a stickler for being together on the holidays, even if it were mostly for appearance's sake. She fingered her long white braid gently.

"Where are you going to be?" she asked tentatively.

"I haven't actually told my parents yet," he began and she instantly felt a slight twinge of alarm as she wondered if that was why he was here, "but I want to stay at the villa in Florida," he added.

"Oh?" She raised her eyebrows.

Brandon looked down for a moment as odd emotions played along his face, "I met someone like you," he murmured finally, looking at his hands.

Lilly smiled to hide her surprise. What did he mean? If he meant an older lady, what was he telling her for and if he meant a girl....? No, he was the one that ran after so many different girls. She knew he wouldn't tell her about it. He knew how she felt about his habits. Perhaps that is why he hadn't visited in so long. She sighed silently to herself, and waited for him to continue.

"She works hard and has a good set of morals," he commented and grinned up at her. "Let me have it about my drinking and stuff," he added, and looked out her living room window, a distant look in his blue eyes.

Lilly smiled again. Perhaps he had met an older grandmotherly figure in Florida that reminded him of her. But no, he would never go where older ladies with morals like hers frequented. Was she a new worker perhaps?

"She's also a Christian," Brandon stated quietly.

Lilly raised her eyebrows slightly, then smiled softly, "Tell me about her," she requested quietly.

Brandon looked up at her, a strange expression on his face and sighed. She frowned wondering about the almost agonized expression that haunted his eyes. "I was supposed to be forgetting her," he mumbled off handedly like he was talking to himself, "but I can't," he stated even quieter and looked down.

"She's a new housecleaner at the villa," he finally stated looking up at her. "She's working there to put herself through college. She's taking psychology," he began and Lilly listened quietly and rather intrigued as her grandson wove a story about a girl that seemed too sweet to be real. She was surprised and shocked to hear the tale, but began silently thanking God that He had sent someone like that for her grandson.

For a long time she had been worried that he would do what his mother had done. Lilly and her husband had been fairly wealthy since he had been a doctor, and although she had never focused on their money, apparently their daughter, Melissa, had. She had even forsaken her parents' religion and set out to find for herself the richest man, no matter the cost. Happiness and love hadn't even been considered, and Lilly often wondered if her daughter hadn't visited for so long because she didn't want to think about the fact that her mother had been right all along.

She listened to Brandon's story and smiled wistfully. God knew what He was doing, even if Brandon had no clue. God was using this girl to call Brandon to Him. She would have to meet this girl Mandy, for even if the girl had no idea what she had done, Lilly knew that this was the start of a wonderful change in her grandson's life. And even if Brandon didn't understand what was going on yet, she could tell by the way he talked that he was falling in love.

Lilly finally leaned into the couch, a slight smile on her withered lips. She could finally relax, because God was still calling to her grandson, and this time, through the help of a rather remarkable young lady, it seemed that her grandson was finally taking notice.

Brandon stretched out on the couch in his private jet. He'd left the airport an hour ago. Twenty minutes before he had said "goodbye," to his grandmother. He sighed, a soft light in his eyes. He'd enjoyed seeing her this weekend, but she'd seemed so eager that Mandy was the perfect girl for him that he frowned. He was still hesitant about the whole matter.

Besides the fact that she wouldn't date him, Brandon had also decided to forget her. Course that had proven harder than he'd thought. And what had he been saying? He'd not completely made up his mind to spend Thanksgiving in Florida, but every time the thought entered his mind the stronger it became.

He cringed as he thought about telling his father. The man wouldn't be happy, but it wasn't like his father really cared. Last year he'd been called away during the meal to attend some stupid business meeting. Maybe he should tell his dad that Lilith broke up with him and he needed personal time.

He knew that his father still must not know about it, or there would have been a terrible storm. Thankfully neither of his parents checked out their children's social media pages or things would have come out a lot sooner. Maybe Lilith was too proud to tell her family that he had broken up with her, and had lied, saying it was the other way around. He wondered if her parents had been as mad at her as he knew his would be at him if they knew the truth. He clenched his jaw tighter.

Then his thoughts switched, and Mandy entered his mind. She would not approve of him lying though. What should he tell his father? That he wanted to stay in Florida and... no, perhaps he should end there. He couldn't complete the rest without lying or angering his father. But he was, he finally decided, with determination, going to Florida for Thanksgiving.

Chapter Twelve

"BEFORE WE GO TO our last day's assignments, I have an announcement," Mrs. Harper declared still looking down at her clipboard.

Mandy and the other girls looked up to see what Mrs. Harper had to say.

"I know you were all told that you would get Thanksgiving off," she stated, finally looking up her brown eyes frowning, "but I am going to have to ask that one of you volunteer to stay, as Deborah is going to be coming," she announced.

Mandy glanced around at all the other girls. They were all looking down or away from Mrs. Harper. She knew that they were looking forward to their Thanksgiving breaks, since they all had to be working Christmas, when the whole family would be coming to stay. She loved her family, but also knew that they would understand if she missed one Thanksgiving. Besides Allie and her husband were going to be at his parents, so she wouldn't be the only one absent.

"I'll stay," she said softly and the other girls looked relieved.

"Thank you Mandy," Mrs. Harper growled trying to smile, "You may all head to work now. Remember your break starts Tuesday after work."

All the girls nodded and left. Mandy was glad that the other girls would get to leave tomorrow, but sighed as she thought about being left behind. Then again, this would be a good chance to observe more people, such as the ones home for the holidays. Perhaps she could even observe Deborah, Brandon's sister. It would be interesting to see what she was like, she decided.

Mandy smiled lightly and wondered if she would be anything like Brandon. All her portraits told her that she would be quite different. She always looked more melancholy than her younger brother and less forceful than her older one probably was. Even in the pictures with her husband she didn't look very happy despite the smile plastered on her face.

She wondered about Deborah's husband. Mrs. Harper hadn't said he would be coming. Maybe she was coming here to get away from her husband, Steven Carter. Mandy paused as she passed a picture of the couple on their wedding day. Allie, her own sister, had looked radiant on her wedding. Brandon's sister looked more like she had an upset stomach. Mandy sighed. This poor messed up family. Money certainly didn't buy happiness, she decided.

Mr. Harper's hazel eyes glittered with love as his wife leaned over the chair and kissed him. She gently took the newspaper from his hands and laid it on the table. "We need to go to bed," she ordered smiling softly. He chuckled. Some people thought his wife was cranky, but they never got the chance to see her with him. She was very sweet.

"Just a few more minutes," he teased, and she smirked, rolled her pretty brown eyes, and went to fix him a warm glass of milk. He started to pick up his paper again then paused. He leaned back in his chair with a frown, and pushed his glasses up on the bridge of his nose.

"Molly?"

"Um?" she poked her head around the corner to see what he wanted.

"I thought you said that Brandon was coming," he inquired.

She nodded her short brown hair, freed from the ponytail holder that it stayed in during the day, framing her round face, "He is."

"But I heard that you told the others that Deborah is coming," he stated pursing his lips and forcing the smile lines around his mouth to disappear.

Molly looked down slightly and sighed heavily. "You know I hate the way those girls act around him."

"I thought you said that Mandy didn't," he asked anxiously.

"They aren't all like Mandy," she smiled ruefully.

"If only huh?" he teased and her snort came out as more of a laugh.

She stepped into the kitchen again, and then walked out, carrying his blue mug with his milk in it. She handed it to him. He took it with his slender hands and smiled up at her as in invitation to explain her reasoning.

"I didn't want them volunteering just because they want to flirt more with Brandon," she huffed, sitting down on the edge of the couch and leaning towards him.

He nodded, "Speaking of Brandon, why is that boy coming or did he say?"

Molly frowned, causing the worry lines along her forehead to deepen, "Didn't say," she commented, and leaned back slightly.

"Well I wish the boy would stay with his family," he commented gruffly in a slight imitation of her.

Molly smiled slightly but ignored the tease, "It would have been nice for everyone to go visit family, but I guess we can't always get what we want," she stated.

"Wasn't Andréa going to visit her daughter, and Oliver was going to go see his sister."

"I think we were the only ones that were going to be staying," she added.

His mouth turned up gently as she stood up again, "Think we should visit family next time?" he asked and pulled himself out of his chair to follow his wife.

"Who?" she asked looking back slightly at him, as they walked towards the bedroom.

"My brother perhaps," he suggested as he followed her.

"Well that would be the logical choice since that's the only family we have," she replied sarcastically.

"We could still adopt," he breathed, and paused as she opened their bedroom door.

She frowned again, "Maybe if we were still young," she murmured.

He furrowed his brow and ran a hand over his thinning dark hair. Was she regretting their decision? He put his hand on her soft shoulder and turned her slightly, "Regrets?" he asked looking into her brown eyes that still played with his heart.

She looked down slightly, then back up at him and finally smiled, "no," she said frankly, "We chose not to take the only option we had for children and I'm still just fine with that," she stated.

He chuckled and pulled her into an embrace, "The Taylor children were more than enough huh?" he teased.

She laughed, and pulled herself out of the embrace far enough to look up into his face again, "I thought they would never grow up," she joked.

"Sometimes I don't think the boy has yet," he commented.

Molly laughed again. He liked the sound of it, "Maybe not," she agreed softly, and then leaned back into him, resting her face against his chest. He sighed contentedly.

Ryan smiled as he plopped down next to Mandy who brushed her beautiful dark brown curls out of her face. She was so pretty and he knew he would have to get something before too long or he'd go crazy. He'd been charming her for two weeks now, but she'd still shown no signs of giving in to his game.

Maybe she really was oblivious to her beautiful blue green eyes, sultry smile, and sexy body, but it hardly seemed possible. In his experience, girls as gorgeous as she was, knew it and took advantage of it.

But then again, maybe it was because she was a Christian. Some of them were harder to get to. He'd lied and said he was one to, and she'd seemed to grow less reserved around him after that, but he still had a lot of work to do. She'd better be worth it.

"So I thought you were leaving?" he asked running a hand through his brown hair as always to accentuate the muscles in his arm.

She grinned at up at him totally oblivious to his showing off, "I was," she admitted and looked down at the ocean, "but things changed."

"Oh," he nodded, discretely checking her out again, "What happened?"

"Someone decided to come home at the last minute and so housekeepers are needed," she stated a wistful look in her eyes.

"But that's not fair," he protested, "They suddenly just tell you that you have to stay."

"Actually they asked for a volunteer," she admitted calmly looking up at him.

Ryan looked into her eyes trying to read what she was saying there. Was she really that good or did she have ulterior motives to stay. "So why did you stay?" he finally asked.

"I didn't want any of the other girls to miss being with their families," she stated nonchalantly, shrugging her shoulders and then looked out towards several children playing near them on the beach.

"What about you?" he asked, a glint in his eyes as he studied her face, wondering if she were telling the truth.

She just shrugged her shoulders again, "I figured I could miss this once," she commented, and he wondered if perhaps she might enjoy being away from her family during the holidays. "I will miss them though," she added, and his dark eyes frowned.

Well escaping her family must not be the reason she was staying, "So who's coming?" he asked casually.

"Daughter," she stated, turning to look at him a questioning frown on her face, "I think it's strange though, because she's married and I never heard anything about her husband coming."

Ryan wasn't about to explain it to her. He understood only too well about getting away from family. His parents ran away from each other all the time when he was a child before they finally divorced. Being a Christian, she really must be quite old-fashioned or naïve. But that was okay, he wasn't worried about catching her with his game. He just had to seem more like a conservative Christian. He gazed out towards the beach.

"So, I guess you don't have anything planned?" he inquired changing the conversation.

"For Thanksgiving?" she asked still looking up at him. Her eyes seemed to be searching him and he tried his best to keep an open, happy expression. He nodded. "Don't you?" she asked, a slight frown creasing her brow.

Ryan stilled. He had to play this very carefully. "Of course for dinner I will be with my family," he stated trying to sound happy about it, "but I thought maybe you'd like to do something together, like maybe tonight?" he added, looking back down at her and into her eyes.

Brandon trotted down the beach. He was having a hard time suppressing the grin at the anticipation of seeing Mandy. He'd gotten into Florida and hurried to the house, but it had seemed deserted. He'd forgotten that a lot of them would be gone, and was almost afraid she'd be away too, and his trip would be for nothing, until he had spoken with Mrs. Harper. She told him that Mandy had stayed and she was out on the beach.

He wondered briefly if she'd volunteered to stay because of him, but decided all of them would have volunteered to stay if they knew he was coming. Maybe

Mrs. Harper had specifically asked Mandy to stay. He'd have to thank her for that if she had.

He was glad that he'd been able to come here without too much of a fuss from his father. Amazingly, his father had been more preoccupied with matters that he himself would have to attend to on Thanksgiving, so having his son gone hadn't seemed to be too much of a problem.

He neared the public beach and scanned the crowd. He frowned. She was lying on a towel and a good-looking guy was sitting in the sand beside her. He moved closer to them.

"... to do something together, like maybe tonight?" he heard the guy asking as he looked into her eyes. Was this guy asking her out or something? His eyes narrowed, and he could feel his blood begin to boil.

Mandy pursed her lips into a frown. That was a good sign. "I don't think that's a good idea," she replied as he strode up beside them.

"Why not?" the guy asked in a tone that sounded way too cocky for Brandon's taste.

"Do you drink?" Brandon queried in an acid tone as he moved to where the two were, "she won't date anyone that drinks," he proclaimed narrowing his eyes at the guy.

The guy stood up quickly, and scowled "No," he said, "and who are you?"

Brandon looked down at Mandy whose eyes had become blue green saucers, "I thought your sister was coming," she stammered.

He shook his head, "Nope, she's not coming," he softened his expression as he spoke to her, ignoring the other guy momentarily.

"So you're the boss huh?" the guy retorted, his dark eyes glittering.

Brandon narrowed his eyes as he looked over. Mandy stood up brushing the sand from herself, "Um, Brandon this is Ryan. Ryan this is Brandon," she tried to introduce them quickly.

"So you know who I am, so just who exactly are you?" he drew out each word sarcastically, but inside his stomach was rolling. What if she liked this guy? His heart squeezed painfully.

"A friend," Ryan sneered.

Mandy's eyes frowned as she looked from one to the other in confusion. "May I ask what's going on here? Do you guys know each other?" she asked, motioning from one to the other of them.

"No," Ryan answered, and shook his head, and his expression softened slightly as he looked over at Mandy "Your boss here apparently thinks he owns you?" he retorted glowering back at Brandon.

Brandon seethed. "And you don't?" Ryan was a couple inches shorter than him and Brandon straightened up slightly using his height as an advantage as he stared the guy down.

Mandy eyes narrowed and she scowled at both of them, grabbed her stuff and stated, "Well, since you are both under the false assumption that either of you have any kind of relationship with me, I'll be leaving, so you two can duke it out," she spit out, then flipped around her gorgeous mass of curls floating around her and strode down the beach.

Ryan's face softened slightly into a sarcastic, know-it-all smirk, "Taking advantage of the help are we?" he snickered.

Brandon gritted his teeth, gave him a fierce look then growled, "No, but if you ever do, I'll hunt you down!" With that he whipped around angrily and followed Mandy's retreating figure. The faint sound of malicious laughter seemed to follow him down the beach.

Why in the world had that happened? Mandy wondered as she slammed the door to her room and plopped herself down on the bed breathing hard. She had only known both of them for such a short amount of time. Whatever could have possessed them to be so jealous? She sighed, and flipped over.

She glanced at the clock and groaned. She had to go back to work. Mrs. Harper had told her everything that needed to be done that morning so she hurried to work without going to any meeting. She would not need to see anyone for the rest of the day, so she could fume in silence, she decided.

Maybe Brandon was still not getting the picture. And she'd not had the chance to explain things to Ryan before Brandon had shown up acting like a bull seeing red. And Ryan himself was certainly a puzzle. "Oh Lord, I am so confused."

He'd shown up two weeks ago and been all sweet. He'd been content to sit beside her and talk every day or just sit quietly while she observed. He seemed like a pretty good guy, and he was a Christian, but there were still too many things she needed to know about him before they could date. It was still too soon.

She smiled to herself, as she sprayed Windex on the mirrors. It was nice to have found guys interested in her though. So it happened quite a bit, but it was always nice to be liked. She couldn't help but be a little flattered, even if she never did date either one of them. She began wiping off the liquid with a paper towel. Strange, she realized how happy she had been to see Brandon. The corner of her mouth slid up on its own accord. She wished that she could stop thinking about him. "What is wrong with me?" she continued to pray inside her head.

She stilled with her hand up against the mirror. Someone was watching her. She turned to see Brandon's dark blue eyes boring into her. His expression was unreadable. "I'm sorry," he confessed softly, his deep voice causing her heart to beat a little faster.

She looked into his eyes for a moment, then nodded, "You're forgiven," she stated. His eyes widened slightly. Maybe he was used to people holding a grudge, she decided and turned back to finish the mirror.

Brandon walked in and sat down in a chair near her. She sighed. Was he going to sit and stare? He knew she hated that! She looked over at him. His eyes were on her. She felt herself growing hot. She frowned at him. "I hate it when you do that," she commented, and put away the towels and Windex in the basket she'd brought into the room.

A slow smile crept up onto his face, "Sorry," he answered unrepentantly, his eyes still on her.

"If you were really sorry, you'd stop," she implored, picking up the furniture polish.

He chuckled, the low rumble causing Mandy to catch her breath, "So you stayed huh?" he commented, changing the subject.

"Um," she frowned, looking down trying to forget the feelings he elicited, "not excited about it, but I did volunteer," she stated, spraying some polish on the dresser in front of her.

"Wanted to see me?" he teased.

She made a face at him as she reached for the cloth, "Actually Mrs. Harper told us your sister was coming. You honestly think that I would have stayed and Brandy wouldn't have if she had known you were coming?" she retorted.

She heard him chuckle, and then stand up. She began rubbing the furniture polish into the dresser with her cloth a bit too fast. She felt him come closer and turned her head slightly to see. Big mistake! His face was inches from hers. She swallowed hard, and her pulse began to pound in her chest. She had to stay calm. His eyes were watching her lips a strange longing in them and she found herself licking them self-consciously. Mandy suddenly had the feeling he was going to try to kiss her.

"I need to get back to work," she said breathlessly, looking around, "Alone," she stressed.

Brandon smiled slightly, "I'm glad you stayed," he breathed and Mandy felt herself going hot. She turned back towards the dresser using the solid feel of it underneath her hands to steady herself.

Brandon stood where he was for a moment. She could feel the heat from him radiating into the skin of her back and smell his musky cologne. She felt her breath coming quicker, but forced herself to stand with her back to him as she continued working. And then, he was gone.

Chapter Thirteen

EDWIN CASTLE SMILED AT Andréa as she padded in bringing yet another dish. They were all eating their Thanksgiving meal together in the small dining room. Brandon had already been taken his meal in the large dining room and now all of them could eat.

"Miss Mandy," Andréa said as she set the dish down, "The young senor want you to eat with him," she stated in her rich accent.

Edwin looked at Mandy. Her eyes twitched, and her mouth was frowning. He smiled to himself. Brandon was finally chasing a girl that was worth it, but she didn't seem happy about it. Poor girl, everyone was watching her. She looked at Mrs. Harper.

"Go ahead dear," she barked flippantly, waving her thick hand as if to dismiss any doubt, "It's not good for the boy to be alone for Thanksgiving and frankly I doubt he'd want to spend it with any of us ancient ones."

Edwin raised his brow. Now he was puzzled, and he could tell he wasn't the only one. Everyone had their mouths open, and eyes wide staring at Mrs. Harper with expressions that told him they thought she had sprouted wings or something. She'd never have agreed to let any of the other housekeepers eat with Brandon. He smiled to himself and looked down at his plate. Maybe Mandy had affected her too, if Mrs. Harper was actually worried about how Brandon felt.

Mandy still had a frown on her face, but she piled some food on her plate and headed out anyway.

Edwin smiled at Andréa as she sat down beside him. Mandy was a good girl, and something inside him was telling him that she was just what Brandon needed. He let his mind wander from her and let it settle on the woman beside him.

Andréa was very different from his late wife, but she had a good heart and she was so cute with her short dark hair that framed her sweet round face. He'd need to make his move soon, he decided.

Andréa smiled slightly at Edwin. He had become very talkative of late, and strangely she had found her stiffness melting. She looked at the door that Mandy had walked out and smiled to herself. Mandy was a sweet girl. She was always smiling and had asked to be taught some Spanish.

Everyone else had just seemed annoyed that Andréa didn't know the language when she arrived. She had learned fast, but not fast enough. She had been forced to learn a lot of things fast, she decided, and put a forkful of potatoes into her mouth. She pursed her lips slightly, and thought. She should have added more salt. Oh well, too late.

She would have visited her daughter during the holiday if Brandon hadn't come. She smiled slightly, thinking of her beautiful daughter. Of all the things her ex-husband had done, the only right one was giving her their daughter. Then he had run away before she had even been born. She bit into the cranberry sauce. Perfect.

Edwin asked her a question. She turned towards him, her mind trying to switch from her Spanish thoughts into English quickly. "You were going to see your daughter weren't you?" he'd asked.

"Yes," she agreed, despising her thick accented voice but Edwin's smiled.

"What is her name?" he asked.

"Alejandra," she replied and thought about her wonderful daughter who had fallen in love and married an American who was in South America on vacation when she had turned eighteen. Later they had found a way to bring her over to America to be near them.

"That is a pretty name," he commented, then added softly, "I love the way your mouth rolls over the word," and Andréa's eyes whipped around to stare at him. He was looking into her eyes with a strange intensity and Andréa found herself very unsure of herself. She swallowed hard. After all the years of pushing other men away, why did she suddenly find herself growing attracted? And why to this man?

Brandon's stomach churned as he waited impatiently wondering if she'd come. Mrs. Harper would probably say something about propriety even if she wanted to. He sighed. Then again, she probably didn't even want to.

The last time he'd seen her had been yesterday. His heart pounded just thinking about it. After she'd turned his back on him he'd left the room, but kept an eye on where she was all day. He'd watched her walk to her room after supper and hadn't seen her since.

He grew warm thinking about standing so close to her. He'd breathed in the sweet scent of her and stared into her blue green eyes and almost lost himself. He's stared at her lips and wanted so much to kiss them. She'd turned away from him and he'd wanted to wrap his arms around her and hold her close. He'd never felt that before, the urge to just hold someone, protect them. He'd sensed her struggle, before she turned away.

Did she feel something for him too, or was it just their close proximity, which he'd decided was what her problem had been last time. He'd stood staring at her back and her long dark braid, and almost lost his resolve to walk away. But he had. Why was this girl affecting him like this?

Brandon clenched and unclenched his fist as he watched the doors. Movement made him snap to attention as she stepped into the room. He felt himself suddenly growing hot. Her hair swayed slightly as she came in and walked towards him. Her long curls fell around her. She was frowning.

"You came," he stated, hoping to understand why she was upset.

"Mrs. Harper thought you'd be lonely," she commented and plopped down in a chair near him.

Brandon brows furrowed. Was she serious? "Are you kidding?"

She shook her head, a slight smirk beginning to light her eyes. "Her exact words were, 'it's not good for the boy to be alone for Thanksgiving, and I doubt he would want to spent it with any of us ancient ones,'" she stated, then looked into his eyes.

Brandon grinned. Mr. Harper had always called him, "the boy." It was sort of a pet name that he'd never minded. Maybe Mrs. Harper was getting soft. Or maybe it was just Mandy. She affected everyone, he decided.

"They look out for you, ya know," she commented, her beautiful eyes softening into a smile, "even if you don't return the favor," she added softly, looking down at her plate, and closing her eyes. Brandon realized she was praying. He paused feeling slightly uncomfortable.

Brandon frowned, and when she finally raised her head back up he inquired, "What's that supposed to mean?"

"Why did you come here?" she insisted, picking up her fork.

He shrugged, ignoring the question. Needn't let her know it was only because of her. "Well, your plans messed up theirs," she stated softly, and lifted a forkful of mashed potatoes to her round mouth.

Brandon frowned, as he picked up his fork too, "What do you mean?"

"I'm not trying to be unkind," she added, after swallowing, "but do you ever think about what everyone else does when you are not here?"

Brandon twisted his lips in puzzlement. Now that she mentioned it, he'd never cared. "No, I guess not," he admitted. But suddenly he was curious.

"Everyone but Mr. and Mrs. Harper were planning to go somewhere else," she commented, looking into his eyes and emphasized, "to be with family."

Brandon grimaced, and looked away. He suddenly felt bad that he'd never thought about the lives of the people that worked for him, for his family.

"Why did you come, Brandon?" she implored again, her eyes searching his face.

He looked up into her blue green eyes, and felt his heart melt, at the gentle look that seemed to compel him to tell the truth. Their depths seemed to drag the truth from him. "To see you," he finally admitted, his voice coming out in a hoarse whisper.

She smiled softly and looked down at her plate, "We discussed this before," she replied, and put another bite of potatoes in her mouth.

"I know," he sighed and looked down at his plate again, knowing he shouldn't stare at her mouth. She even ate gracefully.

"So why am I in here?" she emphasized the last word, and finished her bite and pursed her lips.

"Because I need company," he teased, glancing at her mouth again as she dabbed it with a napkin.

"I think we need to keep our roles in perspective," she murmured. "You should be eating with your family, not your housekeeper." Brandon clenched his teeth. He'd rather eat alone than with his family.

Mandy frowned. The moment she had mentioned his family, Brandon's humor had left. It was hard to understand a family that was exactly opposite her own, but she felt the need to listen and understand him, like she always did with anyone she knew was hurting. "Lord, help me say the right things," she prayed in her mind.

"You're cuter than my brother," he attempted to tease her, but it fell short. They ate in silence for a few moments, before she broke into the quiet.

"Tell me why you're not fond of your family?" she inquired, and picked up her cup of juice to sip on.

Brandon looked at her for a moment contemplating. "I bet you're really close to your family, aren't you?" he replied, an almost envious smirk on his face. She nodded. "So you're not going to use this as more of that, 'our morals are different' stuff, are you?" he asked quizzically, waving his fork around to be dramatic.

She laughed. "The family you are born into is not of your choosing, only what you do with it is your choice," she stated, looking into his eyes again to emphasize. "Morals are a choice."

"But what about the fact that you grew up with parents that have morals like you. I grew up and have morals like my parents. Don't you think morals might be partly hereditary too?" he inquired, before shoving a bite of cranberry sauce into his mouth.

Mandy smiled, impressed by his insight. "A person is shaped by hereditary and environment," she began, "So yes, you learn morals from your parents, but as we grow older we have to decide for ourselves if they are good or bad. After a certain time, morals become our own choosing."

Brandon nodded as he finished his bite of cranberry sauce, and smiled. "I see you've thought about this before," he quipped.

Her pretty round lips turned up into a smile again, "Yes," she agreed, "I've often thought that people who grow up in the best of environments have the best advantages, but they can never be as strong."

Brandon's eyes frowned. "What do you mean?"

"Adversity breeds strength," she recited from the well of ideas that spilled over in her mind, and paused to see if Brandon understood yet. His brows were still furrowed.

"People that go through the roughest times either break or become strong. I never had many problems. I am not as strong mentally as my friend, Devon."

She saw him frown slightly, but she ignored it. "He was abused as a kid," she stated, feeling the pain of that thought even as she spoke. "He chose to come out of it and not be bitter, and not fall into the same cycle. It will be a struggle when he gets married and has children, but his resolve is strong never to be like his father, and I know he will let God help him keep that resolve."

Brandon nodded in understanding. "I see, so you can be strong in your beliefs because you were raised that way, but your friend is strong in his beliefs because he was raised in a bad environment and resolved to be different."

"Yes," she agreed a light in her eyes. "It takes more strength to go against how you were raised," she added.

Brandon nodded again and looked down at his place. "So you're saying that I'd be stronger if I chose not to be obsessed with money and tyrannical like my father and fixated with beauty and appearances like my mother?" he bit out in acid tones.

Mandy just smiled slightly in concern. She watched him for a few seconds. He clenched and unclenched his jaw in anger. "If you do not like how they act, why would you want to be like them?" she asked softly.

Brandon looked up at her and their eyes met. His deep blue eyes seemed to be pleading and Mandy couldn't turn her eyes away. It was as if he was saying he needed her. But that was all wrong. She shook her head to clear her thoughts and looked down. He didn't need her. He needed God, she thought with resolve. "My brother and sister are becoming like them," he finally retorted softly and looked away too.

"In what ways?" Mandy asked, allowing him to talk about what she knew was bothering him.

"My brother is becoming just like my father. They both work at the office twenty-four seven, and my brother is becoming just as unfeeling as my father." He sighed, and shoved a bite of turkey into his mouth. He chewed it several moments and swallowed it before he spoke. "I remember when we were young, he'd play games with me, but the older we got the more he wanted to be with our father. Even when he was ten, I can still remember him saying, 'I'm not taking advantage of people, I'm just taking care of myself,' just like my father always says."

Mandy eyes studied him and she could see that it bothered him. "Do you agree with your father's saying?"

Brandon sat in silence for several moments before he spoke, "I guess I have in some ways," he admitted, glancing over at her. "I never liked the saying, but I realize now that I've actually been following it though."

"Realization is the first step," she declared with a little wink.

"You mean like that old G.I. Joe slogan, 'Knowing is half the battle,'" he recited, smiling.

Mandy nodded, thankful she even knew what he was talking about because of the old cartoons her parents had shown her. Their laughter slowly died as they ate in silence for a few moments. She looked over at him and found him watching her. Mandy smiled slightly. She wondered why he insisted on doing that. It bothered her that she was affected by him more than anyone else she had ever tried to help. But she didn't know what he was about, what he really wanted from her. His reputation suggested something that she did not like, and was not willing to give. And recently he had started looking down at her mouth on occasion and she knew what that meant. Even though she grew warm just thinking about it, she knew it couldn't happen.

Plus, she could never seriously think about getting involved with anyone who didn't have a relationship with God like she did. But that didn't mean she couldn't use this opportunity to teach, to witness, even if her heart was trying to play tricks on her just now.

"Why did you come to see me?" she asked again.

Brandon looked down at his plate, and then back up at her, his brows puckered, "You intrigue me," he admitted. She stared at him, wondering what he meant. "You know I haven't had any alcohol since I saw you last," he added softly.

Her heart lurched unexpectedly. What was he trying to tell her? "I know you think I take advantage of people, and have bad habits, but people can change you know." His deep blue eyes seemed to be pleading with her.

She stilled. Was this what she was waiting for? "I know" she agreed, and looked down, "I know."

"So you don't think I could change for you?" he asked, in a challenging tone.

She smiled up at him, "You don't know me enough to change for me," she stated softly, but her mind was in turmoil.

"So give me the chance to get to know you," he pleaded.

She looked down and ran a finger over her nose. She didn't know what to say. She'd never thought about being in a situation like this before. She'd always known what kinds of men she would and wouldn't date, but she'd never expected one of those that she wouldn't date to say he'd change for her.

But then the warning bells sounded again. He still didn't have a relationship with God. "I don't think you quite understand everything yet," she paused.

"So help me understand," his eyes pleaded with her.

She looked at her cup and picked it up, "I couldn't date anyone who wasn't a Christian like me," she stated quietly and then sipped her juice.

He nodded slowly and a sad smile crept onto his lips. "I had a feeling you would say that. My grandma is a Christian, and she use to tell ..." his words trailed off, and he looked across the room momentarily.

She stared at him for several moments, trying to focus on praying, and trying to ignore the muscles in his arms as he brushed a hand through his hair. She looked down at her plate again wondering what to say then realizing she should be praying about it instead. "Please Lord, help me with this temptation," she prayed in her mind, "And Lord help me be an instrument and say the right things."

"So, do you think you could at least talk with me some," he asked, looking almost hopeful, and she frowned momentarily, wondering if he were for real, or if this was just another ploy. She sighed, then looked up at him and smiled, realizing that this might be her answer to prayer.

"Maybe," she said quietly, and then looked down at his plate. "You are done eating now, and so am I, so I think I should be going," she added and picking up her plate, went out the door.

Trevor put up both arms and yelled as he and his friends were flung straight down, the coaster they were on, twisting and turning on its downward track. "I love this one," he yelled out.

Brandon laughed, as he clutched the arm handles that were over his chest. "Me too!"

A couple moments later the ride stopped and the boys got out. Trevor laughed again as their other friends piled out from behind them. John and Gavin looked almost sick, but they were laughing too.

"It's a shame Rick couldn't come," Brandon murmured to the group.

Trevor shrugged, "He's having to face the real world soon."

"Not until graduation," John stated. "He needs to let loose and have fun while he can."

"Try telling him that," Gavin retorted with a snort.

"So tell me why you didn't invite any girls to our After-Thanksgiving-Trip?" Bobby asked his dark eyes glittering.

Brandon smiled over at him with a shrug, "Less people to pay for," he teased, as they headed out of the dark tunnel leading them away from the ride.

Trevor laughed sarcastically. That definitely was not the case. The Taylor's could pay for all of their friends and acquaintances to come to Universal with them and have no problems at all. It was only the five of them, though since Rick wouldn't come. It was pretty strange.

"So didn't you have the hots for some housekeeper the last time you were down here?" John asked nonchalantly rubbing a hand over his light blonde spiked hair.

Trevor watched as Brandon gritted his teeth and said, emphasizing each word, "Her name is Mandy."

"So why didn't you invite her?" Bobby asked offhandedly.

"Invite a maid," Gavin laughed at Bobby, as they walked out into the light. "Maids are for playing with, not spending money on."

Trevor kept silent, but he saw Brandon's jaw tighten rock hard. Gavin missed it though and kept yapping, until Brandon said forcefully, "I did invite her."

Trevor raised his eyebrows, "She didn't want to come, or was she working?" he asked.

Brandon didn't answer. "What's so special about this girl?" Gavin asked narrowing his dark green eyes.

"She intrigues me," Brandon stated quietly, then ignored them as he stopped at a stand to buy cotton candy.

Trevor's light brown eyes followed Brandon. Then he turned to watch the other guys. They didn't seem concerned. Gavin was again joking about how the girl must be fine and Brandon just needed to get with her. Maybe that was it.

When Brandon was done buying his cotton candy Trevor walked beside him as they wove their way through the park towards the next ride they had decided to go on. "Hey man, do ya think perhaps you should just sleep with this chick and then the intrigue would die, like it did with all the rest?"

Something flickered in Brandon's eyes, but he didn't answer, so Trevor let it go. But during the rest of the day he watched his friend. What was up with this girl and why did Brandon seem so different?

Ryan watched Mandy for a few moments. She was actually sunbathing. It was strange. She'd never done that before. Maybe that spoiled rich kid had gotten to her. He sneered. Who did that guy think he was moving in on his territory? He'd probably not even been living here year round but expected every girl that worked for him to swoon. Well, he'd have his fun first and then that Brandon could have her.

"Hi," he said softly sitting down beside her. She looked up and smiled. That was encouraging, "Sorry," he added, trying to sound sincere.

Her full lips curled up again then she lay her head back down. "It's okay," she stated.

"You actually sunbathing?" he asked incredulously.

"Resting," she commented with a yawn, "I have this afternoon off, so I decided to enjoy the sun."

"So do you think perhaps we could try having that conversation again that we started a couple days ago?" he asked raising a brow.

"Which one?"

"The one where I was asking you to go out with me tonight?" he teased, and leaned back to rest on his elbows, so he was closer to her.

"You asked me about Wednesday night, not tonight," she commented, flipping her head over so that she could look up at him. Her gorgeous curls flew all over her body and he caught his breath momentarily.

"Yes, but we got cut off," he clarified a grin in his dark brown eyes.

"Not before I said, 'no,'" she answered, a smile in her voice.

"But I hadn't gotten my chance to rebuttal," he countered.

One side of her mouth turned up, and she shook her head slightly. "So that's another, 'no,'" he asked.

"Yes," she agreed, propping her chin up on her hands. Ryan frowned. Maybe she was going out with Brandon or something. Most girls didn't turn him down.

"Why not?" he asked, then couldn't help the slight bitterness that seeped out, "I'm not as rich as Brandon?"

She turned her head towards him again and narrowed her eyes. She shook her head slowly and looked back out towards the ocean that she was facing. "Though what Brandon said is true," she answered softly.

"Well, I don't drink," Ryan lied. At least he hadn't yet today.

Mandy looked up at him again, "I like to date only guys that have the same morals I do," she answered.

"And you think I don't?" he asked, trying not to sound shifty.

"The point is I don't know you enough yet to know," she answered. "I know you said you are a Christian, but not everyone who claims to be really is," she ended with a sigh.

"So how are you going to get to know," he asked, deciding to take a less defensive approach, "if you won't go out with me and find out?"

"Well, we're getting to know each other more each time you come out here and we talk," she commented, grinning up at him.

This girl really was aggravating, he thought, but smiled down at her. How long would he have to keep coming out here, wooing her, before she'd give him what he wanted? This girl certainly wasn't going to give in quick, so she'd better be worth the wait.

Chapter Fourteen

DESIREE TWISTED HER SHORT brown hair in her fingers and laughed softly to herself. So she wasn't being very subtle now, but she had to get Brandon. It was now or never. He'd not come to the club at all in the last few days that he'd been around and she hadn't been invited to the amusement park today, so getting him to go somewhere with her this evening was her only chance.

She knew it was harder to say, "no" in person, especially when she was dressed up in such a sexy red dress. Brandon had to take notice. She knew she looked good. She smoothed her dress absentmindedly. She pulled up into their drive and to the front gate and waited. The butler answered and she identified herself then waited for the gates to open.

She drove up and parked and then walked up to the house, her tall stiletto heels clicking on the cobblestone walkway. The butler opened the door and ushered her into the den. She sat down and crossed her legs. She knew the butler was going to announce her unexpected visit to

Brandon. She twisted her hands in her lap, trying not to be impatient.

Brandon came in shortly and ran a hand through his blonde hair. He was so cute and muscular. She sighed. "Hi," she stated eagerly trying not to make it obvious that she was batting her long eyelashes at him, "Sorry for just showing up," she cooed, "but I knew it would be harder for you to say 'no' in person."

Brandon raised an eyebrow, "Say 'no' to what?" he asked still standing in the doorway.

"Did you just get back from Universal?" she asked, deftly changing the subject.

Brandon half smiled and nodded. "A half an hour ago."

"So aren't you going to invite me in and give me something to drink?" she teased, standing up.

He smiled more fully. "Where are my manners?" he teased. "Come on," he called motioning with his hand, "and I'll get you something to drink."

She grinned to herself. So far this was going as planned. They headed to the living room which was next to the kitchen. She sat on the sofa, and Brandon stepped out a moment, returning a moment later. "Most of the staff is on break today," he commented, "but the cook or some other staff member will bring us soda momentarily," he commented. He sat down in a chair nearby. Her brows furrowed. She'd left plenty of room on the sofa for him.

Then his words sank in. Soda? Since when did Brandon entertain guests with soda? It had always been wine or champagne. "So what's this that I'm not going to say, 'no' too," he asked, leaning forward in his chair.

"Well, I know you've been busy and all, but I thought perhaps you'd like to go see a movie with me?" she cooed, and rubbed one of her arms unconsciously.

Brandon laughed, "All this for a movie huh?" He leaned back and rubbed his chin slightly with one hand, as if in contemplation. Better think of more to entice him.

"Perhaps," she teased, "And perhaps afterwards I could show you my new place? You haven't seen it yet, have you?" she let her voice become slightly deeper.

Brandon shook his head and frowned. "I'm pretty tired after the amusement park though. Perhaps some other time?" He looked up at her and smiled slightly at the suggestion.

Desiree grit her teeth and tried to force a smile. "But you'll be gone again soon," she protested, and then ran a hand along her face, "I promise I won't be rough," she teased seductively.

Brandon frowned again, and then looked up as the door opened to their left. Desiree watched the look on his face go from annoyance to an almost peaceful joy that angered her. Who could make him look like that? She wondered and she whipped her head around.

A fairly beautiful girl with long curly brown hair and bright eyes had walked in carrying a tray. The maid? He was giving that look to a maid? She'd never seen him give that look to anyone. Her blood began to boil. She could feel her hands becoming fists.

The girl came in and gave them both drinks. She smiled sweetly at Brandon. Then the girl walked over towards her and Desiree glared at her as she served her. The girl kept on smiling, though, even at her. Did she know something or was she really that cheerful all the time? Maybe she was trying to get into Brandon's bed and from the look on his face, it must be working.

"So what's going on here?" she hissed suddenly.

The girl looked confused, and Brandon gave her an odd look, one that seemed to hold a slight tinge of warning, but she ignored it. She had to be right. "What do you mean?" he asked slowly.

"You know getting involved with the help," she emphasized the word, "is a bad idea. They're mooches."

Brandon's face grew red and the muscles in his jaw and in his biceps tightened. She had to be right! She looked over at the girl. She still looked slightly confused and not at all angry. That was strange.

"Thank you Mandy. That will be all," he said sweetly to the girl who nodded and smiled at them both before leaving. Maybe she didn't understand English or something.

The moment the girl stepped out of the room Brandon turned on her in fury. "How dare you!" he bellowed through clenched teeth.

She was surprised. He'd never acted this way before. When she'd heard other friends of his tease him about messing around with the help, he'd never gotten angry. Maybe she had wounded his pride with the way she had said it.

"I'm sorry Brandon, I never meant to imply that you can't make your own choices or say you have bad taste. I mean, I'm sorry if I hurt you," she added quickly, trying to sound sincere.

"You have no right to assume anything," he spit out angrily. "She's my friend and what you said was downright mean. So unless you'd like to apologize to her, you can leave," he declared evenly, staring at her from narrowed eyes.

Desiree brows went up in shock. A friend? She could leave? What was wrong with him? And apologize to that maid? She'd rather die! She got up and headed for the door.

Maybe Brandon would come to his senses later, but for now, there were other men to chase.

Brandon was still so angry he could hardly see straight as he headed through the door Mandy had gone out, the second Desiree left. He'd not expected this.

Course he'd not expected a lot of things. He hadn't expected Desiree to come by and in an attempt to be nice, she'd taken her suggestions to far. Then he hadn't expected Mandy to come through the door or the wave of inexplicable joy he'd felt at seeing her. And he certainly hadn't expected Desiree to get nasty and Mandy to act perfectly calm. He strode into the kitchen.

He needed to find her and apologize since Desiree wouldn't. He looked around and saw her putting away the soda. She was humming. He furrowed his brow perplexed.

"I'm sorry about that," Brandon stated quickly as he strode towards her. He felt an unexplained desire to be near her.

She whirled quickly, looked up at him and shrugged. "Why are you apologizing, you didn't do anything?"

"But she had no right and I'm sorry if what she said hurt you," he stated, stopping as close as he dared.

Mandy shrugged again and smiled with the corner of her mouth. "You know that saying, 'sticks and stones'?" she began, and turned to grab a glass of juice that she had apparently poured for herself. Brandon nodded. "I don't really care what she thinks, so even if it were true, nothing she says can bother me."

Brandon stared at the girl his eyes widening as she smiled up at him. "So does nothing faze you?" he asked bewildered.

She laughed, and sipped her juice before answering, "I just don't let what other people think of me affect how I act, or affect who I am, because the only thing that matters is what God thinks, and He loves me no matter what!" And with that she smiled broadly at him and headed out the door with her juice.

Brandon plopped down on a barstool. He realized that he had been worried all his life what others thought of him. His mother had been obsessed with what she looked like and both she and his father were always more worried about what others thought, rather than what they were really doing.

He rubbed his jaw slightly. It had never really mattered to them how many women he dated, as long as they were pretty and rich or influential. They had never cared that he drank as long as it was in the best clubs with the richest friends. That rule about not messing with the help, well that had been passed on to Mrs. Harper because of appearances too. What housekeeper made lots of money or had influence with people in power?

He tightened the muscles in his arm as he ran a hand through his long hair. His father would insist he cut it soon. He sighed. Once more it was all about appearances. He'd always said that long hair did not look professional and one of his standing needed to look professional. He pulled at the ends of his hair slightly.

As he sat there and thought about it, he realized that there was no one he actually cared about enough to worry about what they thought of him. Not really. Well, maybe his Grandmother Rathsmasen. He did not like disappointing her so much, he realized, but then she wasn't the kind that cared about money. She cared about God, like Mandy.

He thought about Mandy and drummed his fingers on the counter. She was so sweet and yet so strong. As he thought about her intriguing ways, he realized that he actually cared what she thought of him too.

Then his thoughts shifted to her comment about God. Was she for real when she said that God loved no matter what? Then why did He have all those rules that people had to follow? Those rules were impossible, and there was no way he could ever be as good as Mandy and follow all of them.

He sighed. Maybe God only loved the good people like Mandy, he thought, pulling at the ends of his hair again. But then again, why did he even care what God thought, surely God didn't actually care about him, he decided. But somewhere deep inside a strange craving began to gnaw at his mind.

Mandy smiled as Brandon stood over her towel, blocking her sun. She'd stayed in her room most of the morning, since she was told she could be off then. She was going to have to help Andréa in the afternoon with the supper preparations.

"Hi," she said, and continued to watch the couple on the beach. She jotted down a few notes. She would need to go to work soon.

He sat down cross-legged beside her. "So, observing more couples?" he asked, and leaned towards her so he could say the words softly. Her heart began pounding. She nodded, "This one any better?" he asked, placing his elbow on his knee. She smiled at him, and nodded.

They sat in silence a few moments, but Mandy's mind was racing. She began to think about how Ryan would come and do the very same thing. He'd usually stretch himself out though, his elbows in the dirt. Strange, but this felt nicer, even if Ryan was a smarter choice. "Lord you have to help me," she breathed inside.

"You off?" he asked.

"Only for another twenty minutes," she stated, trying to concentrate on what she was writing.

"Well I have to leave tomorrow," he announced and Mandy felt a sudden twinge of disappointment. She scolded herself. It was best when he was gone anyway. "Would you maybe allow me to take you out once more?" he pleaded, "Tonight?"

Mandy paused a few seconds in prayer trying to strengthen her resolve before answering, "I have already told you 'no' Brandon," she stated softly, unable to look in his eyes that were at this moment begging, she knew.

"Actually the other day you said, 'maybe,'" he teased.

She smiled and looked up at him. She had to admit, he was persistent. "What I said was that maybe we could talk together some," she stated, and looked into his eyes, almost against her will. His dark blue ones were boring into hers and for a moment she almost lost her resolve. Her pulse was quickening and he was making her dizzy with emotion. This is wrong, she thought and dragged her eyes away, "I can't go out with you," she said quietly, "not yet," she almost added, but stifled that thought, and looked up with a smile, "Is there anything you want to talk about? Like maybe I can explain to you what I believe, or about God?" she asked.

He shook his head a sad longing in his eyes that Mandy suddenly hoped was for something other than her. Then he picked up some of her dark curls in his hand and rubbed them between his fingers his heart in his eyes, "I had to try," he teased, and then he said his "goodbye" and left.

She couldn't stop her heart from beating fast. She'd had a few boyfriends in her life, but no one had made her feel so adored, just by such a simple touch. What was wrong with her? She had to remember what the real issue was here. He needed God, not her! "Lord help him to hunger after You!"

Bobby smiled at John, and said, "Your turn," and gestured toward the smart phone in his hand.

John frowned. He usually loved calling up Brandon and getting him to hang out with them at the clubs or parties, but ever since this girl, Mandy, had gotten to him, Brandon was acting strange. He didn't want to drink and didn't want chicks.

What could he say to get Brandon to come to the club with them in an hour without revealing that he had a hot new girl that he wanted Brandon to meet? Brandon kept saying he didn't want other girls, but he knew once he saw Cassandra, Brandon would forget about the housekeeper. He'd definitely be thanking him later.

"Hey buddy," he declared after Brandon picked up the phone. He rubbed his spiked hair briskly for a second.

"Hey John," Brandon answered lightly, "What's up?"

"Just wondering if you'd like to go clubbing in a few?" he asked quickly.

There was a long pause, "You know drinking isn't my thing anymore," he heard Brandon say softly.

"That's okay," he shrugged, "You don't have to drink," he reminded his friend.

"Hum?" Brandon paused again, "What about dancing?" and John could tell he was teasing. Maybe there was light at the end of the tunnel after all.

"None of the old girls necessarily," he joked back, "You can dance with brand new ones."

Brandon grew quiet again. "I don't know," he stated broodingly. Maybe not. John clenched his jaw and thought quickly.

"At least come hang out with us man," he implored. "We even got Rick to come out tonight."

"Well?" Brandon paused.

"Do you even have anything planned?" John asked suddenly.

"No."

"So you'd rather stay home alone and do nothing, than hang out with your friends?" he teased.

"Well no," Brandon laughed back.

"Then let's go," John cajoled with a smile.

"Okay, okay," Brandon admitted defeat and asked where to meet them.

Good! This was good. He'd gotten Brandon to meet them at the club, and he knew Cassandra would be more than happy to fulfill her part.

Cassandra Singer laughed with Stacey, but her eye was on the door. She couldn't wait for John and Brandon to arrive.

"I've seen him before," Whitney giggled, "and he's so cute," she emphasized with her black eyes.

"Be glad you are getting to meet him," Cassandra announced in a steely voice, her eyes never leaving the door. "I didn't have to invite you, you know?"

"We know Cassie," Lindsey crooned, in a sugary tone, "Thanks."

Stacey pursed her thin lips, making them look smaller. "Course you're only getting to meet him because of one of his friends," she stated jealously.

"And you're only getting to meet him because of me," Cassandra voice dripped with cynicism, and she turned towards her friend, her blue eyes glittering. Everyone stilled. The two stared at each other for a few seconds before Stacey looked down, mumbling an apology.

The other girls began to chatter among themselves while she watched the door. So Brandon had some girl problem that she had to distract him from, John had said. She frowned. Bandon was actually obsessed with some girl. As far as she'd heard, girls were usually obsessed with him.

She could help him though, she thought, her lips curving up into a luscious smile. She knew what to do. She ran a hand through her long straight platinum blonde hair and smiled again. She knew she was very beautiful, with her gray blue eyes, long lashes, and perfect features. No guy could resist her. She knew the only reason she hadn't been invited into Brandon's circles before was lack of wealth. She knew her beauty would eventually be noticed though. And it had. One of Brandon's closest friends had noticed in fact.

She and John had met several months ago and had a bit of fun, but then they'd grown tired of each other, but

Cassandra still knew that he'd eventually introduce her to other people and soon, Brandon. And then to her surprise he'd called up and practically begged her to take Brandon. She smirked to herself.

John and Bobby walked in. She'd met Bobby three days ago. Then three more guys strolled in behind them and all five headed for her table. She smiled at John wondering where Brandon was.

"Hey honey," John said, and kissed her cheek. "He's coming soon," he stated softly in her ear when he saw her eyes looking toward the door.

"This is Trevor, Gavin, and Rick," John introduced, as he stood, and waved his arm to include the other guys with him. She smiled seductively and introduced her friends. She could tell all the men were impressed with her, and she smiled to herself. Good. Snagging Brandon would be easier when all the other guys wanted her too. Men were so competitive.

Just then she saw him walk in the door. He was as gorgeous as she was. He had a perfect body, wide shoulders, and muscles galore. He had piercing dark blue eyes, just like in the pictures she'd seen of him, but he was even more perfect in person. He sauntered over to their table and said "hi" to his friends, then ran a hand through his light blonde hair before using it to shake her hand as introductions were made.

"Nice to meet you," she commented calmly, forcing herself to leave off the "finally." He was watching her. That was good. She could tell he liked what he saw. John looked happy. This was working perfectly. They all talked amongst themselves. Pretty soon the rest of them were on the dance floor, except for her and Brandon.

Alone at last. They talked of trivial things for a few moments and Cassandra wished he'd ask her to dance.

"So I heard Stacey call you 'Cassie,'" he commented, looking up at her with a smile. "Do you prefer that or Cassandra?"

She liked the way his deep voice said her name. "Cassandra," she murmured, in low tones. They kept talking, but she noticed that he kept looking away from her. He seemed to be getting more and more distracted. What was happening? Everything was going great at first, but it seemed as if he were becoming slowly unimpressed as they continued talking. Was she not saying what he wanted to hear?

She tried more flattery. He got even more distracted. She told him more about herself and asked more about him, but nothing seemed to work. Forget talking then. Talking was only a type of foreplay anyway. "Want to dance?" she finally asked. Close contact was good.

Brandon frowned, and she saw a muscle in his jaw twitch. "I don't really feel much like dancing?" he remarked.

What was going on here? She knew he still thought she was pretty. After the look he'd given when he'd first met her, how could he not? "Would you like a drink then?" she asked.

He shook his head, "I don't drink," he pointed out, and she almost laughed. Was he serious?

"You know Cassandra," he began, and took one of her hands. Was he finally making a move? "You've been great, but I've got to leave early in the morning, so I'd better go."

Cassandra was stunned. He was leaving? What had happened? She watched him get up and tell his friends, "bye." What was she going to do now? She narrowed her eyes. She'd better have another chance. Perhaps Brandon really was just tired. She didn't think so though, and then she wondered again about the girl that Brandon was supposedly obsessed with. Maybe it was true.

Richard Sanchez watched Brandon walking toward the door and frowned. It had been a long time since he'd felt like he could take time away to be with his friends and now it seemed like something was wrong. He was the only one having to take over a huge business the moment he graduated while the rest of them always had fun. He watched the door close on Brandon and wondered why his friend was acting like he didn't want to just kick back and have fun anymore.

He'd heard Bobby say it was because of a girl, but that couldn't be what the hungry look in Brandon's eyes had been about. He'd seen the way all of them had looked at Cassandra. He knew what being hungry for a girl looked like. So what was going on with Brandon?

"Well you tried," Bobby stated to John.

John just shrugged. "His loss," he stated, but his eyes darkened slightly.

"Hey Rick," Trevor stated, coming over with a blonde and a red-head on each arm, "you met my friend Charity?"

Richard smiled appreciatively at the blonde and then looked back over at Cassandra. Gavin was headed her way. Richard shrugged. Any blonde would do, he thought and smiled at Charity. She grinned and came strutting over to him and he draped an arm over her shoulder.

A quick flash of regret coursed through him as he led her away to a private booth. What was it about Brandon's look of longing that had awakened the feelings of longing he'd kept in check for so long? But there was never anyone or anything that satisfied, so why was he stressing? He smiled over at Charity and pushed down his feeling determined to enjoy another fling.

Chapter Fifteen

DONNY SMILED AS HE tugged on the wheel slightly and pulled into the driveway. It was still relatively early, but he preferred mornings. He parked his car and headed to his room to put his stuff away. He wondered what Mandy had thought of Deborah. He smiled to himself.

She was probably very different than all the stories Mandy had told of her own family. Donny's green eyes sparkled. Mandy was a great girl. She was so sweet and funny. She was really pretty too. He should go see what she was up to.

He headed into the villa and heard voices in the kitchen. He paused. It sounded like Mandy and Brandon. Brandon? What was he doing here? "...won't be back until Christmas," he heard Brandon say.

Mandy's reply was too soft for him to hear. "I'll miss you," he heard Brandon say and Donny clenched his jaw. Was that rich kid trying to hurt Mandy? He'd better not be still trying to hit on her. He probably only wanted to use her them move on. He'd heard stories about Brandon doing that all the time. That made his blood boil, because Mandy was too nice for that.

He heard Mandy laugh, "You'll miss the rejection?" her muffled voice sounded playful.

He couldn't hear Brandon's reply, but then he heard footsteps coming toward the door. He stepped back and pretended to be walking toward the kitchen as Brandon came out, saying, "Bye," over his shoulder.

"Bye," Mandy repeated and Donny could see she was seated at one of the barstools. Brandon saw him and nodded once as he went by. Donny headed into the kitchen.

"Hey Windex girl," he called out, keeping his tone light.

"Hey Mulch Boy," she teased, grinning at him as he came in and sat down beside her. "Fun vacation?"

"Yup," he laughed then put the back of his hand against his forehead, feigning sorrow. "So, sorry you got stuck here!" Then put his hand down as she giggled, and his brows furrowed slightly, "Hey, I thought the daughter was supposed to be here," he stated, watching Mandy out of the corner of his eye.

"Me too," Mandy shrugged with a laugh, "I guess Mrs. Harper got it wrong."

"Apparently," he teased, rolling his eyes, and then asked her about her break.

She told him about getting some time off and explained what she had done. She never did say anything about Brandon. He frowned slightly. Maybe he hadn't bothered her, but then again, what was with the comment he'd overheard?

"So what did Brandon do all by himself here?" he asked, trying to sound casual and leaned his head on his skinny fist.

She laughed and explained that he'd gone to Universal and to see friends for a few days. "Where did he eat his Thanksgiving meal?" he tried again to sound indifferent.

"Here," she stated and a smile played at the corner of her mouth as she looked up at him, "Mrs. Harper thought he'd be lonely and sent me to eat with him," she started to grin, "Can you believe it?"

Donny's eyes widened. He didn't think it was all that funny. "Mrs. Harper?"

"That's what I thought when she told me. I couldn't believe it," she responded through fits of laughter.

Donny tried to laugh with her, but he was also very upset. What could all this mean? And what if Mandy was starting to fall for his cunning ways? Maybe he'd better make a move?

Brandy pulled into the drive just as the limo carrying Deborah away pulled out. She drove her car and parked it, then headed to the kitchen. She smiled to herself as she thought about Alex. They'd had so much fun over vacation. Then her brown eyes narrowed into slits as she heard Donny and Mandy talking in the kitchen. Now she had to come back here, and her whole mood was ruined. She glared at the closed door, but didn't go in.

"So you want to go to the movies with me tonight?" she heard Donny asking.

Brandy cringed, and gritted her teeth. She was supposed to have gotten to Donny before Mandy did. But, she never got to see him though. How could she combat that? She glared at the closed door but stepped a tad closer so she could hear better, and decided to re-double her efforts.

"Sure," Mandy answered, "and let's invite Alexis," she added. Brandy's mouth opened. She couldn't believe what she was hearing. Maybe this girl really was clueless, she decided.

"Okay," Donny agreed. He didn't sound disappointed, so maybe she still had some hope in getting him away from Mandy.

Brandy pushed on the door slightly, and stepped into the kitchen. "Hi," Mandy called. She faked a smile at the girl and smiled almost seductively at Donny. His eyes glittered in confusion and got off the barstool he was on. "See ya later," he called and headed out the door.

"Bye," both of them called after him.

Brandy's face changed the second the door was shut. A muscle in her cheek jerked. She grit her teeth, and then put a smile on her face to turn and face Mandy, who of course was smiling. The little fake. She'd get her yet. She grabbed a can of soda, and left again. She'd have to figure something out soon, she resolved, or she'd go mad. That girl had to be put in her place.

Ryan walked up the path towards the Taylor's home. He'd decided that he'd come see Mandy here, now that he'd figured out where she worked. Maybe she'd be more willing to say "yes," if he caught her right after she got off. He glanced at his watch. 3:55pm. Perfect.

"Hello," he called to a slim older man, with dark hair peppered with silver, who was trimming the hedge down near the gate at the end of the path.

The man looked up at him quizzically. "May I help you?" the man asked a slight frown in his eyes.

"I'm looking for a Mandy that works here," Ryan answered, trying to smile kindly at the man.

"You a friend of hers?" the man demanded eyeing him closely.

"Yes," he replied with a broad smile.

The man put his clippers down, and opened the gate for him. "Come with me," he stated and turned towards the house.

Ryan followed him towards the villa. At the back door he paused and looked back at him. Just then the door opened and three girls stepped out. All of them stopped short and starred. He smiled at them. He was use to that reaction.

"Where's Mandy?" the man asked them.

"She's just getting off work, Mr. Zeismer," a red-head commented. "I'll be happy to take him to her," she added sweetly.

Ryan smiled at her. He knew what she was after. She was probably a female version of him. He smirked slightly. Good, familiar territory. "Thanks," Mr. Zeismer muttered and turned away.

"My name is Brandy," the red-head bat her eyelashes up at him.

"Ryan," he answered smiling down at her with a knowing expression.

"I'm Connie," one of the other girls added behind him and he turned slightly to smile at the girl with light brown hair. The blonde was already leaving.

Brandy turned toward Connie and he could see her jaw clenched. He knew who was in charge here! "I'll meet you in my room Connie," she commanded forcefully, then turned her back, dismissing her friend. She took him by the arm and led him into the house. Ryan looked back at Connie. He couldn't tell if she was angry or simply disappointed. No matter. He liked girls that couldn't be pushed around by anyone but him.

He looked back down at Brandy. She was gorgeous with her red hair, and seductive eyes. He knew that she was a girl that got what she wanted. Maybe he'd have to keep this one on the side. She'd be a good distraction.

"So where did you and Mandy meet?" she asked.

"At the beach," Ryan replied.

"Um," she hummed it suggestively.

Ryan chuckled, and almost said something provocative in return, but Mandy rounded the corner. Her brows raised momentarily and then she smiled at him. He grinned back.

"Thank you Brandy," he stated and the red-head smiled seductively again and whispered "anytime," before she walked away her hips swaying. Ryan would have loved to watch her go, but he had to force his attention to turn and smile again at Mandy.

"What are you doing here?" she asked a flash of confusion in her bright eyes.

"Thought you might be interested in dinner and a movie perhaps," he asked.

Mandy laughed, "What happened to getting to know each other first?" she teased, "Four more days is hardly enough time."

Ryan laughed, and draped his arm over her shoulder lightly, "How about if you take a walk on the beach with me right now and we can talk?" he proposed.

"I promised Alexis I'd go do something with her tonight, so how about if we do that tomorrow evening?" she suggested, trying to walk in sync with him.

Ryan nodded, deciding Alexis must have been the blonde. How sweet, he thought sarcastically. Alexis must be Mandy's charity case. "Sure," he agreed aloud, "See you tomorrow then?"

"Sure," she smiled and walked with him out of the house. He undraped his arm and headed back down the path, with a wave.

Brandy was waiting for him. He smiled knowingly. "I'm a better catch," she teased a glint in her eye.

"Better or easier?" he asked suggestively.

She raised an eyebrow. "Well, that depends," she pursed her lips and smiled provocatively. His brows went up.

"Oh?"

She turned and looked over her shoulder at him, "Which would you prefer?" She let her tongue glide softly over her lips.

Ryan smiled slowly, and watched her walk away. Her hips swayed and her bright red hair sent flames through him. Now here was a girl who could satisfy him after encounters with Mandy left him frustrated.

Mandy giggled as Alexis pretended to swoon onto her bed, a hand at her temple. "And then when he comes to save you, play dead," she crooned with a tease as she lay on Mandy's bed, her legs and arms in the air in the "dead cockroach" position.

Mandy laughed so hard she fell onto the bed beside her friend, "You are too funny," she announced through her fits of laughter, "Why don't you ever let anyone else know how funny you really are?" she asked growing more serious and standing up again to fix her hair.

Alexis turned over onto her stomach and propped her head up on her fists, and half smiled up at Mandy. She groaned softly, and Mandy felt sorry for her. "My mom just tells me to stop being so silly and grow up," she replied.

"That's not very good advice," Mandy countered, turning to look at her, "You know of all the people I know, the ones who act the silliest and smile the most always look the youngest and have the most fun," she added.

Alexis smiled wistfully, "I know, but I doubt any guys would like my humor either," she stated, "I'm not funny the way you are. You're jokes are more... more... well, intellectual or something."

Mandy laughed, "Now you're just being crazy," she replied and rolled her eyes. "My jokes are just as silly as yours."

Alexis tried to smile. Mandy turned to pull up another curl, and looked at Alexis through the mirror. "I just don't catch guys' attention like you do," Alexis sighed, and stared wistfully at the dark curls that Mandy was piling on her head. Mandy didn't want the girl to be envious of her.

"I bet you have and just don't know it," she countered staring at Alexis's porcelain features in the mirror.

Alexis shrugged her shoulders, "You're just trying to make me feel better," she countered softly, and then changed the subject, "So where are you and Ryan going to eat at?" she asked.

Mandy sighed to herself. Alexis always changed the subject anytime they started to discuss her looks. She wished she knew what to do to convince Alexis that she really was attractive, and not just on the outside.

She really loved this girl and prayed for her constantly. Mandy had talked to her about God a few times, but just like when they began to discuss looks, Alexis would change the subject. She had said she was a Christian but strangely never wanted to talk about it.

The girls chatted for a few moments longer, about trivial things, while she got ready, then Alexis headed for her room. Mandy grabbed her purse and headed to the den to wait for Ryan.

It had been a full week since Ryan and she had first started walking on the beach every evening, except for Tuesdays. She still reserved Tuesdays for her evening out with Alexis. She wasn't sure if it was too soon, but she figured at least they'd only be eating and not sitting together in a dark theatre.

She smiled to herself. Ryan was a good-looking guy with his brown hair and light brown eyes. He was very muscular and he had a good heart. Mandy frowned. She thought he did, though sometimes she was just as undecided about what she really thought of him as she was about Brandon. They both made her nervous, and she didn't know why. She wasn't usually nervous with guys. "What is wrong with me, Lord?"

She sighed and focused on Ryan again. He'd told her about his little sister and all the times he had babysat her when she was a child. He'd told her about how he had refused to follow the crowd when they tried to get him to smoke and take drugs. She frowned. She wondered what his friends were like though, because she realized she had never met them. You could tell a lot about a person by their friends. But he seemed like an all-around great guy and he was athletic too. Mandy liked people who enjoyed the outdoors as much as she did.

Brandon liked boating. She sighed. Why did she have to keep thinking about him? She needed to concentrate on Ryan. She tried so hard during their walks, but every time Ryan would tell her something about himself and his past, she'd think about Brandon and wonder about what he was like at that same age. But the one thing she couldn't dispute in her mind, as she realized she was growing more and more attracted to Brandon, was that Ryan was a Christian. She sighed to herself. "Lord you were supposed to be helping..."

The doorbell rang cutting off her prayer, and Mr. Rathers went to answer it. Poor man, he should be off by now. She went out to meet Ryan. She smiled at Mr. Rathers as she went by him and down the front stairs. His eyes narrowed. Mr. Rathers was a rather protective man. He treated Brandon almost like a son, and maybe he was trying to look out for her too.

"You look stunning," Ryan breathed and grinned at her.

"Thanks," she said and walked with him towards his car, "You look good too."

He grinned again, and then opened the door of his yellow Mustang for her. She got in. He went around the car and slipped in too. The ride was a short one, but the meal was good.

They talked softly through the meal and Mandy couldn't help comparing this date with her meal out with Brandon. She smiled faintly, her "un-date," she decided.

Ryan was charming and sweet. He wasn't funny and ... well downright obnoxious like Brandon. Why was she fascinated by Brandon? He really did seem different than when she'd first met him in October. He seemed a little less stuck up and more aware... hum. Aware of what, she wondered. Could her talk about God have really affected him, she thought then frowned as she remembered the way he had shook his head at her suggestion that she talk with him about God. She pursed her lips and tried to smile at Ryan.

With the meal over, Ryan quite reluctantly drove her home. As she sat in his car, Mandy looked out the window and wondered what it would be like to be riding again in Brandon's Ferrari, the smell of his subtle musky cologne filling the car. She sighed again. She had to stop thinking about him.

Chapter Sixteen

CONNIE GLANCED UP AS Brandy walked into her room. "She aggravates me," she fumed through clenched teeth.

"Mandy?" Connie asked tentatively, sitting down in the chair.

"Of course, Mandy," Brandy spit out and Connie cringed.

She knew Brandy's plans to take away every one of Mandy's interests wasn't working very well. She never talked to Donny, who always seemed to be out working or with Mandy and her unfashionable friend. Both of them seemed to hang on Mandy any time they could.

Of course they never saw Brandon, which they had finally learned was at the villa over Thanksgiving and not Deborah. Brandy about spit flames when she had found out. She had decided that Mrs. Harper had planned it ahead with Mandy and they were all against her. Connie thought that an absurd idea, but didn't dare disagree with Brandy when she was in one of her moods.

The only one that seemed to be succumbing to Brandy's charms was Ryan. It had been two weeks since he'd come by that first time, proving he was real, but nothing really had happened. She knew that Ryan had shown interest, but it was hard for anything to happen without Mandy knowing.

Connie knew it wouldn't be long though until Brandy would catch Ryan alone again, "We need to come up with a better plan," Brandy stated a hard glint in her eyes.

"Like what?" Connie asked looping her light brown hair behind her ear.

Brandy groaned and flung herself onto the bed, "Do I have to think of everything?" she fumed.

Connie frowned. What would make Brandy happy? "How about putting plastic wrap on her toilet?" she suggested.

"Oh my goodness," Brandy spit out, and looked over at her, distain in her eyes, "You are so childish! I want her gone for good!"

Connie cringed again. She hated it when Brandy acted this way. Nothing could please her. She used to be so much fun to talk about guys with, but now she was only interested in ways to sabotage Mandy. Maybe she should think of something really devious. She furrowed her brows, and rubbed her small forehead trying hard to think.

"Accuse her of something really terrible," she suggested, wishing Brandy would like one of her ideas.

Brandy was still for a moment, and then looked up at her a slow maniacal smile creeping onto her lips. "That's it!" she announced, "I've got the perfect plan!" she added, her brown eyes glowing.

It was a week before the Taylor's would arrive for Christmas. Alexis smiled to herself as she headed to the kitchen to get her lunch. She passed by the front door and looked out. Donny was still putting mulch around the front flower beds. Her full lips turned up as she watched him wipe sweat from his brow with the back of his arm. His short brown hair was sticking up slightly in the front from all the times he'd done just that.

"Ready for lunch?" she heard Mandy say behind her and she forced herself not to jump as she whirled around and gave her friend a smile. She glanced at Mandy's face, hoping she hadn't noticed that she had been watching Donny.

"Yep," she agreed quickly and headed towards the kitchen, Mandy at her heels. They got their food and a few moments later, Donny came in, "Hey Windex Girl," he teased Mandy.

Alexis bit her lip. "Hey Mulch Boy," Mandy joked back. They looked at her momentarily and she tried to smile all the while her heart was constricting. She wished that Donny would tease her too.

"Hi, Alexis," he said, and she smiled at him trying hard not to stare into his intoxicating green eyes.

"Hi Donny," she replied. She forced her gaze away. The two girls left the room together, and headed for the temp.'s housing. When they got there, Mandy paused instead of heading into her own room. "Why don't you join me on the beach today?" she insisted.

"Oh no," Alexis answered. Mandy was a sweet girl to keep asking. Others would have given up by now.

"But you don't burn in the sun and you look great in your red swimsuit," she countered, "Why not?"

Alexis paused. Mandy had never pushed before. Maybe she really did believe that, because she had never lied at least not to her knowledge. It was a shame others didn't believe that too. "I can't," she stated finally and opened her door.

"Then may I join you?" Mandy asked, her lips inching into a smile.

Alexis smiled back, "Sure," she agreed and Mandy followed her into the room. She'd done that several times, like anytime it rained, but she usually didn't just up and decide to eat with her for no reason. Alexis's hazel eyes glittered with curiosity.

They sat down at the little table in their room and began eating their burritos. "Andréa sure makes great food," Mandy commented through mouthfuls, "Um yum!"

"Yep," Alexis nodded. They ate in silence for several moments.

"I think Donny would love your sense of humor," Mandy stated quietly, breaking the silence. Alexis shuttered and looked over at Mandy apprehensively. Did she know?

"Really?" she asked softly looking down at her hands as she wiped them with a napkin.

Mandy laughed. "Of course! He loves being silly. Even you know that!" she stated as she cleaned up the mess she'd made eating.

Alexis felt a lump rising in her throat. She tried to swallow. A few moments passed in silence. "I bet he'd love more than that about you," Mandy observed softly.

Alexis swallowed hard. She must have noticed her watching him, "You know?" she asked, a tear forming in her right eye.

Mandy smiled, "Of course. He's a great guy! Go for it!"

Alexis frowned, "But he likes you," she began, hated tears starting to roll down her cheeks. She scrubbed at them furiously.

Mandy leaned over and took both her hands into her own, "Alexis," she stated, "He does like me, as a sister or maybe a good friend," she began, "He does not like me the way you like him." Alexis gulped.

"Are you sure?" she implored pulling a hand away to scrub more at her tears with the back of her hand.

"Positive," she affirmed, "He asked me out that day because he was afraid Brandon was going to hurt me in some way."

Alexis's brows furrowed, "He told you that."

Mandy smiled with the corner of her lip, "No, but I figured it out very quickly. I mean Brandon had just left and he was suddenly getting protective, but in a brotherly way," she added quickly. "He had absolutely no problem when I invited you to come along too."

Alexis felt her heart constrict. She looked up at Mandy and smiled slightly. "Positive?" she asked, a light beginning to grow in her eyes.

Mandy laughed, "Positive!" and then with a grin she added, "And I can help you think of ways to swoon for him!"

Alexis laughed and laughed as her friend fell out of her seat and imitated her "dead cockroach" impression. They talked for a long time after that and Alexis finally allowed the dam to break loose and talked to Mandy about God.

It had always been hard for her to think of God as a loving father when all she knew of one was her own who was so verbally abusive to her and her mother. Through her tears Mandy had explained that God was not like that. He had never wanted her father to be like that either.

Mandy was a dear friend and with her help she gave her life back to God again. "Thanks Mandy," she smiled at her friend through the tears in her eyes, "It's great to have a persistent friend," she added, and wondered momentarily at the strange expression that flickered in and out of her best friend's eyes.

Charles Taylor punched in more figures into his tablet as he sat back in the limo. It was good to be in Florida for Christmas, if only for the warmth. He had a lot he had wanted to get finished with before the holidays though, but his father had insisted that he get home first and be sure everything was being taken care of.

He gritted his teeth. Of course it was! Charles knew that and so did his father. They had a very capable staff. This was just Robert's way of punishing his son, and all because a deal went bad that Charles couldn't have stopped. He sighed and slammed his tablet down. His father was not a very forgiving man.

Oliver pulled the limo into the drive and Charles waited until they were stopped before he got out. He headed up to his room and paused as he walked in. This place always brought back memories. He'd grown up here and then when he was twelve they had purchased the California home. It wasn't until he was in his late teens that they had moved to New York. He went into his room. It was the place he loved the most because it was facing out to sea.

Sometimes he dreamed of getting on a boat and just sailing. He'd keep going and not look back. The wistfulness in his eyes slammed shut and he focused again on the reality before him. It was just a silly childish fantasy. He was a responsible adult with things to do. He didn't have time for games, not like his little brother. His brow furrowed. Brandon was still a child in so many ways. He never seemed to grow up. He had fun and played, while he and his father provided the money that Brandon spent.

He sighed again, and stood by the window overlooking the ocean. He wished he had the time to stand and watch the waves roll in as he had as a child. He'd grown up way to fast. He ran a hand through his short brown hair. Someone had to help their father and that someone certainly wasn't Brandon. His little brother had decided on something more artistic like his mother's career. It figured that he'd take the easy path, computer graphics. Hah, like Brandon even cared that much about it.

Charles brushed a short strand of brown hair from his face and wondered again why Brandon had gotten the best looks. His hazel eyes had never drawn the attention his brother's blues had. Not that he needed the women that flocked to his little brother like bees to honey. He didn't have time for girls.

His smart phone rang so he picked it up. "Hello," he answered.

"Hey Charles, long time, no see," the voice at the other end called out.

"Duritzen," Charles announced, grabbing his tablet as he talked, "What are you up to?"

"Oh, come on, you know what I'm up to man. Come on over! The girls are great," he laughed.

Charles smirked. Collin Duritzen had always been good for his sanity. He'd been his best friend growing up and had always loved having fun. Collin had been the only thing to keep him from becoming a complete workaholic.

Course that was only when he was in Florida. He set up his laptop on his desk near his tablet, and pulled out several files as he talked.

He let Collin convince him to hang out at the club with him and soon he got into his BMW and was heading out. It was still early Friday afternoon, so he knew that he would have a few hours before the rest of the family showed up. Maybe after the club he could even get some more work done. He smiled slightly.

Charles got to the club quickly and went in to find Collin. The man was with several girls, as always. It was time to let loose a bit and have fun like they'd done as teenagers, Charles decided, trying his best to forget about the problems that were constantly tugging at the back of his mind.

"So how's your little brother?" Collin asked, waving at someone behind him.

Charles didn't turn. Brandon was one thing he didn't need to think about, "Don't know," he commented and took a swig of his wine. "How's yours?"

"Trevor's been telling me about Brandon's new interest actually," Collin replied.

"You probably know more than I do then," Charles replied. Shrugging off the conversation, he turned to watch some girls on the dance floor.

Collin persisted. "Apparently she got him to stop drinking," Collin stated almost casually.

Charles raised his brows. There was nothing casual about that! Charles turned to look at his friend. "You're kidding! Brandon loves his alcohol!"

"From what I hear he's been sober for like two months now," Collin replied and turned to watch the brunette that was passing.

Charles watched as Collin reached out and pulled the girl onto his lap. Charles frowned at the thoughts in his mind. Maybe Brandon was trying to woo some girl and decided to "change" for her for a while. He'd never gone for two months without alcohol though. He turned once again to look at the dancers. His brother never did anything he didn't want to do. Charles scowled. Something seemed strange.

"So who is she?" he asked casually still looking away from his friend.

Collin looked over at him and the girl on his lap left. Collin shrugged, "That's the strange part. Don't recall ever hearing her name, but I think Trevor said she was some housekeeper of yours."

Charles grimaced. Great! His father hated that. Course he knew his little brother had gone behind his father's back before and didn't care about obeying much, but he hoped Collin was wrong. He sighed. He'd better warn their father if it were true. They would have to deal with *another* of Brandon's indiscretions.

Chapter Seventeen

MELISSA TAYLOR FIXED A stray piece of brown hair that had blown loose as she stepped into the house. This place always smelled salty, no matter how clean the staff kept it. She wrinkled up her small nose. She had grown up in the Midwest and lived there until her father decided to move them to California when she was seventeen. She had never gotten used to the humidity of this place.

She looked back at her husband. Robert hadn't stopped to give her a hand out of the limo, but Oliver had. Despite the fact that Oliver was paid to do such things, her husband would have done it at one time. She lifted her head slightly with pride refusing to feel sorry for herself. Robert had opened car doors and pulled out seats for her while they had been dating.

During the first year of marriage he had stopped. The last bouquet of flowers she'd received from him had been on their anniversary, but she knew the secretary had probably ordered them anyway. She sniffed. Course Karen was probably sleeping with her husband too, but she didn't really care. Not anymore. The right side of her eye twitched slightly. She didn't love Robert anyway. Not any longer.

She walked into the living room and glanced at the couch. Deborah was sprawled out reading a magazine. Robert walked in behind her. "When did you arrive dear?" she inquired of her daughter.

"Thirty minutes ago," she stated without looking up. "Charles is here too," she said and motioned that he was upstairs.

"Where's Steven?" Robert demanded.

"Not here," Deborah replied in a very nonchalant tone, but Melissa noticed the twitch near her daughter's right eye. Melissa gritted her teeth.

"What does that mean?" her father growled.

"He's not coming," Deborah emphasized still looking at her magazine.

Melissa glanced at her husband. She saw the glint of anger in his hazel eyes, and the clenching and unclenching of his jaw. This was not good. She looked down at Deborah, who was still trying hard to seem calm, but Melissa knew her daughter was anything but. "Do you realize how bad it will look if you two don't spend the holidays together?" he asked in a barely controlled tone.

"See and I knew no one would ask me 'why?'" Deborah exploded. "It's all about how it will look for you and never what I'm going through," she whined.

"Fine," Robert glared impatiently, "What happened now?"

"I think he's cheating on me," Deborah whimpered, self-pity dripping from every word.

Melissa gave Robert a fleeting glance. Hardly any emotions were on his face. She knew what this meant. Her left eye twitched. "Well, have you been doing your duties as a wife?" Robert insisted his steely eyes on Deborah.

Melissa snorted in disgust. He was putting the blame all on her. Well, two could play at this game. "Maybe he got boring," she countered maliciously.

Deborah's hazel eyes glittered with hurt and anger as she looked up at the two of them. "And maybe I grew up with parents that don't really care about what I think. Instead they use every opportunity to fight with each other," she cried out.

Brandon could hear the commotion the second he stepped inside. He sighed heavily. His family was at it again. He could hear his father's deep tones scolding, his mother's high-pitched yelling, and his sister's whining voice. Where was his brother, he wondered. He usually took their father's side, and Brandon took his mother's while Deborah whined and cried the whole time about life not being fair.

His blood began to boil, and he strode towards the living room. This is why he hated being home for the holidays! He grabbed the handle in his hand, ready to yank it open. He froze. "It takes more strength to go against how you were raised," Mandy's quiet voice echoed in his mind. It was like a cold shower. Thoughts of her cooled his rage faster than he thought possible. His lips curled up of their own accord. He took a deep breath, and stepped into the storm.

"You still shouldn't have gone to separate places for vacation," his father barked quickly, a permanent scowl furrowed into his brow as he glared at his daughter.

"It does look bad," his mother was saying through clenched teeth, "Even if there was a good reason," she spat out, her eyes on his father.

"Hi," he called out cheerfully. "Merry Christmas!"

All three of them turned and stared at him like he'd just turned purple and sprouted wings. He chuckled to himself. "What are you so happy about?" Deborah asked in an accusing tone.

"Christmas isn't for another six days," his father stated blandly and looked away.

"What girl brought on that grin?" his mother hissed with a condescending look. A strange glint of jealousy glittered in the back of her eyes. He ran a hand through his slightly shortened hair.

He laughed. He couldn't help it. Everyone eyed him again. He smiled at them all. It was amazing how different and cynical his family was compared to Mandy. Maybe that was part of the reason he loved being near her. She was always happy. "Aren't you all a cynical grouchy bunch," he accused lightly.

"Well your sister didn't stay with her husband," his father charged, looking back at his daughter with an almost indifferent expression. It was strange that he didn't really care about her, but instead about her appearances. Brandon sighed to himself.

"Even you must realize how bad this looks," his mother proclaimed, her last word becoming shriller with emphasis.

Deborah shot up and flung her magazine down. "Nobody cares that he's sleeping with someone else do they?" she flung out, self-pitying tears in her voice, and stomped out of the door.

Everyone followed. "Stop right now," his father bellowed as Deborah got to the stairs. "We are going to finish this before you run off to your bedroom to cry!"

Deborah stopped and turned towards them and gave her father such a look of consternation that Brandon cringed. A movement caught his eye and he looked up. Charles was standing at the top of the stairs and his hazel eyes were narrowed in annoyance. When Brandon saw him, he started down the steps. Brandon decided he'd been planning a retreat until he had been spotted. Why did his parents expect them to join in arguments, he wondered, just as the realization dawned.

"Hey dad," Brandon called out softly. His father looked over at him, fire in his eyes at the chance that his son was going to argue. "Why does it matter what people think?"

All of them turned suddenly and stared at him with an expression of confused skepticism. They probably thought he'd lost his mind. He snickered to himself. "We don't want a bad reputation," his mother scolded, in a tone that said she was dismissing the matter.

"You're just saying that because you're involved with one of the housekeeping girls," he heard his brother sneering from behind him.

"What?" his mother and father cried at the same moment, and turned upset eyes his direction.

"Are you sleeping with one of the help?" his father accused, narrowing his eyes to slits.

Brandon's face hardened, "No," he stated firmly, ever muscle in his body tense.

He saw a movement and looked up into the balcony and his heart seemed to stop. Mandy was standing there her heart in her eyes. His parents were still yelling at him, but he didn't hear them anymore.

Deborah suddenly yelled out, "You care about him more anyway, so I'm just going to leave!" and ran back into the living room.

He glanced over at his parents and stated calmly, "Go finish up with Deborah and then come berate me later," he added and began climbing the stairs.

He could sense their struggle, but strangely they obeyed him. He tried his best to walk calmly up the steps, but his eyes were searching. Mandy was no longer at the railing. He looked on the landing and found her sitting in a chair in the corner!

He walked over and she looked up and smiled faintly. "Everyone told me that I should not be in the house when the whole family arrived, but I hadn't finished with one room yet," she shrugged, "I started to come down the steps when Deborah came flying out. I tried to go out the other way, but your brother came by."

He smiled down at her and then knelt in front of her. "I'm sorry," he breathed. "I'm sorry about *all* that you heard," he added, searching her eyes.

Mandy frowned and took both of his large hands in her small ones, "Brandon," she breathed softly, and his heart turned over, "Everyone may think you are the lucky one, but I know better," she murmured so softly it felt like a caress. "I'm sorry that you have to go through all this."

Brandon felt captured. He felt captured by this wonderful creature that understood and cared. "How can you be so, so wonderful?" he asked, feeling that no word could describe her. The heat that always came with her touch was strangely ignored and all he could concentrate on where the strange new emotions coursing through his body.

"I'm not actually wonderful by nature," she snorted quietly and her lips turned up. He frowned. What did she mean? "I am this way because I let God take over my life," she whispered softly, her heart in her eyes once more. And suddenly he realized that it was true. A sudden wave of longing swept over him. He realized that he would give anything to have what she did. He lifted one of his large hands from hers and lightly touched her silky cheek.

He wanted more than anything to understand her, to know her in every way. His heart squeezed. But more than anything he wanted that same inner peace and joy that always radiated from her. Was it really God that had given that to her? He breathed in her essence and realized he wanted to capture this wonderful creature, the same way that she had come softly in and captured his heart.

Robert growled. He'd leave those two whining women to sort this out. He needed to take care of Brandon anyway. That boy's indiscretions would be the death of him. He stopped momentarily to let the pain pass. He grimaced. What was with all the nonsense about why it mattered what people thought. Brandon knew as well as any of them that it mattered a lot. Reputation helped sell his company, the company that provided for all that ungrateful boy's needs.

He plodded up the stairs and stopped short. There was that boy now caressing a girl's face in his very home! His blood began to boil! Right in front of him! How could he? "So this is who you're having your indiscretions with?" he bellowed.

Brandon started slightly. Then he calmly turned around and stood up. How could the boy be so calm when he'd caught him with the girl? He could feel his ulcer acting up again, and the pain in his stomach churned his anger even hotter.

"No dad," Brandon replied, very calmly, looking him straight in the eye. "Strange though," he added, "That you would think that." He laughed sarcastically, "because of all the 'help,' as you put it, that I *have* messed around with, it's strange that you would catch me with the one girl that I never have messed with." And with that his son strode away.

Robert stood there in shock. Was his son for real? Then he looked at the girl who had stood up. She was a pretty thing and strangely her face was serene. The words "You're fired," were on his lips to say, when something flickered in her eyes. Was it concern? For him?

"Father's always want the best for their children," she commented softly and Robert stood and stared as she turned and walked away. He wasn't sure what had just happened, but something about that girl confused him. It was as if she were commending him and scolding him all in the same breath. But what confused him the most were her eyes. She had not looked worried or afraid. She had a strange peace about her and what else? Had she looked up at him with pity? Why would *she* feel sorry for *him*?

Chapter Eighteen

MANDY LET THE SAND run through her toes as she paused in her walk to enjoy the childish sensation. She let the wind blow her dark curls around her and tickle her face. It felt good to have a few hours off, after the scene she had unfortunately seen and even taken part in Friday night. She'd been kept busy in the kitchen all weekend so far, except for her few moments of "haven" when she'd gone to church. Fortunately she had not seen any family members since.

"Enjoying the beach?" the deep voice resonated in her chest as he spoke. She felt herself getting tingly.

She turned and smiled up at Brandon. She hadn't seen him since that night either. He'd touched her face and stared at her and she'd found herself wishing he would kiss her. She was almost glad when they had been interrupted. "Yes," she murmured softy, "though this breeze is rather cold," she stated.

Brandon laughed, "Not really," he teased, and draped a heavily muscled arm around her and pulled her close.

Mandy fought down the crazy sensations and tried to focus on their conversation.

"You've been in New York though, so of course you don't think so," she retorted with a smirk forcing her voice to sound normal. She didn't fight his embrace, knowing her words had only given him an excuse for an action he would have done anyway. "I've been here all my life!"

"On the beach?" he raised a brow in fun.

"Of course," she joked back, as she felt his side press up against her as they walked. He was definitely warming her up!

He laughed and looked down at her jeans and bare feet. He was in shorts and a tank top as always. He looked good in them, like he belonged.

They walked in silence for a few moments, and Mandy found that her arm dangling between them was uncomfortable so she wrapped her arm around his back. "You getting a break?" he asked with a new light in his eyes.

"Yep," she replied, "Same as always," she looked out at the ocean, wondering if she was doing the right thing, but not feeling completely wrong about it.

"So you don't have off this coming weekend huh?" he asked, looking down slightly, a frown in his eyes. She let her eyes wander up and find his, and her mouth turned up slightly.

"With you and your family here, none of us do," she stated then looked back out at the ocean.

"What about after work?" he asked, and turned his gaze out to sea as well.

A wry smile tickled the edge of her lips. "You trying to ask me out again?" she teased, and he looked down into her face. She met his gaze.

"Maybe," he grinned. Their eyes locked for several seconds, and Mandy had to remind herself to breathe. Her heart was racing way to fast. She forced her eyes down and stared at the sand. There was a pause for several more seconds. "Do you have Thursday off?" he asked breathlessly, breaking the silence.

"Christmas?" she clarified, "No."

"When do you guys get a break?" he implored, pulling at the ends of his blonde hair with his free hand.

She bubbled with laughter for a moment, "Not a lot with *you guys* here." She teased.

"So when *do* you have off?" he tried again, a slight grin inching up his face.

"Actually we are working longer hours and different shifts so at least one housekeeper is around at all times," she stated finally, ending their silly game. "As you know we don't just clean," she smirked.

"I know, I know," he ribbed, "You bring juice when we're entertaining," he remarked, raising a mock glass.

She laughed, "Yes, and on Christmas when your family has that big party here, we're all going to be working a lot! And bringing around lots of *juice*," she emphasized the word in a silly way.

His mouth turned up in an amused grin. Mandy found it hard not to stare at it so she looked away. "So you still didn't answer my question," he accused playfully, "When *aren't* you working?"

She couldn't handle being this close anymore, she thought, and broke free from him. Feeling playful she began to run up the beach. She could feel his footfalls behind her. He was gaining. A strong arm snaked out and grabbed her around the waist. She let out a shriek. "Still playing hard to get are we?" Brandon accused breathlessly and wrapped both arms around her and pulled her around to face him.

Mandy's breath froze inside. She realized the playfulness may have been a mistake. Now she was even closer than she'd intended. She looked up into his blue eyes that seemed to be probing hers. "That was never my intention and you know it," she scolded huskily.

Brandon stilled and his eyes seemed to bore into hers. Mandy felt her pulse begin to race even faster. "I know," he murmured, and loosened his grip on her with his right hand and brought it up to her face.

Mandy fought to control her emotions, as heat poured into her cheek where he was touching. He looked down at her lips, and she parted them instinctively. "No," her mind was screaming, but her body didn't want to respond. His mouth slowly moved towards hers and she felt herself breathing a prayer. Suddenly the hold was gone and she looked away, "My current schedule is from eight to eleven and then again from three to seven," she stated blandly, still breathing hard. "I mostly have to help Andréa in the kitchen."

He nodded and stared at the side of her face as she looked out towards the sea again. He seemed to be searching for something, but she refused to look back into his eyes. He finally dropped his arms. She felt a sudden chill and her jaw tightened. "Why Lord," she thought. "Why does he have to feel so good... and safe even?" She sighed.

They began walking slowly along the beach, back toward the house. "Any other breaks?" he inquired, acting as if nothing had happened.

"Um, after this weekend we are all getting a bit more time," she rattled off her voice slowly returning to normal.

"Really, when?" he asked too quickly and she could tell he was watching her from the corner of his eye.

"On Sunday Alexis and I get the whole day off, and Monday Brandy and Connie have off," she stated.

He nodded, and she could see him beginning to smile from the corner of her eye. "So could you perhaps spend a bit of time with me?" he asked.

"Is this your new way of asking me out?" she teased slightly.

"Is it working?" his mouth turned up into a grin that broke through the strain that had been etched on his face.

Mandy's mind paused, waiting for the prickling of warning to ring through her senses, even as her legs kept walking up the beach. Nothing. "Lord?" she whispered. Brandon was watching her. "Is six too early?" she suddenly heard Ryan's voice in her mind. She groaned. She looked up at Brandon with a sigh. She didn't want to have to tell him. She stopped walking abruptly and he stopped too. His eyes lost their sparkle as he watched her face.

"What?" he asked, his blue eyes clouding over like a stormy day.

"I can't go out with you Sunday evening," she stated and fished for a way to state it, "I have plans," she mumbled, softly biting on her bottom lip.

"Oh?" Brandon's brow raised and he reached out with one hand and lifted her chin up until her eyes met his. Mandy could see emotions flickering in his eyes. "With whom?" he asked, getting to the heart of the matter.

"Ryan," she replied softly, and his eyes narrowed and he let go of her chin. She looked down again.

A muscle in his jaw twitched, and he looked up at the beach in front of him again and nodded bleakly. "So what did I miss while I was gone?" he asked through clenched teeth.

Mandy glanced up at him and sighed. Why did it matter so much that he seemed wounded? "He's been hanging out on the beach with me everyday till last week when he started a new job," she stated quietly looking down at her feet as they started walking again. "And we went out a couple times," she added reluctantly.

Brandon looked over at her, the sorrow evident in his eyes, "I see," he said sorely, "So what does this mean?" he asked so softly she could barely hear him.

"We've been getting to know each other," Mandy stated trying hard to keep emotion from her voice. She hated hurting Brandon more than anyone else, she realized, and groaned at the implications.

He stopped walking and she paused in mid stride. She turned and stepped back to where he was. He looked into her eyes, and she couldn't pull hers away. His grip on her heart was growing she realized as it began racing. His eyes brooding, he moved closer, diminishing the gap between them.

He raised a large hand and paused centimeters from her face, "Can we still get to know each other too?" he breathed, "I really do want..." he paused, and lowered his hand, not touching her.

She felt suddenly bereft. "What does this mean Lord?" she breathed inside as his eyes focused on her again, pleading somehow.

"I have some questions...?" he began then halted. "About... well... I was wondering," he stammered.

Mandy watched him, all the while praying that he was finally searching for the right thing. He looked up at her again, a hunger filling his face. It was a yearning than she had never noticed before. "I have questions about God," he finally spit out quickly and looked down at the sand beneath them.

She smiled slowly, afraid if she spoke she would choke. She silently thanked God, and nodded. Brandon's eyes smiled only slightly as he reached up with his hand and this time began to touch her cheek, ever so softly. His heart was in his eyes as he stared into hers. Ryan never looked at her like this, with the intensity that showed her how much he felt. "What do I do God?" she prayed. "Is he really in love with me?' She shook the thought away, not sure if she was ready to digest it yet.

He reached out slowly and caught a strand of hair that was blowing in her face. He gently brushed it back. Why did this man make her feel things she'd never felt before? He smiled slowly. "Thank you," he murmured, and they began walking again.

Brandy pressed the phone closer to her ear, rolled onto her stomach on the bed, and hissed quietly, "You sure you got it?"

"Yep," the voice affirmed.

She smiled maliciously. Everything was going perfectly. "Remember it has to be at exactly eight because the family gets back by eight thirty."

"I got it," the voice stated impatiently, "You know you owe me."

"And you'll get what you want very soon," she murmured seductively, turned off her phone, then flipped onto her back with a devious smile as her red tresses fell around her face.

She looked over at Connie. Her friend wouldn't look her in the eye and was biting her lip. Brandy rolled her eyes. It had been Connie's idea, so what was her problem? Brandy smiled to herself, and put her arms behind her head, resting on them. She had simply perfected that idea. Her *friend* had better not be getting cold feet now, she thought sarcastically.

"Trust me, this will work," she asserted with a smirk, and Connie looked up from the chair she was in and pretended to smile.

"I know," she hesitated, "but are you sure we should?" she added looking down at her shoes and biting at the inside of her cheek.

"What?" Brandy scowled, sitting up suddenly. Connie jumped slightly. She could be so infuriating. She had probably even started to like Mandy. She gritted her teeth. The traitor! Everyone liked Mandy best, but not for long, she narrowed her eyes and smirked.

"I'm sorry Brandy," Connie sniveled, fidgeting, "You're right. I shouldn't have said that." Brandy pursed her lips. Connie was getting jumpy.

"Is there anything wrong with this plan?" she asked coolly, leaning back on her palms.

"Oh no," Connie conceded. "It's great! A perfect way to get rid of Mandy."

Brandy smiled menacingly and snorted in disgust. Connie had been fun for a while, teasing her, laughing and sharing. Recently she's become clingy and obnoxious. That was probably all Mandy's fault too. Well, no matter, the problem would soon be taken care of.

Alexis rubbed her feet and sat down on her bed. "Boy am I tired," she stated.

Mandy plopped down beside her. "Me too," she added yawning. "So glad the family didn't decide to bring the party back here this evening."

Alexis yawned too, "Me too," she looked over at her friend, who seemed almost preoccupied. "What's wrong?"

"Huh?" Mandy looked over with furrowed brows.

"You've been acting strange," she accused.

"Really?" Mandy muttered quickly. Too quickly, and looked down.

"So, you've been listening to everyone else's problems, how about you let me listen to yours now," Alexis stated softly, eyes on her friend.

Mandy smiled up at her and laid her head back against the bed. "Okay," she sighed finally, "okay."

Alexis leaned back as Mandy poured out everything that had happened between her and Brandon. Alexis smiled. She had realized something was going on, but strangely Mandy had never said anything. She had started thinking she was imagining things. But this sounded serious. Serious like how she felt about Donny.

"And so far this week during my three hour break he's come out and walked with me," Mandy declared with a happy sigh.

"Kind of like Ryan?" Alexis asked.

Mandy paused, and one side of her face twitched into a frown. "Yes and no," she began.

Alexis round face froze, trying not to grin. Should she tell her friend that she preferred Brandon? Brandon had smiled at her like she was cute. Ryan was... She had only seen him once, and he had ignored her. She didn't like him much. There was something about him. "I feel more comfortable with Brandon actually," she stated and Alexis smiled, "Which is odd since Ryan and I seem to be more alike."

"Opposites attract," Alexis commented.

Mandy laughed, "Maybe," she agreed. "At first I thought I just felt sorry for him and wanted to help him. I pray for him all the time." She paused and Alexis watched her. She was staring up at the ceiling, as she searched for the right words, "But the more I'm with him the more I'm drawn to him, his personality, the strengths and weaknesses."

Alexis smiled, "Like I am with Donny," she sighed a silly, happy sigh, and Mandy laughed.

"Actually the thing that gets me the most is that he is starting to ask me questions about my relationship with God, I mean he seems genuinely curious. And Ryan and I never could talk about God, or rather, never do," she frowned slightly.

Alexis smiled, "So what's the problem?"

Mandy laughed, "You'd think I'd be all happy huh?" she replied and Alexis grinned and raised her brow in question, "I guess I just want to know for sure that he is not doing this because he is still only trying to get with me, you know?" She shrugged.

Alexis patted her leg as Mandy stretched out on her stomach on the bed. She looked up at Alexis, who said, "So what are you going to do about it?"

Mandy grinned impishly and looked over at Alexis with a grin. "He's taking me out Monday night," she stated, and Alexis began to laugh.

"So you finally agreed to go out with him?" she sighed, "That's great!"

Mandy laughed at her enthusiasm. "So you think that it's a good thing? I have prayed and prayed about it, but I don't feel like I should say 'no' anymore. Does that mean I am just not listening hard enough? Why would God suddenly tell me to go out with him?" Her quick monologue almost made Alexis laugh again, but instead she took her friends hand in hers.

"I don't know Mandy," Alexis stated, patting her friend's hand. "But I do know that if you keep trusting Him, and praying," she paused, knowing she still had so much to learn, "I know God will lead. He always leads you. I know. I have seen it!" she added, looking into her friends face.

Mandy's bright eyes lifted and she stared at her. "You think so," she asked and Alexis nodded.

"Maybe this is just more of a chance to witness," she added.

Mandy frowned, "So why doesn't He keep me from feeling… well… so much, if that is all it is?" she implored.

"I don't know," Alexis stated, "Just trust, right?"

Mandy nodded and gave a little sigh. In the back of her mind she kept thinking that perhaps Brandon would become a Christian and that is why things were working out the say they were. Alexis smiled to herself at her little romantic dream for her friend.

"So what are you going to do about Ryan?" Alexis asked looking over at her.

Mandy bright eyes darkened. "I just don't feel right with him anymore," she commented. "I think I will stop going out with him after Sunday night."

Alexis nodded. "Good," she said, "I prefer Brandon anyway," then her eyes got a mischievous glint, "So, now all is well in paradise?"

Mandy laughed, "So how is your paradise coming?" she countered.

Alexis blushed as she thought about Donny, and then she laughed, "I don't know actually. I've tried to be more open and talk and be myself around him like you said," She frowned, "but I don't know what he thinks yet?"

Mandy's eyes glittered with mischief. "I know what we can do to find out," she crooned impishly.

Donny strode across the front porch and headed into the villa. He was glad the family was on the yacht this evening and everyone was getting a break. Mrs. Harper said that they could have from four until eleven off, but they needed to be back in case the family needed anything when they got home at eleven-thirty.

He opened the front door. He needed to go see what Mandy and Alexis were doing. Maybe they could all go out and see a movie. He was sure the theater would be open even though it was Christmas Eve. He glanced at his watch as he walked through the villa. He was off late. It was already 4:35. Maybe the girls had already headed out.

He went and knocked on Mandy's door. He waited, but there was no answer. He headed to Alexis's room and paused. He heard giggles inside. He smiled. Those two girls sure were fun to be around. They were both sweet and funny, though it had taken Alexis a lot longer to prove just how amusing she really was. She was a strange creature actually. He'd not really noticed until recently, when she'd finally started talking more. He rather liked her.

He knocked on the door. "Coming," he heard Mandy say, but a gorgeous blonde opened the door.

Donny stilled abruptly and stared, his mouth opened slowly as he suddenly realized it was Alexis. She had her gorgeous blonde locks piled on her head, with several curls down framing her perfect rounded face. She had on a tight red dress that stopped at her knees and high heels. Gold hoops dangled from her ears. He gulped. He couldn't speak.

"Hi Donny," she murmured softly and he looked up into her hazel eyes. They were smiling and inviting and he couldn't stop his thoughts. His heart began to pound strangely. Why hadn't he realized how beautiful she was before?

She'd always been cute even in her baggy work clothes and the loose t-shirts she wore when they went out, but now she was downright breathtaking, "Hi," he managed to squeeze out.

"Hey Mulch Boy," he heard Mandy laughing as she came to stand beside Alexis, "We're going out to the movies? Want to come?"

"Uh sure," Donny managed, trying to drag his eyes away from Alexis for a moment. "Let me get dressed," he stammered and with his mouth still hanging open, he turned toward his room. Laughter erupted behind him and Donny grew red as he realized what had happened.

"Those girls," he muttered to himself with a slight grin, as he also realized *why* they'd done it. He ran to his room. He couldn't wait to go to the movies now. He smiled and thought about Alexis, and found his mouth going dry. What a great job this was turning out to be, he thought with a grin.

Elise ran a hand down the smooth bowl and picked it up, pulling it out of the cupboard. Everyone was off, even her, but she didn't have anywhere to go even though it was Christmas Eve. So she had decided to get some things down and be ready for tomorrow, after all the family would be having a massive party here. She paused as she heard laughter coming down the hall near the kitchen.

She could tell it was Alexis, Donny, and Mandy, and she smiled to herself. Those three had become best of friends in their time at the villa so far, and Elise was happy. She had only a few more months left to work before she left, and was happy that she had known a few good workers during her time here.

She pulled down a platter and stilled as she thought about Mandy. That girl had changed so much around here, she would almost be sad to go now. Elise had come to the villa over a year and a half ago and the place had seemed cold, and the people, very closed.

Elise knew that as a Christian she should witness to them all, but she had been afraid, not knowing what everyone would think of what she had to say, so she'd just kept her mouth shut and gone about her business. She did a great job, didn't complain, and made sure no one ever had a thing to complain about her either, but there was something missing.

After Mandy had been at the villa a month, Elise realized what it was. Mandy shared her faith, and didn't bottle it up. Mr. Castle had become a Christian, and several of the others had renewed their faith, and Elise discovered that Mr. and Mrs. Harper were Christians too, and she never even knew because she had been afraid.

She plopped down on the barstool and put her face in her hands. "Oh God," she prayed, tears slipping from my eyes, "I should have spoken of you, and not been ashamed.

I should have been brave, even if no one here had turned out to be a Christian!"

She raked a hand through her dark hair and sighed. "Please forgive me, and give me the strength to share my faith with others from now on," she pleaded, rubbing at the tears that were falling. She bowed her head once more and silently prayed for more faith.

It was still and quiet in the room, and Elise smiled to herself as she felt a peace that she hadn't felt in years fill her. She knew that she would need to start up her morning Bible studies again. That was part of the problem, she knew. She needed to stay connected to God.

"Thank you Lord, for always forgiving, always taking us back," she sniffed, a smile forming on her face.

Chapter Nineteen

BRANDON SIGHED AND STRETCHED out in a chair in the den. He needed a quiet moment. The week had gone by so fast and he'd hardly had a chance to catch his breath.

Strangely his father hadn't said another word about Mandy, and she'd not been fired, so he decided to let it lay too. He'd enjoyed his walks with her every day, but that was the only time he ever seemed to see her. The first weekend his family had each done their own thing and found their own friends, thought Sunday night he'd had that walk on the beach with Mandy.

Monday had been a charity gala down town and Tuesday his father had informed them that he was going to the country club that afternoon and they all knew that meant they were supposed to go and mingle too. Then they'd taken the party back to their place that night.

Wednesday was the Christmas Eve party on the yacht, and then there had been the Christmas party at the villa. Everyone in his family was making a habit of getting up late and going to bed late, so no one really noticed that he got up earlier and walked with Mandy at eleven. He drummed his hand on the arm rest.

He'd seen more girls this weekend that annoyed him with their clingy ways, he felt, than in all his years of dating. He snorted knowing that wasn't really true. He had just finally noticed how annoying they all were. His mind drifted over all the girls he had once thought were so hot. Now, he realized they were like candles and Mandy was like the sun. Who'd want to go back to the dim, dull, witless chicks after being with her? He frowned. Today his parents said they'd be resting, meaning he could too. But he couldn't, not really. Mandy was going out with that Ryan character in just two evenings. Something about the guy didn't feel right.

The door opened and Mrs. Harper walked in, dust rag in hand. She looked startled to see him. "Thought you were all still sleeping," she huffed gently.

"Couldn't sleep," he commented, and rubbed softly at his temple.

He could see she was trying not to smile. She had been the closest he'd had to a nanny while growing up. He had almost forgotten about all the good times he'd spent with her, because she'd grown older and grouchier. He sighed to himself. That was probably his fault though, because he'd grown distant and bratty.

"Thanks for worrying about me," he stated, running a hand through his blonde hair, and then smiling up at her.

She turned and smiled slightly, "You were always the one that needed the most worry," she teased brusquely.

Brandon laughed, and she smirked and turned back to her dusting. He stilled as he watched her. He looked at her hands and realized that they were motherly hands. They were hands that worked, hands that cared, like his grandma. The perfectly manicured hands of his own mother could never quite compare. Here were hands that he felt sure Mandy would call, "giving." She had used that word to describe God too. Giving.

He stared at Mrs. Harper's hand, and thought that she should have had a child. Instead she and Mr. Harper had poured out their time and effort on them, on him. He felt a lump in his throat. He rose and went towards her. She turned, a questioningly look on her face. "Thank you," he muttered and wrapped his arms around her. She stiffened in surprise. "Thanks for being my second mother," he whispered as he embraced her, and he felt her slight shutter.

He let her go and saw a tear fall down her cheek. "She got to you too, didn't she?" Mrs. Harper asked hoarsely.

Brandon smiled trying to reign in his own sheen of tears, and nodded, "She came to this rich place, and showed us how to be rich people," he observed.

Mrs. Harper laughed huskily, "Yes she did and I think you are finally rich enough for her," she kidded softly. Then she turned and headed out the door.

Brandon eyes followed her, and his lips curled up slightly. He turned around and sank back into the chair. He sat thinking a few more moments as he let his emotions cool, then he headed towards the kitchen. He pulled on the ends of his hair as he walked. It was closer to lunch time, but his family would be waking up soon and wanting breakfast. He opened the door and headed for the fridge. He'd just find something for himself, and not bother the staff.

He thought about all that Mandy had been teaching him as he grabbed some food and went upstairs to eat. She had such different views of God than his parents, or friends. But if her God was like her, than perhaps he was ready to stop running from Him.

"You know that theory of taking no more than you give?" she had asked once. He'd nodded, and she'd said, "That's what God does. He keeps on giving and giving."

"He gave us life, and a choice. Then when humans chose the wrong path, He sent His son to die so that there was still a way we could live with Him someday. He gave and gave, and all we have to do is give one simple thing to Him."

"What is that?" he'd asked, as he strolled along beside her.

"Your life," she'd breathed, "Your will," she had added as her brown curls whipped around her in the breeze.

"That's two things," he'd teased, folding his arms on his chest.

"Kind of," she had smiled up so sweetly that he'd put his arm around her and hugged her.

She'd laughed at him and they had begun to run down the beach like they had the first time. He enjoyed teasing her, he realized. It was funny that he had accused her of being a tease. She loved to tease but she was definitely not one. Everything she did was open and honest. He hadn't been able to tease other girls like this. Course he hadn't talked very seriously with other girls either.

He walked into the bathroom to wash his hands after he finished eating. Mandy was different, because she was giving too. She was like the God she worshiped. He remembered other snippets of conversation they had had over the last few days.

"God didn't give us rules and expect us to do it on our own," she had told him when he'd complained. "He gave us those rules to follow to keep us happy. Were you happy when you were sleeping with a bunch of women?" she asked bluntly and he'd almost blushed.

He couldn't look into her eyes, but he'd admitted, "I thought so while in the heat of passion, but afterwards..." He'd hung his head. "No, no I wasn't."

"Well God said to commit yourself to one person, because He knew you would be happier in the long run," she stated plainly. "Same goes for drinking, and other things like that. He knows what is best for you, mentally, physically, and spiritually." She had stopped to look at him with intensity. "Not to mention, if you love God, and we should because of how much He loves us and has given to us, then our natural response will be to just do what pleases Him."

He'd frowned at that and she'd immediately continued, "Think about your Grandma Rathsmasen," she commented. He was glad that he'd told her about his grandma. They were so much alike. "When you were a child, why did you love her?"

Brandon shrugged, "She was such a great person, doing wonderful things for me, watching out for me, and well, scolding me even," he'd laughed. "I knew she loved me!"

"And did you want to please her?" she'd asked.

"Sure," he nodded, "When I was a child," he'd frowned as he thought about how he'd been as he'd grown older.

"So that's like God," she ended, "Get it?" she'd smiled and he'd laughed slightly at her enthusiasm.

She had a great way of trying to show him what she meant. He let his mind continue to wander as he finished up in his room and walked down the hall. He had just reached the landing when the gate buzzed. He waited to see who it was, thinking of Mandy and her teasing.

She loved to tease him as much as he did her. She was so fun to be with, and so beautiful. He caught his breath, afraid to think along those lines, for fear they would get him into trouble. It was strange how she made him want to be different, how God made him want to be different, but he couldn't stop the urges he felt for her. Course they were not just the same kind of lustful feelings he'd had for other girls. They were.... He let his thoughts trail off as Oliver opened the door.

Ryan stepped in. Brandon gripped the railing and gritted his teeth. He could feel his blood beginning to boil. What was he doing here? Oliver led him into the den and left. Ryan was trouble, he knew, but he couldn't hurt Mandy and tell her to stay away from him. He sighed. Since when did he care about the feelings of others above his own? He wouldn't say anything to her if Ryan made her happier. His heart squeezed. It would kill him though.

A moment later Oliver came from one of the other rooms, and Mandy was trailing behind him. He started down the stairs and stopped outside the den as Oliver was coming out. The man looked at him. His eyes glittered with understanding, even though the change in his face was ever so slight. Then the man walked by and out of sight.

Brandon clenched his fists and put his ear up to the door. He had to know what this guy was about. He had to know if his gut feelings were right or wrong, because he couldn't let anything happen to Mandy. He loved her! He froze, with the sudden realization. His insides began to roil as he listened and heard Mandy say, "I'm still working Ryan," She sounded distressed. Brandon ground his teeth together.

"I know," Ryan announced smoothly, "I just came by to remind you to be ready by six on Sunday," he stated.

Brandon clenched his fist, "I will," Mandy responded and he could hear her words growing louder as she moved towards the door. "Bye," she said, "I'll see ya."

Brandon dashed into the hallway as quickly as he could and heard Ryan mumble something back just as the door opened. Brandon stepped out of sight as the two came out and Ryan headed out the front door.

Brandon watched Mandy's face as she walked towards him, back towards the room she was cleaning. She had her head down, and she was watching her feet as she walked. She looked confused. Was that a good sign, he wondered. He stepped from around the corner and she almost smacked right into him.

"Sorry," he murmured as he caught hold of her to steady her.

She looked up at him and smiled. Her eyes were sparkling slightly, but she seemed confused. "No problem," she remarked and tried to step by him. He moved back into her way.

She looked up at him with a mischievous grin, "Are you trying to dance with me?" she teased this time her whole face lighting up. Yes, like the sun!

Suddenly he couldn't think. "Maybe," he breathed, looking down into her eyes. He put his arms back around her and pulled her close to him.

"Brandon?" she whispered looking at him her eyes probing. Her intensity captured him all over again. Her breath was coming in short gasps, and he found himself staring at her round lips. They looked so soft and sensual. "I have to go back to work," she begged unconvincingly.

Brandon leaned towards her and her eyes rolled back slightly. His lips brushed hers very softly but the sensation made him weak. He pulled back slightly, so that he could still feel her breath on his face. They were both breathing hard. He wasn't playing fair, he knew, but she'd felt so wonderful, wanted so to be near her. No woman had ever tasted so sweet.

She pulled away from him but not before he'd felt her heart pounding. "Sorry," he whispered. She just smiled gently and turned to go back to work.

He stood and watched her, knowing that he wanted to spend his life feeling that sweetness, loving her gentleness. When had his life taken such an abrupt turn? Had he never loved a woman until now? He found himself smiling with an incredible joy until his thoughts shifted. He frowned again, his mind back on Ryan. A muscle in his jaw twitched. Ryan had better not hurt her or he'd make good on his threat.

He thought of her being with him. Alone, in his car. His stomach churned. He gritted his teeth. He couldn't handle the thought. What if something happened to her? He pulled at the ends of his hair furiously suddenly resolved that he would protect her no matter what the cost. He knew what he would do, he decided, his hand hardened into a fist.

Ryan beamed at Mandy again. She smiled slightly and lifted another forkful of desert into her mouth. She seemed distracted. No matter, he'd get what he wanted shortly.

He briefly wondered if she'd ever think about why he hadn't asked her out again yet. Maybe that was what had her so quiet. Their meal was over soon and they headed back out into the car.

He headed right and flipped on the radio. No need to talk and keep up the charade since it was ending soon. She stared out the window. Finally she realized the direction they were going. "Where are we headed?" she inquired, turning worried eyes in his direction.

"We've got awhile until the movie starts, so I thought we could drive around," he stated smoothly.

"We could just wait at the theatre," she retorted stiffly.

"Actually I have a nice little place in mind where we're going to wait," he countered and pulled down a dirt road through the palmetto and pine trees that created a secluded little make-out spot.

"Ryan," Mandy announced sharply, "I don't want to wait here," she emphasized.

"Well I do," he quipped smugly. He was going to enjoy this. Even if she fought, and didn't give him what he wanted, he'd still get his dues. He pursed his thick lips. After all the time he'd spent on this little game with her, he couldn't believe how much better the rewards were going to be, even better than he'd expected when he'd started this thing.

Ryan drove to the end of the road and stopped in the small clearing. The moon was only a sliver in the sky so shadows still lurked. He smiled to himself. He put the car in park and leaned over towards her. She leaned away from him frowning. "We are not going to do whatever it is you take girls here to do," she proclaimed calmly.

"You think I do this a lot?" he insinuated with a laugh.

"I do now," she retorted in disgust.

"So why did you not figure me out sooner, Miss Psychologist?" he sneered.

"I guess I was giving you the benefit of the doubt," she grit out, shaking her head, and looking out at the darkness surrounding them.

"You're just used to being around good Christian people," he mocked.

"Not really," she stated calmly and looked up at him a sad expression filling her eyes. He snickered. "There is no such thing as good or bad people only good or bad choices," she added and looked out the window.

Ryan rolled his eyes. He didn't need a lecture, "Whatever," he spit out, "Know what all the other girls did when I brought them here?" he inquired leaning closer to her, a glint in his eye.

She turned disdainful eyes on him, "Let me guess, they all wanted you?" she replied sarcastically.

He nodded. She was quick at this game, but not quick enough. "Well, I don't," she stated forcefully. "In fact, after tonight I was going to tell you that I didn't want to go out with you anymore."

His eyes narrowed, and he pressed his lips up to her ear and murmured menacingly, "I don't care what you want," then he leaned back and laughed all the while watching her. She looked straight ahead, but he could see her jaw tightening in fear, and her lips seemed to be moving slightly. Maybe she was praying. He laughed to himself. It wouldn't help!

"Take me back or I'll get out," she threw out. He lunged at her pretending to grab at her but really grabbed her purse. She opened the door and flew out in one swift motion.

He laughed, looking down at the purse in his seat knowing her phone was in there, revved his engine back on, and sped back down the dirt road. He'd still get what he wanted, he thought. He swerved onto the road as a car's headlights passed by headed in the other direction. Things were going perfectly!

Chapter Twenty

DEBORAH SNIFFED, AND RAISED her slender hand up to touch her forehead. She could feel a headache coming on. She hated her family when they treated her this way. None of them really cared. She sighed. Brandon seemed sympathetic of late, but then he'd still been more preoccupied with other things.

It was strange though that he'd not been flirting with any of the girls at all this weekend. She narrowed her eyes. Maybe there was something to this new housekeeper thing, which Charles had mentioned, after all. It was strange how quickly that one had died down. Either he'd gotten his way or the matter had been dealt with.

Deborah walked into the house and up to her room. Their dinner out had been dull and painful. Brandon was off with friends and Charles and her father had been discussing business as usual. She went into her bathroom and opened the medicine cabinet. She grabbed out her bottle of Advil and swallowed two tablets without water.

She couldn't believe Steven was cheating on her. She recalled how passionate and fun things had been when they had first met. He was a rich businessman and the family approved. She furrowed her brow. He had actually been sweet during their first two years of marriage, but then he'd grown more distant and stayed away from home more and more.

Deborah looked down at her vanity. She pressed her palm to her temple and sat down. She looked into the mirror. She glanced at her pretty blonde hair and delicate features, just like her mother. She frowned. Those same features hadn't kept her mother happy. She glared into the reflection of her own eyes. They were a dark blue, contacts covering up the hazel color she detested. She knew she still looked gorgeous, but for some reason that was not good enough. She pulled the pins out of her hair and let it fall around her in silken waves past her chin.

She looked down at the contents strewn across her vanity's counter and thought about the times that Steven had run his hand through it when she'd pulled it down. They'd come home after a long evening out, and she'd pull the pins out and he'd pull her into his chest and run his hands up through the back of her hair. She had melted then.

She sighed. How long had it been since he'd done that. She suddenly focused on her counter and frowned. Where were the gold hoops she'd worn yesterday? She'd left them right here. And where was her diamond bracelet? Hadn't she taken that off here too? Her eyes searched the contents of her vanity as she realized that all of her expensive jewelry was missing!

Deborah stood up and glanced around the room. Perhaps she had put it away while she was drunk and didn't know. Now which day had she drank too much? But the hoops, they should still be there. Her dark eyes searched everywhere, as a deep panic settled in her stomach. She had over several hundred thousand dollars' worth of jewelry that she couldn't find. Where was it all?

She headed downstairs. She heard her parents muffled tones coming from the den. She knew they were arguing, but she didn't care. They looked up in annoyance when she came in. She ignored the looks. "I can't find my jewelry," she stated in alarm.

Her father frowned. Her mother's eyes widened. They both assured her they hadn't noticed her jewelry anywhere else, so they called Oliver in. Her father asked him to get all the staff together. Deborah went to sit by her mother. She felt better with her father in charge. Her mother put a slender arm around her. She smiled slightly, and her mother nodded once as Mrs. Harper motioned that the last staff member at home had entered.

"My daughter's jewelry is missing," her father began, not wasting time on preamble. Her mouth turned up dryly. Her father could get things done, she decided, even if he didn't care about everything that was happening to her.

"Did any of the housekeepers move it?" he asked, then frowned. Two girls were sitting on the setae across from her. The redhead looked familiar. The other girl did too. They shook their heads. She looked around, realizing why her father was frowning. "Is there someone missing?" he demanded looking up at Mrs. Harper.

"Yes, two of my housekeepers have the day off," Mrs. Harper replied brusquely.

"Mr. Taylor," Deborah glanced over and saw that the redhead was addressing her father. She narrowed her eyes. Did she know something?

Her father's hazel eyes turned and penetrated the girl. Oh what was her name? "Yes Brandy?" her father inquired. Yes, that was it.

"I think I know where it might be," she started, and then paused, looking around slightly. Deborah frowned. Everyone was looking at her intently. The girl looked up at her father and responded sweetly, "I saw Mandy, one of the other housekeepers with some jewelry a tiny bit earlier. Maybe she moved it."

There was a gasp and Deborah looked up at the other staff members. Most of them looked in shock, and Mr. Castle looked upset. One guy was even glaring at Brandy. Deborah frowned. What was going on?

"Mandy wouldn't have moved anything unless instructed to," Mrs. Harper stated hoarsely.

The other housekeeper finally spoke up in a soft whiny tone, "But she is poor and always talking about how much she wants to go to school."

"Mandy wouldn't steal, Connie," the guy accused, his eyes narrowing. Connie wouldn't look at him, and seemed to be biting the inside of her cheek. Deborah frowned.

"Well we can solve this quickly," her father stated, "Oliver go get me the spare keys," he demanded, "Did this girl, Mandy go anywhere in particular on her break?" he asked offhandedly.

"She went out with a boy named Ryan this evening," one of the other staff members answered, but Deborah didn't even look to see who had spoken. She stood quickly and headed toward her father.

"Then let's call him up," her father stated, grabbing the phone and handing it to Mrs. Harper. "If she's still with him then she couldn't have stolen anything," he added harshly.

It was funny how everyone scurried around to do as her father bid. She'd get her jewelry back in no time, even if this poor pathetic maid had stolen it. She smiled. Mrs. Harper had found a way to locate the boy's number and soon Ryan was called.

Deborah listened with interest as Mrs. Harper asked the boy a few questions, and then her father impatiently grabbed the phone. "What time was that?" he growled. "Thank you. I may need to call you again," her father ordered and told the boy "bye."

Deborah looked up inquisitively. "She was dropped off here at eight," her father queried. Then he looked over at the staff members. "We got back at eight-thirty. Did anyone see Mandy at eight?"

Everyone shook their heads except Brandy. "When did you see her?" her father huffed, his eyes narrowing.

"At eight-fifteen or so," she began one side of her mouth turned up with a strange hint of mirth. "That's when I saw her with some jewelry."

"That was over thirty minutes ago," Deborah cried out. "Where is she now?"

"Someone call her," her father commanded.

The boy who'd glared at Connie went and got his phone but apparently no one answered. Everyone started talking at once. Oliver came back right then with the spare keys and her mother rose and stood beside her and her father. Her mother put an arm around her as her father held up his large hands. "Quiet," he ordered.

Deborah watched as her father instructed everyone to wait until the family, Mrs. Harper, and Oliver checked out Mandy's room. She frowned again. It was strange how uptight all of the other staff members were about this when it didn't even concern them. She shrugged, and headed toward the staff housing with her parents.

"Which one is Mandy's room?" her father demanded of Mrs. Harper.

Oliver opened it and they all walked in. It was fairly neat and orderly. Deborah pulled out of her mother's grasp and ran to the girl's small table. A bit of gold was gleaming at her. "This is one of my gold earrings," she cried.

Melissa had never been more upset. They had never had anyone steal from them before. Mrs. Harper had always chosen so carefully. Perhaps that was why she kept on saying that the girl wouldn't have done it. It didn't look good for her judgment. She pursed her thin lips.

She paced in the living room while her husband called the police. She passed her daughter and smiled encouragingly. The officers would be here in any minute. They had better hurry and find that girl and the rest of the jewelry soon. What if she sold it or something? She walked to the sofa and looked down at her daughter. She looked distraught. She bit her lip and patted her daughter on the arm. "We'll get it back dear," she soothed.

Charles had been in his room during the whole fiasco, but now he was down in the living room with them. He was pacing too. His determined expression looked just like his fathers. She smiled slightly at the resemblance, and then ground her teeth, as she realized that wasn't always a good thing. If only Brandon would come home too. He was more like her, and besides, a family needed to be together during a crisis like this.

She heard the sirens and Oliver went to open the gate. He seemed distressed. Actually they all did. It was odd really, but almost all of the staff seemed upset and couldn't believe this girl would do such a thing. It was always the ones you least expected, she decided grimly, and ground her teeth.

The police officers came into the house and the questioning begun. Brandy and Connie were brought into the living room, and Ryan was called again. He was asked to come over as well. She caught herself tapping her foot as she waited. She hated the nervousness in the pit of her stomach. She hated this waiting.

If only her youngest son would come home, she thought again for the hundredth time. Where was he? She couldn't remember where he had said he was going. Had he even given them specifics this time, or only said he was out with friends? It was getting late though, shouldn't he get back soon, she wondered, thinking maybe she should call him.

She heard the front gate buzz, and sat down on the couch with her daughter. It was probably Ryan. Her son would not need to buzz. She patted her daughter's knee, feeling comforted even as she comforted her daughter. Deborah seemed calmer now that they knew who had taken her jewelry. She looked up as Oliver ushered a good looking young man into their living room.

He seemed very confident and that restored her sense of hope. Connie had seemed so unsure of herself this whole time, and she was beginning to feel insecure too. She looked over at the police officers and her husband sitting at the small table. The girls were on the other side. Ryan went to join them. He glanced at them both once, and nodded, as if he'd only just met them. Maybe he had.

Melissa frowned. Why was Connie acting so nervous though?

The police officers asked the boy questions and Robert was handling everything. She was glad for him in situations like this. He was always so sure of himself. She looked up at her son Charles again, and sighed. He was becoming a replica of his father. There were times like this that she was proud of their drive, but other times, when she was the one being run over, it didn't feel good.

She sighed and looked the other direction toward the door. If only Brandon… and it was as if her thoughts willed him, for just then the door opened, and he stepped in. She could feel some of her tension ebbing away. She smiled at him. His brow was furrowed.

She stood up and went to him, "We were robbed," she replied shrilly to his unspoken question.

"There she is," Brandy suddenly cried out, and Melissa looked behind her son to see a girl, "That's Mandy."

Brandon stiffened. "Go arrest her," Robert commanded sternly, and Brandon stepped back in the way, blocking the pathway out, a very hard expression on his face.

"What is this all about?" he asked harshly. "Why is she being arrested?"

"That girl of yours," Robert stated, a note of steel in his voice, "robbed your sister." Melissa looked back at her husband. What was going on here? There seemed to be some strange tension between the two that she hadn't noticed before. Whatever had happened to Charles' statement that Brandon was with one of the housekeepers? Suddenly her eyes widened and she looked back at her son.

The girl in question stepped in the doorway, her pretty eyes widened slightly in surprise. She had long curly brown hair and she seemed very pretty. Was this the girl, and if so, why was she still working here? Robert had said he had dealt with the matter!

"When? How?" Brandon was asking his father as he reached to take the girls hand. The girl looked around with questioning eyes for a moment before she took her son's hand.

Melissa frowned. Her son really had been involved with this one! Why hadn't Robert fired her? She could feel her own anger rising to match her husbands. "While we were out," she heard herself saying stiffly.

"At eight-fifteen," Robert corrected.

Brandon's face softened slightly. Melissa was baffled as her son's face slowly began to lighten and the corner of his mouth turned up. He looked back at the girl, and the smile he gave her was so peaceful that Melissa was suddenly struck with a sharp pane of jealousy. She had never seen quite that look before on her son's face. She felt her gut tighten. Her son led the girl into the room. "Before you arrest her," he began calmly holding up his other hand towards the officers who had risen when Mandy had entered, "Let's all sit down and see what she has to say for herself."

Melissa frowned. Well that did seem to be fair. She glanced over at Robert. He was scowling at Brandon, but he nodded in agreement. Charles, she noticed had a smug expression on his face, as he came to sit beside her and his sister while the girl spoke.

Mandy and Brandon went over to the table and sat down in the chairs beside it. Melissa looked up at Mrs. Harper and Oliver who were standing nearby. They both seemed upset still. She shook her head and focused on the girl. She could see why her son liked her. She was very pretty, and strangely she also looked very serene. Once more Melissa felt the jealousy, but she pushed it aside. No one could really be that peaceful in a situation like this.

"So what do you have to say for yourself?" Robert demanded of the girl coldly, "We found some of the jewelry in your room."

Melissa expected her youngest son to react to that, but he had leaned back in his chair and his expression was almost as calm as the girls. She pursed her narrow lips. She looked back at the girl as she began, "Ryan and I had a date. He picked me up at six."

"Yes," Charles interrupted from beside her, "He told us that already. Start with the part about his dropping you off at eight." She noticed Robert's proud smile at their oldest. Yep, just like his father.

Mandy laughed slightly, "He dropped me off all right," she stated with a laugh that surprised Melissa, "in the middle of nowhere and without my phone," she added with a sigh, directing herself toward the officer and not Charles. "We were supposed to have gone to a movie at eight, but he drove me down this dirt road and tried to..." she paused as if looking for the right words. Melissa saw Ryan scoff. "He left me there," she ended, looking up and into her husband's eyes.

Melissa frowned. She seemed so sure of herself. Ryan began refuting her story to the officers and suddenly Brandy asked, "So then how did you get back here so fast?" just as her husband asked, "Can you prove it?"

She looked over at both of them. Brandy was glaring at the girl, but her husband, strangely had unclenched his jaw. He always kept his jaw clenched when he was upset. Did he perhaps believe Mandy? Melissa looked back at the girl in question.

Mandy was smiling slightly and she had looked over at her son. Brandon was still holding her hand. She furrowed her brows. He was glaring at Ryan. He apparently believed Mandy, and what if she were telling the truth? She looked back at Ryan. He seemed like a good enough boy, but as they had all found out this evening, looks could be deceiving.

"Yes," the girl murmured. She seemed so calm and unassuming that Melissa suddenly found herself actually hoping she was telling the truth.

"How?" one of the police officers asked.

"I got picked up," she began.

"Likely story," Brandy scoffed, cutting her off. Melissa frowned. She began disliking that girl. Why did she have to be so rude?

"By whom?" the other officer asked after holding out a hand to quiet Brandy.

"By me," Brandon said softly. Melissa gasped. Everyone else was looking at her youngest son with the surprise she felt. Her youngest suddenly turned cold eyes on Ryan, "I was the car that passed by just as you got off the dirt road. I had followed you both all evening, because, funny thing," he retorted in a steely sarcastic tone, "I didn't trust you." His face hardened even more, "Guess I know why huh?" he stated cynically.

He looked down at Mandy who looked up at him with a calm smile. "I almost lost you, and I'd have not found Mandy for a long time if I hadn't noticed your car pulling out of that dirt road." He stated still staring at the girl. They seemed to be communicating without words, Melissa thought. Her chest tightened. She and Robert had never been able to do that. She felt moisture in her eyes.

She looked away, as her son ended, "I found Mandy at the end of that road at exactly 7:54."

All eyes turned toward Brandy, Ryan, and Connie. Melissa glared. She had never liked that redhead anyway. So where was her daughter's jewelry? She narrowed her eyes.

Chapter Twenty-One

MANDY SMILED AT MRS. Taylor who grinned almost gleefully as Brandy and her cohorts were taken away. The rest of the jewelry and Mandy's phone had been recovered in Brandy's room.

"We all need to talk," Mr. Taylor growled and she was ushered into the den along with the rest of the Taylor family.

Everyone sat down and Mandy glanced around at this family. She wished they were more like hers, especially for Brandon's sake. Her family meetings were nice, even when someone was in trouble. Everyone knew how much they were loved, but here, it was so stiff and painful.

Mr. Taylor glanced at his son and then at her. "Brandon," he began, "I am proud that you were heroic and helped out in this delicate situation. Things could have been a lot worse, especially for Mandy here, who was innocent." She smiled at him. The man did care about his family even if this seemed more like a business meeting than a family discussion. He just cared in a different way than her father did.

"Thank you dad," Brandon replied stiffly. Mandy could sense his tension from across the room.

"I think though that you need to put an end to your relationship," he said the word distastefully, "with our housekeeper." Mandy glanced over at Brandon, wondering what he was thinking.

A few hours ago she had known exactly what he'd thought. She'd been fairly scared and lost, and she had prayed and prayed. She had begun to walk back down the path, and was starting to feel more at peace when headlights had emerged from the darkness. The car had screeched to a halt, and Brandon had flown out. He'd rushed to her, and grabbed her up in his arms. "I'll never leave you again," he'd declared.

She'd clung to him and felt so safe. She'd felt safer than she'd ever felt. It was right, and it was so wonderful. He'd touched her cheek gently and she had felt fire, as she thought about his kiss, and almost thought he would kiss her again until his eyes had clouded and he'd asked what had happened. She knew he was upset with Ryan.

He had not touched her again until he'd grabbed her hand in the doorway. They had driven around for a while and just talked. He had told her that he had finally prayed for the first time. He'd prayed for her. She was touched. It had felt good to just talk to him, and she knew that everything was going to work out.

He had asked what had happened. He had told her how he felt and what he had gone through, and then they had talked of other things until she was calm and Brandon was satisfied that Ryan hadn't hurt her in any physical way. Then they had driven home and chaos had erupted.

Mandy watched Brandon now as he sat in silence for a moment. She'd know what that look had meant when he'd stared into her eyes in front of his family, and she wondered if he would be strong enough to be truthful again. He seemed at peace. She relaxed. He looked up at his parents. "Do you know what it really means to give?" he asked.

His father snorted and his mother looked confused, "We give to charities every..." she began, but Brandon waved her off.

"Do you know what it feels like to be trusted?" he asked looking into his father's eyes. The right corner of Mr. Taylor's eye twitched and he looked down slowly. "Do you know what it's like to feel completely safe?" he inquired, this time looking at his mother. Mrs. Taylor bit her lip and Mandy thought she saw a sheen of tears as she hung her head.

Brandon's eyes glanced her way and the expression pulled at her. She smiled gently. "I do," he stated, staring into her eyes with such intensity that Mandy felt weak. "I do," he repeated and smiled, the promise back in his eyes again. Mandy felt her heart constrict. She loved him. She just couldn't help it. She looked down as he looked back at his family. "She may be just a housekeeper to you, but she's richer than anyone I've ever known," he stated.

Mr. Taylor looked up puzzled and gave her a strange questioning look. "She follows the rules," he stated with a soft laugh.

"What rules?" Charles asked.

"Never take more than you give," he said, and then added softly across the room to her, "See I did learn something." She grinned.

Mandy glanced over and Mrs. Taylor was watching her, a strange hunger in her eyes.

"Why is that the rules?" his sister asked skeptically.

Brandon smiled patiently at his sister, "Because Someone knew that in the end, that would make us the happiest," he began with a small laugh, "This girl came into our house and you can ask anyone of the other staff members," he waved his hand around, as if to emphasis, "she changed them all."

Mandy frowned, shaking her head slightly. No, what was he talking about? She hadn't done it! "Oh Lord, does he still not get it?" She didn't want to be put on a pedestal just because she listened to people. She just wanted to be a good psychologist someday. And it was God that had changed everyone, not her!

"Did you notice that Mr. Castle is more outgoing and Andréa is happy? Oh, and Mrs. Harper isn't so grouchy. Oliver smiles, did you know that he could?" he laughed.

Everyone began talking at once, "Oliver smiles?" "Mrs. Harper has always been grouchy though?" she heard.

"What did you do to get Edwin to be cheerful?" Mr. Taylor asked looking down at her.

Mandy shrugged her shoulders, "I didn't do anything. All I did was listen to him tell me about his wife." She began to stutter, "I didn't know that Mr. Rathers didn't smile," she added confused.

"You see," Brandon said with a huge grin. She looked over at him perplexed. "She cares so she listens to people and makes them feel special. That's why she is richer than anyone. Richer in the only way that really counts; She loves people!"

Mandy began to shake her head, No, it was all wrong, they were going to think it was all her... But before she could say anything Brandon held up his hand, and got up from the seat he'd been in and came to stand by her. He looked over at his family, "She taught me that it is about giving and not taking. I haven't been with any girl since I met her actually," he stated and Mandy looked up at him. She could feel her face growing warmer. Had she really affected him that much? No, it wasn't her. She frowned, but Brandon only smiled, and nodded slightly, as if reassuring her that he wasn't through.

"And I hear you haven't been drinking since then either," his brother spoke up, a hint of awe in his voice.

Brandon's lips turned up and he nodded slowly. His family was watching her again. Her insides began to quake slightly. She looked down, wondering if she should say it, or if Brandon really was going to say something. She could feel his eyes looking down at her too. She looked up at him. His eyes were twinkling. He had changed so much. She shook her head slowly in wonder and silently thanked God as he looked back over at his family.

"But then I found out why she is the way she is?" he commented still looking into her eyes.

"I thought you said it was because of the rules," his brother snorted.

Brandon smiled at his brother, a look of pity in his eyes, "Yes, it is, but for a long time I thought she was different because she was just better than everyone," he looked down with a teasing glance at Mandy, then looked back up at his family, "and I started to fall in love with her because she was different than anyone I had ever met." He looked down at Mandy again, and Mandy could feel her face growing red at his admission. "But something made her different..."

"What?" Deborah asked.

"Actually I guess I should say Someone?" Brandon commented, looking up at his sister.

"Who?" his father demanded.

"God," he said softly, and looked down at Mandy again, ignoring the sounds of awe and disgust that were erupting from his family.

"So she's a Christian?" his brother's mocking voice sounded from the chair he was in.

Brandon nodded and looked back at his family, "Yes she is, and I am happy to say that I want to become one too," then looked at his mother, "I think Grandma Rathsmasen will be happy about that, don't you?"

His mother's face lit up with a sad smile. "Yes," she nodded, looking down at her hands in her lap, "Yes, she will," she commented, and Mandy could hear the wistfulness.

Mandy stood abruptly and went over to Brandon's mother, and knelt in front of her, and took the lady's manicured hands in hers and murmured softly when she looked up, "It is never too late to go home," and smiled sweetly.

Mrs. Taylor's eyes began to mist and she reached out a hand to Mandy and brushed her hair gently. "Thank you dear," she choked out.

Mr. Taylor stared at the two and shook his head, "Her being a Christian still doesn't stop the fact that she is a housekeeper, and I can't have you messing with one."

Brandon sighed heavily, "Don't you understand what I have been trying to tell you," he groaned, "She is a Christian meaning she won't be messing with me, as you say, because she feels it is morally wrong."

"Why?" Deborah asked, turning startled eyes towards Mandy who had stood back up and headed back for the chair she'd been in.

"Because it says so in the Bible," Mandy replied quietly, "In Ephesians 5:5 it says that fornicators, or people that have relations," Mandy blushed slightly and went on, "like that outside of marriage will have no 'inheritance in the kingdom of God', which means, heaven."

"Oh yeah, and you Christians believe in heaven," Charles snorted.

Mandy smiled slightly, "What do you believe in Charles?" she asked so quietly and unassumingly that the man seemed slightly taken aback.

He stammered slightly, "I, well, I… I believe in myself?"

"And do you fail?" she saw a muscle in his jaw twitch, but he didn't answer, "God never fails," she stated quietly, and then smiled broadly, "I guess I would rather put my faith in Someone I know will never fail me," she raised her hand when Charles appeared to want to protest, "Even when I don't always get the answer I think I should," she ended.

Deborah looked puzzled, "You mean like when we pray and don't get what we want?" she asked.

Mandy nodded, "So you see, since I follow God, I won't do things that will displease Him."

"That's right," Brandon added, then explained to his family about why we should love God and follow him, just as she had done with him, even using the example she had with his grandma. She smiled as she listened to him.

"I guess the fact that she wouldn't let me do things with her like everyone else, drew me to her at first. I thought it was just another challenge," he commented, "but in reality it was the ultimate challenge," he teased, looking down at her again.

Mandy laughed slightly, but Mr. Taylor was frowning, "I still don't like you being with a housekeeper," he spat out the word as if it were a swear word.

"Why dad," Brandon asked, and Mandy could see his hand tighten on the chair beside her as he tried to stay calm, "because she is not rich or influential?" His father gritted his teeth. "Don't you think it is better that I found someone of substance than someone with substance?"

Mr. Taylor brushed back a strand of hair, and Mandy looked at him, feeling sorry that he was so worried about appearances. "Found?" he finally asked. "Does this mean you think you won't grow tired of her like all the rest?" he finally asked with a snort.

Brandon laughed and looked straight into his father's eyes as he declared forcefully, "I'm sorry that I haven't done very well in the past, but I won't be giving this girl up ever! This is the girl that I have waited my whole life for, short as that may be." He looked back down at her and the intensity was there in his eyes again. "I plan on being with her forever," he stated and this time, Mandy knew as she looked into his eyes and saw the hunger there, that it was a promise.

Brandon couldn't believe he'd actually gotten his way on this! His parents must have been affected by Mandy already too. His mother sure had understood what Mandy said, and she had been crying a lot today saying she needed to visit her mother. He smiled to himself as he pulled on his shoes. He wasn't going to push his luck and tell his father about this double date though.

Last night he'd been floating on air when his father had agreed to let him date her. He'd have done it anyway, and everyone knew it. He smiled to himself. He ran his fingers through his hair and smiled. Maybe he'd cut it even shorter just to thank his father. He'd spent a very interesting evening yesterday, he thought.

It seemed like the whole last few days had been an emotional roller coaster. He had been upset to see Ryan then intoxicated by the kiss. Then last evening he'd felt determined as he'd followed them, and frantic when he lost them. The moments had dragged on sucking his life with them. He'd cursed the drawbridge that had gone up letting Ryan pass and not him. Then he'd immediately apologized for his dirty words and begun to speak to God for the first time ever.

"Please God, I know you love Mandy, and so do I," and he'd paused wondering what he should say to impress God, then realizing, even as he thought it, that there was nothing he could say that would, so he'd bared his soul. "Help me please! Don't let anything happen to her," he'd breathed haggardly. And he'd kept it up even as he felt the fingers of panic crawling up his spine as he'd driven.

He started praying that God would give him the kind of peace he had seen in Mandy's face so many times and amazingly, the stress seemed to start seeping from his body. But then he had seen the car, and the terror had returned when he'd realized Mandy was not in it. He'd started to call Ryan every foul name he could think of as he spun his Ferrari around and raced down the dirt road, and then got upset with himself that he'd trusted in God to help him then fallen back into his old habits so soon.

He began to pray for forgiveness again, and at the same time that Mandy was okay. His relief at finding her unhurt had about caused his undoing. He had leapt from the car and held her, vowing never to let go.

It had felt so good to hold her, protect her. He wanted to never let that moment pass, and she must have felt the same, for she clung to him just as tightly. Then he'd felt heat crawl up his body at the nearness of her, and he'd pulled back and looked into her eyes. His hand had reached up to caress her face, and her eyes flickered. He suddenly remembered Ryan!

What had he done to her to make her flinch? He had let go, and vowed not to touch her again if she was afraid. His emotions were in turmoil as he pictured the awful things that could have happened. He'd actually started praying again, but this time that God would avenge her. He laughed now as he thought about it.

They had talked in the car, and his emotions subsided as she talked and he realized that everything she said about being okay and unharmed was true. Besides Ryan hadn't had the time to do the terrible things he'd thought of. He had relaxed and finally shared with her what he had gone through himself. She had been so happy when he'd told her about praying, though he left out the last prayer he'd prayed for vengeance. Then with a smirk, he realized that even that prayer had strangely been answered.

When they had driven home Mandy had stayed calm through everything that had happened there, and somehow she had made him strong. He couldn't give her up, no matter the cost. He needed her, almost as much as he needed God, he decided. He sighed. It had been an interesting day.

It was evening now, and yesterday's emotions seemed far away. Mandy would get off work in twenty minutes and they would be leaving to see a movie soon. His father had made it very clear that the relationship would only happen if it didn't interfere with her work. Brandon had laughed and said, "She won't let me around when she's working." So, he'd had to explain that one, but he didn't mind. It only made them respect her more.

It was strange that such a girl had come into their world and turned things completely around. He knew it would take a while and some of his family would never really change, but he had. He'd keep on praying for them anyway.

He thought about the first time he'd seen her, right here in his room. He laughed at what a spoiled brat he'd been. It was amazing that so much had changed in such a small amount of time, and the funny thing was, he wasn't the one that had made the changes. God had. He sighed contentedly to himself. It was time to ask Mandy one last thing.

He opened his door and headed to the foyer. Mrs. Harper was walking up the stairs as he was going down, "Hey rich boy," she huffed softly, a teasing smile on her face. Brandon grinned. He walked down the stairs and Oliver smiled slightly at him as he went out.

Mandy was leaning against the railing, waiting for him. She was so beautiful. Her dark curls hung loosely to her waist, and her blue green eyes were sparkling. "Ready?"

"Yep," he agreed, and they headed for his Ferrari. He opened the door for her and then went around and got in.

"Next time we'll have to take my car," she stated with a grin.

He just laughed. So maybe he wasn't completely changed, but he was getting there, he decided as he opened the door for her. He went around and got in.

"So why did you tell me to have Alexis and Donny meet us there?" she asked.

Brandon gave her a sheepish look, "I didn't tell my dad and I don't know how he'd react if he knew I was double dating with the staff," he admitted and cringed.

"Brandon," she scolded and he laughed. She was so cute, even when she was perturbed.

"Besides this is a good chance to have you all to myself," he beamed. He drove down the driveway and stopped before pulling out onto the road.

Mandy smirked at him, an invitation on her face. He leaned over and touched her face gently. He stared into her eyes and felt the words he'd planned to tell her begin to slip his mind. He smiled and leaned back. "I'm going to go to school here," he said.

"Hum?" she asked bemused by his befuddled words.

He grinned at her and his thoughts returned. "I mean I am going to be going to school here in Florida in January," he stated.

She smiled impishly at him. Brandon leaned over towards her again, and suddenly all humor was gone. He reached out and cupped her cheek, and pulled her face closer to his, "I meant it when I said 'forever,' you know," he breathed. "I love you so much."

Mandy's eyes glistened. Her heart was in her eyes as she spoke, "I know," she whispered, "And you know, against my will, I've fallen in love with you too," the soft smile lit up her face.

Brandon laughed and leaned closer until their lips touched. He felt fire again and he knew she felt the same.

They pulled away breathless. "You're funny, you know that?" he teased.

Mandy began to laugh. Brandon loved the sound of it. "Wait till you meet my family!" she hooted, and threw her arms around him and kissed him again!

He laughed at the thought, and then stilled again, "One last thing," he commented, and she looked up at him, her heart in her eyes, "You said that you could never date anyone that wasn't a Christian," he smiled slightly, and she nodded, a puzzled expression on her face. "Well, I want you to help me," he begged.

She frowned, "With what?" she asked.

His brows furrowed slightly and the side of his mouth turned up into a self-conscious smile, "I want to become a Christian, I mean, I know I already said I wanted to be one, and all, but could you help me know what to do to actually become one?" he begged.

Her face lit up into a beautiful smile as she turned to him and grabbed both of her hands in his, "Pray after me," she instructed.

Brandon smiled sweetly at her and closed his eyes, "Dear Lord," she began and he repeated, "Please forgive my sins and mistakes, and come into my heart today." She paused for him to repeat what she had just said. "Keep me from temptation, and give me the strength to do your will. Help me to have faith and to find ways to get to know You each day," she paused again, "Amen."

"Amen," he echoed, then smiled up at her. "That's what I needed to pray?" he asked.

She laughed, "I improvised," she teased, "But I do know that God just wants to come into your heart each day, so ask Him. Oh, and you'll want to get baptized," she stated growing more serious, "But in the meantime your job is to learn to do His will," she added.

He laughed, "And that would be by reading the Bible, right?" he stated, then got an impish look on his face, "or listening to you," he teased.

"Oh no!" she laughed, "Don't ever think that I know enough," she added.

"I know that I love God because I love you," he said, and she frowned. "Sorry, I guess that came out wrong," he teased, "I mean, I fell in love with you because of something I saw in you, and so in reality I was falling in love with what God did in you," he clarified, and Mandy just grinned up at him, and finally they began their trip.

Chapter Twenty-Two

"BUT WHO DO YOU think she is bringing?" Allie began, flipping a strand of dark brown hair behind her ear with one finger.

"I bet it is Brandon," Jenna cooed.

"Don't be silly," their mother scolded from her place on the couch. "I think it is her new friend Alexis," she added.

"I wish Amanda had just told us who it was," Aaron groaned, but his blue-green eyes sparkled, thinking of his sister.

"I still say Brandon," Jenna countered from her place on the floor. She put her Uno cards down for a moment.

"She would have told us if things had changed with him right?" Jason questioned, his skinny form sprawled out on the floor beside Jenna. He sat up and lay a wild card down on the pile in the middle of the living room's coffee table. "I change to green."

Allie's matching light brown eyes frowned too. She couldn't imagine why her sister had said she was coming home for New Years with a friend, but wouldn't be coaxed into telling them what friend. Allie glanced over at her husband, Paul, who was just grinning at his family but not participating in the bantering. Strangely he seemed the most like Aaron in that. She smiled at him and his puppy dog brown eyes melted a bit as he looked at her. She felt butterflies and looked away. Maybe later she could let herself melt at his gaze, but right now she had to keep her head on straight and think. She set down a green two.

"Do you think it is that guy Ryan she talked about a couple times?" their father asked placing a red two on hers.

"Brandon," Jenna said in a sing-song voice and picked up her cards again to see if she had any red.

"It can't be him," Allie groaned. "I know you always liked the idea of the rich boy and your sister, but this is not a fairy tale. And your sister knows better than to get mixed up in things like that."

"He could have changed though," Jenna's hazel eyes misted slightly and she sighed a sappy sigh.

"Oh please," Allie insisted, "Would you focus on the game! It's your turn!"

Jenna just laughed and drew a card. Their mother placed a card on the pile and then added, "Maybe it is Ryan. She wouldn't have started this guessing game if it were just her friend Alexis would she?"

"What about her friend Donny?" Jason questioned as their father leaned forward to put down his card. Allie smiled at them both. Paul made a sound of disgust at the card on the pile. She looked over at him. They were banned from sitting next to each other during games because they were accused of cheating. She laughed. Her family was crazy! She'd never cheated a day in her life. In reality she just had a hard time paying attention when she sat next to her husband.

"Uno!" Aaron called as he sat down his next to last card and covered the last one quickly. "I say its Alexis *and* Donny!" he added.

"Ahh, someone was supposed to have stopped him!" Jason shook a fist in the air in play. "I guess it could be both," he mused and drew a card.

Allie looked at the two cards in her hand, a red seven and a green skip. It was on blue. She drew a card. Who was Mandy bringing?

"Hey everyone!" she heard a chipper voice call from the door. Allie looked up and everyone in the family followed her gaze. A tall, muscular guy stood behind Mandy in the doorway. The family started getting up. Did Ryan have blonde hair? She couldn't remember anymore.

"I was right!" Jenna shrieked, and ran and threw her arms around her sister.

Mandy's laughter bubbled over as she bent slightly to squeeze her sister. "You were huh?"

Jenna turned doe eyes towards the guy behind Mandy and cooed, "Hi, how are you?"

The guy's blue eyes sparkled and he smiled and reached out a hand to shake Jenna's. "Hello," their father boomed before the guy could react and shook his hand next. Allie could see father's scrutinizing look, but the guy faced him head on, as the two firm hands shook.

"Welcome to our home," mother affirmed in a calm voice, and with her hands ushered them all in to sit down.

"And who do we have the pleasure of entertaining?" father questioned as they all parked themselves in the living room again. The guy had settled on the couch next to mother and Mandy. Father moved to sit on the other side of their mother, the game of Uno forgotten on the coffee table between them all.

Allie saw Mandy grin mischievously at the guy who smiled at her then turned to face the family. "This is my good friend..." she began, "Who happened to have a change of heart over the last few months."

Jenna started laughing. "And you said my idea was just fairly-tale like."

Mother shook her head at Jenna, and turned to Mandy and the guy. "Fairy-tales," Jason scoffed, "Puke!"

"Jason," father's voice scolded, a hint of mirth twinkling in his light brown eyes.

"Sorry," Jason mumbled, but he was also trying not to laugh.

Allie could see the guy was a bit startled and knew that it would probably take him awhile to get use to their family, like Paul. She looked over at her husband. Paul's dark brown eyes were on his sister and the guy, and Allie was curious. Her husband was grinning slightly. Her wide forehead creased and her thin brows puckered. What was her husband thinking?

She looked back at her sister, who seemed to be glowing more than usual. "He is my boyfriend, I guess you could call him," Mandy continued and looked over into the guy's beautiful blue eyes. The eyes in question were looking at her with a strange intensity that Allie had only seen in Paul before.

"Nice to meet you Brandon," Jenna cooed.

Allie drew in her breath. Was it really Brandon? Mandy threw her head back and laughed. "I should have guessed that she would know," she teased. "She did keep track of everything from the beginning. She likes puke fairy tales," she stuck her tongue out at Jason who grinned. "She wanted me with you from the beginning," she looked at Brandon from the corner of her eye.

Brandon jumped up and went straight to Jenna and planted a big kiss on her cheek then bowed like a waiter at a fancy restraint, "I knew I'd like you!" he teased. Jenna got slightly red then began laughing so hard tears began to squeeze from the corners of her eyes.

The rest of the family had frozen momentarily, but Jason began laughing too. "So don't tell me you like fairy tales?" he teased Brandon.

"Only ones that involve the King," Brandon remarked cryptically and went back to sit beside Mandy.

She smiled up at him when she sat down, "And perhaps a chase or two," she laughed.

Brandon grinned brightly and added, "And a changed heart."

"So tell us this fairy tale," Jenna begged and clapped her hands in glee, getting into the mood immediately.

Allie glanced at her family again. Her mother's bright eyes were watching Mandy's face. Her father was watching Brandon, who had reached for Mandy's hand. Aaron looked confused, but Jason and Jenna had eager faces. They always did catch onto things the fastest. They loved stories and a good tease. She glanced at Paul again, who had leaned back. He grinned up at her, and pulled her back to lean against his chest. She leaned into him and sighed, her whole body involuntarily relaxing.

"There once was a King who had a lovely daughter," Brandon began.

"I think He had a whole family, a family of shepherds," Mandy teased. Brandon chuckled. "Then the daughter of the King went to live in another place."

"A shack right," Brandon interrupted.

"Really? A shack?" Mandy's eyes crinkled in the corners.

"Had to be if she was living in the palace before," Brandon countered. He turned towards the family and continued the story. "There was a brat who lived in the shack." He smirked as he looked back down at Mandy again. "He thought he was smart, and rich, and had everything he needed."

Jenna laughed, and mother covered her mouth to keep from doing the same. Allie began to smile, realizing where this story was headed. "The brat saw this light shining out of the daughter and wanted her. He started chasing her. He thought the daughter of the King should live like him," Brandon continued and Allie detected his jaw clench slightly in embarrassment. "Then he realized the light shining from the daughter would go out if she did. He decided he would do anything to keep the light in her." Brandon's eyes grazed Mandy's and Allie saw something pass between them.

"The daughter wanted the brat to have the light too," Mandy took up where he'd left off, "but he fought if for a long time."

"Then this dragon came along..." Brandon growled in play.

Jason howled with laughter. "Ah," Jenna clapped, "Tell us more," she begged.

"Did you have to bring up the dragon?" Mandy groaned and then began laughing. She turned to Brandon. "That was perfect. I never would have thought of calling Ryan a..." then she stopped and clamped her mouth shut. With a sheepish grin she turned back to her family. "Uh, so yeah, the dragon kidnapped the daughter, and tried to..." she faltered. A frown creased her brow.

"What did Ryan do to you?" Father suddenly looked serious.

Mandy smiled. "It's okay daddy," she disclosed softly, "Nothing really. The King was with me." Then she began to laugh. "We are telling a fairy tale here, let us continue!"

Their father's eyes relaxed and he leaned back into the couch beside mother. She turned and smiled at him and Allie saw her take his hand. She looked back at her sister's shining eyes. "So the dragon tried to lock her up in this castle," Brandon stated, "and the brat was so scared he finally listened to the King's voice... the voice he'd heard coming so many times from the daughter, and he asked the King for help."

Jenna began to grin. "No more alcohol?" she mouthed to Mandy who just shook her head and winked.

"So the brat became a son of the King too," Brandon continued, "And strangely, like all fairy tales, the dragon and his evil henchmen... women," he corrected quickly and Allie heard Mandy giggling again. "They were all dragged away in chains, and haven't been heard from since. The new son of the King and the daughter of the King decided to visit the daughter's family of shepherds."

"Her father and mother, two sisters, and two brothers, right?" Jason asked with a wink.

Brandon just nodded at him, a grin on his face. "We were hoping..." he floundered and stopped.

"Welcome to this crazy family," Allie heard her husband say. Allie's eyes widened. "I totally understand!"

Brandon smiled at him and Allie saw Mandy whispering to Brandon. She knew her sister was explaining who Paul was.

Father stood. Brandon did too. Allie could see his brow's furrowing slightly. Father turned to Brandon and held out a hand. "Anyone who is a son of the King is welcome to be part of my family," he smiled. Brandon shoulders slumped slightly as the tension was released, and he took father's hand and clasped it firmly.

"Thank you," he breathed, and Allie could see the sheen of tears in his dark eyes.

"So tell us what really happened?" Jenna pleaded.

"Thought you wanted a fairy tale," Mandy teased.

"Aw," Jenna shrugged, "Real romances are always so much better."

Brandon laughed as he made his way back to sit by Mandy. "Sometimes," he countered.

"Yeah, tell us the story of the spoiled brat, the criminal, and the little minion my sister," Jason's eyes glittered with mirth and he stood, poised for flight.

Mandy flew from the couch. "Minion again is it?" she shouted chasing after him, "You are a piece of lint!" she chased him down the hall. Shouts could be heard echoing through the hall as Mandy caught up to him.

Everyone laughed. "I'm afraid your girlfriend will never grow up," their mother shook her head in mock sadness.

Brandon threw back his head and laughed. "Good!" he proclaimed, "I think it is time to go back to my childhood too!" Mandy came screeching back into the living room and jumped into their father's lap.

"Daddy save me!" she wailed.

Father wrapped an arm around her and laughed, "How many times do I have to say I don't get into these things?"

Jason came panting back into the living room and narrowed his eyes. "Cheater, you know I hate trying to find you in the mountains of Switzerland!"

Mandy just giggled as mom and dad made a place for her between them. Once everyone had settled back down Mandy and Brandon told them all the story of what had happened to them over Christmas. Allie snuggled down next to her husband and relaxed. Things were going to be perfect this year, she decided.

The night before had been so much fun, Jenna decided as she lay in bed thinking of their New Year's party. Sure it was probably different than the parties Brandon was used to, but he seemed so happy. Jenna sighed in contentment. Her sister was happy too, and it was all so romantic.

She jumped out of bed and threw her robe over her pajamas and headed for the kitchen. She was about to push the door open when she heard the low rumble of laughter coming from the other side of the doorway. "You getting juice huh?" she heard Brandon saying.

"Yup," she heard Mandy's bubbly laughter. "This is the epitome of entertainment," she could hear her sister teasing.

Brandon laughed again. Jenna rather liked the sound of it. Someday she would find a guy that laughed like that. She pushed the door open slightly and peeked around the corner. Mandy had pulled a glass down from the cupboard and Brandon had wrapped his arms around her from behind.

Jenna grinned to herself and started to turn away. "So I was thinking?" she heard Brandon whisper and she paused.

"Dangerous," Mandy joked.

Brandon laughed, "Especially when it involves you," he admitted. "You radically changed me…" he began, "Well, I guess it wasn't really you, but it was because of you," he added.

Mandy just turned in his arms to look up into his eyes. Brandon stared at her for a moment, "Maybe you should turn back around," he stated breathlessly, "I can't think when you look at me like that."

Mandy just laughed and pulled away. Jenna let the door slide closed as Mandy started walking her way. When she heard Mandy pull out a barstool she leaned against the door again to listen. "What were you thinking?" she asked.

"Well, how long should we wait before we get married?" she heard Brandon ask. She heard her sister start laughing and say something about it being a bit early for that talk, and Jenna decided she had eavesdropped long enough. A big smile caused crinkles around her hazel eyes. She turned. She was happy for her sister. Now, all they had to do was find someone for Aaron and all would be well. She frowned as she thought of Candace. At one time she had seemed like the perfect girl for him. She sighed as she went back down the hall. She pulled her mind back to the present, and smiled. After they found someone for Aaron then it would be time for her and her silly little brother to be all grown up, and then, "watch out world!" she teased herself with a grin.

About the Author

BORN AND RAISED IN Florida, Michelle Noonan has always had a love for romance. She graduated with a degree in education from Southern Adventist University which is where she met and married her husband, Scotland. They have been married 17 years. They moved to several other states in the southeast while she taught where ever God led. Currently she has been called to be a teacher at a small Christian school in Washington State, which she loves. She also loves writing and is always working on a story or two, as well as writing in her journals.

Printed in the United States
By Bookmasters